THE BRIDE WORE BOOTS

by

J. T. Schultz

WHISKEY CREEK PRESS
www.whiskeycreekpress.com

Published by
WHISKEY CREEK PRESS

Whiskey Creek Press
PO Box 51052
Casper, WY 82605-1052
www.whiskeycreekpress.com

ISBN 978-1-59374-975-0

Credits
Cover Artist: Molly Courtright
Editor: Laura Reagan

Printed in the United States of America

WHAT THEY ARE SAYING ABOUT
TORRID TEASERS VOLUME 23:
THE KISS OF THE WOLF

"I love paranormal romance but I've never read a book with a werewolf as sexy as Jarred Forester.

"I would have liked Kiss of the Wolf to be a bit longer so I could relish the ending, but I wasn't disappointed in the least. There are plenty of steamy sex scenes and JT Schultz does a fabulous job of creating a short story you can really to sink your teeth into!"
Kelly Wallace
Love Bites Romance Reviews

"An incredibly sexy story right out of the gate, Kiss Of The Wolf starts off TORRID TEASERS VOLUME 23 with a bang. Werewolf fans will be greatly pleased with this steamy story."
Lori Ann
RRT Erotic

"An extraordinary paranormal tale *Kiss Of The Wolf* is like no other werewolf story I have read. Brianna and Jarred are two alphas that like doing things their own way, and hate having to play second fiddle. I couldn't decide which one of them I loved most, it seemed like they were both vying for top dog or should that be wolf? But they both discovered that in the end being together was preferable to being apart. JT Schultz has penned a fantastic werewolf story and I know I wouldn't mind reading more of Jarred and Brianna in the future."
Sheryl, Sensual Ecataromance reviews
Rating 4 1/2 stars

"Oh were, oh were can my wolf be?

"*Kiss of the Wolf* by J.T. Shultz makes you wish for your very own werewolf to howl at the moon with. Brianna, a lawyer, is looking to free Jarred from a will that states he has to marry. Jarred wants to marry Brianna, but there's just one problem - he is a wolf once a month. Will they be able to bend the will or will Jarred bend Brianna to his will?"

Wendi

Fallen Angels Reviews

Rating 5 Angels

Other Books by Author Available at Whiskey Creek Press:

www.whiskeycreekpress.com

Dedication

To Jan, for taking a chance on a crazy writer.
To my readers both new and old that love a cowboy.

Prologue

"Oh dear, what have I done?"

Madison Bellini lifted a white gloved hand to her chest.

Staring back at her in the floor-length antique mirror stood a woman on the precipice of marriage. And she was shaking her head at Madison in disbelief. She moved her gloved fingers up and over the pearl encrusted bodice to slide along the lump she felt growing in her throat. She was having difficulty breathing. The woman in the mirror seemed troubled as well. She tried to see what her reflection was trying to tell her and barely heard her mother's authoritative and condescending voice.

"Madison, stop that before you hyperventilate. Really, darling. And stop worrying your lip so. Don't you realize how lucky you are to be marrying Edward? Why, every girl in town is after that man."

"And most of them have had him." Madison almost did choke as she heard the mumbled reply from her best friend, Bethany.

"What was that, dear?" Her mother's tone held a sharp edge of warning.

"Um, she was agreeing with you, Mother."

"Hmm. Well, darling, I need to leave you with your…friend. If I don't go and pry your father away from the mayor now, *I'll* have to walk you down the aisle. I swear those two are thick as thieves."

Maddy watched as the door swung wide and she glimpsed the multitude already filling the pews of the huge church. The lump grew.

As her mother closed the door, Madison tried to work a small breath around the boulder in her throat. Again, she peered at her reflection in the grand, full-length, brass mirror. Her pearl tiara matched the expensive necklace around her neck. The pearls sewn into her veil weighed a ton and caused her head to ache. Her satin shoes pinched and hurt her feet. The long, full, meringue-looking dress had cost her father almost ten thousand dollars. Blinking, she stared at herself. She looked just like a porcelain doll. So elegant and pretty, but breakable.

Her heart picked up speed. She was actually marrying Edward Theodore Von Housen III in a matter of minutes. Somewhere in the back of her mind, she always knew this day would come, but why did it have to be today? It was too pretty outside to be stuck inside this church with the cream of society, exchanging wedding vows to a man who no longer held any reverence for her. *Had he ever?*

She thought hard, but not long. She knew the answer. She had gone out with him at her parents' behest. Since that day, their parents had become joined at the hip, or at least the hip pocket. It wasn't like she loved him, but marrying him was now expected. Edward had serious problems keeping his pants on at the country club and it had earned him the nickname Ready Teddy. He wasn't even her type. Their marriage though, was good for both her father's company and Edward Senior's.

Instead of the nervous fluttering a bride should feel, she swallowed hard against the anxiety that churned inside her stomach. Her breathing became ragged and she realized it wasn't nervousness at all that plagued her. It was dread.

"You look flushed, Maddy. Are you okay?"

"I don't think so."

Again she stared at the face of the porcelain doll in the mirror. Soon, the door would open and her father would come to escort her to Ready Teddy . Once more, she asked herself what she was doing. She watched as her friend Bethany furrowed her brows.

"Maddy, this isn't about Sophia, is it? I mean, that was two days ago and it was a bachelor party. Things get crazy at bachelor parties."

"It isn't the bachelor party, Beth."

"Good. Now turn around so I can adjust your veil. It's slipping."

Again, the young woman staring back from the reflection in the mirror seemed to be waiting for Maddy to do something about this situation.

But what?

"Beth, I don't think he…will be faithful."

"Surely, once you two are married…"

As Maddy lifted a perfect eyebrow in incredulity, her features and the one in the reflection finally matched.

"My feet hurt!" Maddy's sudden outburst brought everyone's attention to the satin shoes that she kicked from her slender feet. Bethany giggled, however Teddy's sister actually flipped her cell phone shut with a disgusted flick of her wrist.

"What do you think you are doing?"

Maddy heard the demand for an explanation from her future sister-in-law and spun back toward the anorexic, aloof bitch. Never a golden hair out of place, Celeste was a carbon copy of Teddy and represented all too well the cold, self-serving world Maddy was about to join hands with.

"Need I remind you that you are about to walk down the aisle in front of everyone who is anyone in Calgary in an Alfred Sung gown? Your feet can bleed for all I care. You cannot walk down that aisle barefoot!"

"Oh, don't worry, Celeste. I won't be barefoot." Maddy whirled back to the low bench, spotting her well-worn but cherished cowboy boots.

"Oh, no!" Celeste exploded, grabbing up the satin sides of her bridesmaid dress as she made to block Maddy from her boots. "You are not marrying my brother in those things!"

"Watch me!"

"Get out of my way!" Celeste fumed as Bethany blocked her path to the bench and the boots. "Madison, you will not make a laughingstock of my family!"

Maddy fought the layers of frothy wedding gown to slip her boot over her toes. She almost laughed at the blocking dance Bethany and Celeste were engaged in as Celeste continued. "This wedding is the most important event of the season! It's going to be featured in society columns all over the world. You can't do this to me!"

Maddy wriggled her toes within her leather boots and sighed, leaning back, not caring if she did wrinkle the gown in the process. Celeste's words registered.

"Do *what* to you?"

"You know very well that my wedding will take place next year! If you go down the aisle in those things, we will never get the press attention you are receiving today."

"Feeling better?" Bethany asked, grinning over her shoulder at Maddy.

"Much," she breathed, smiling for the first time. As she felt her smile stretching across her face, she saw Bethany's eyes grow larger. She watched as Bethany mouthed silently, "What?"

Maddy shrugged innocently, kicking her boot-clad feet and sending the frothy shirt flipping up into the air.

Celeste stopped struggling and stared down at her cell phone. "Oh, no!"

"What?" Bethany asked, letting go of her.

"Mother just text messaged. It's starting!" With those words, she flung the door open. Sure enough the strains of the organ could be heard and Madison felt suddenly numb. And perhaps sick. The image of her father coming around the door caused her to tuck her booted feet under her gown and stand.

She wondered if there would be time for a father and daughter talk. One she could cherish forever. Where he talked of how she had grown before his very eyes and how proud he was of her.

She waited as he waved Bethany out into the main chapel.

"Well, Madison." She waited, feeling her eyes begin to itch with emotion. "Let's go, girl. Everyone is waiting!"

What? He sounded as she were holding up traffic!

"Father, I'm not so sure about this."

"Nonsense! You were born to be Mrs. Edward Theodore Von Housen III. Come along now. Can't keep my future son-in-law waiting."

She felt the steady pressure on her back as he propelled her toward the door.

"Madison, where's your bouquet?"

"Um...on the bench."

"Well, hurry it up!"

As her fingers wrapped around the beautiful bouquet, all she could think was how wrong this all felt. Staring down at the peach and white roses, she realized it was all wrong. She hated the color peach and she wasn't even that fond of roses. She thought back on the beautiful and vibrant yellow and purple wildflowers she used to pick at her aunt and uncle's ranch and how she would fashion them into a huge bunch and pretend she was getting married. Yet, in her pretend wedding, she walked toward a strong and handsome cowboy, not a pretentious man whore. This was all wrong.

"I don't want to marry him," she whispered as she felt her world crashing in around her.

"What? Madison, now is not the time for this." His reassuring hand on her arm did more leading than comforting as he led her from the room and into the main vestibule. Maddy tried to make eye contact with her father, but he was checking his appearance in the small mirror above the credenza. Turning, she caught Bethany's look of concern. Before Maddy could say another word, the organ music began, signaling the procession. Maddy watched as they slowly moved past her, each wearing their peach gowns. She had wanted anything but peach. She hated peach. It did nothing for anyone's complexion and it reminded her of the wine coolers she and Bethany had tossed back the other night, the night of the bachelor party.

She felt the touch of her father's hand grasping her gloved fingers and draping his arm with hers. The first chords of the organ struck, startling her and she felt a tightening in her throat.

"Daddy, I don't think Teddy is ready for this. Hell, I don't think I'm ready for this..."

"I know. I heard about the bachelor party, but he's a young man. He will settle down eventually. For God's sake, smile, Madison. All of society is watching."

She was led down the aisle, the peach and white swagged pews resembling a gauntlet of sorts. She fought the urge to yank her hand away and could even feel her father's strong fingers trapping her to him. Nervous, she glanced about and at the same moment heard a gasp from her right. Looking in the direction of that gasp, she saw her soon-to-be viper-in-law staring down in abject horror at Maddy's feet.

The woman's evil eye was actually twitching spasmodically. Beside her stood her soon-to-be father-in-law, an older, yet true version of the man she now saw waiting for her. Waiting for her and casting a glance over to his bachelor party favor, Sophia. Sophia Wainwright, blonde, buxom, and apparently totally boffable. According to rumor, she had been a party favor for Teddy before he had dumped her to begin dating Maddy. Only now she knew the truth. She was still a party favor for Teddy, the swine.

Watch him rock back on his heels as if he has just scored a merger. Oh, that self-satisfied smirk. I hate that. I've always hated that. What am I doing here?

Maddy felt her arm being released and heard the preacher begin to speak. She dared a quick glance to Teddy and found herself waiting for him to even acknowledge her.

And then he did it. He did the unthinkable. He turned once again and looked back to Sophia. The preacher was saying something, but suddenly all Maddy could hear was a loud buzzing in her ears.

Her parents wanted this wedding. She did not. She had gone along with this to make them happy. Make them proud of her.

The priest still rattled on, but it was just muffled, monotone sounds and unclear words. This was it. This was her life, formal pearl perfection. The tornado spun more wildly and tossed her nerves. She couldn't focus. Then, as if she had reached the eye of the storm, a calm settled over her as she looked at her husband-to-be. So good looking, so unfaithful and so consumed with money.

Madison turned and looked at Sophia, who was still crying. Then to Teddy and finally at the priest.

"We're waiting, Madison," Teddy whispered.

An eerie calm settled over Madison. "No."

Teddy's eyes widened and he snapped his head in her direction. "What was that, Muffin?"

A strange stillness fell over her. Edward Theodore Von Housen III was a first-class asshole. Not only did she not love him, she didn't even like him. "I said no. No, you unfaithful, money-grubbing swine. I won't marry you." She felt as if she were gathering steam. "Have I ever told you that I detest it more than a trip to the dentist when you call me Muffin?"

Gasps filled the church fully packed with society's elite. She smiled. "No, I'm not going to honor and cherish you. I don't love you now, so I guess that rules out the whole in sickness and in health part. Frankly, I wouldn't care if you dropped dead tomorrow." Giggling, she realized what she had just said to the man before her. *How liberating was this?*

"There are people watching, Muffin." Teddy's voice held an edge of warning.

"Oh, really? Since when do you care what people see? Or do you think they didn't see you at your bachelor party, and at the country club, with Sophia? Yeah, well, all of society saw you stick your penis in Sophia on the deck of the outdoor pool two days ago, so we're even." Maybe she should not have used the word 'penis' in church but hey, even the priest had one so it wasn't really a big deal, was it?

For the life of her, she couldn't believe how calm she felt in the face of his mounting rage. His face was turning a livid shade of vermilion.

"Now, see here, Muffin."

"I am not your muffin, you supercilious bastard!!"

"How dare you?" Mrs. Von Housen stammered and stepped forward.

Madison turned on her boot heel and looked at the most ostentatious and venomous person she had ever met, next to the woman's son.

"How dare I? Would you like for me to tell you just how I dare?"

For the first time since Maddy had met the pretentious wind-bag, the old viper was speechless...sputtering even.

"I am so outta here." Maddy was saying the words as her boot-clad feet were spinning her toward the huge double doors.

Mrs. Von Housen's talons sank painfully into Maddy's arm, spinning her back. "Y-y-you can't just leave!"

"Oh, yes I can! I'll tell you what I can't do, though." Maddy smacked at the woman's grip with her peach and white rose bouquet, sending rose petals into the air between them. "I can't marry a mama's boy, and I won't marry a philandering pig who reaches for his zipper like he was reaching for his wallet."

"Well, I never."

"Then he must get it from his father!"

Mrs. Von Housen's grip suddenly loosened as the woman sought to cover her own mouth in shock at Maddy's words.

"Excuse me." Maddy swept up her poofy, valanced, gown into her fingers and moved swiftly toward the huge church doors, each booted stride leading her closer to freedom.

She knew someone was running, moving after her, and quickened her pace to a sprint. "Maddy, wait!"

Bethany. Madison halted as her hand felt the cool brass of the door pull. *Oh, no. Bethany, do not tell me I am wrong.*

"You'll need your purse." Bethany shoved Maddy's white satin clutch into her gloved hand.

"Thank you." Maddy hugged her long-time friend.

"You are not leaving here!" Mrs. Von Housen yelled, making her way down the aisle. "You *are* going to marry my Edward."

"Oh, I'd run," Bethany advised as Madison pushed the heavy doors of the church open.

Chapter 1

Madison sucked fresh air into her lungs as she headed her yellow Corvette south. She had the top down and her stereo blaring all the way.

That had been almost five hours ago. She had crossed the border into Montana and had begun to feel the incredible rush of freedom she had hoped for. It empowered her, energized her.

She felt almost giddy as she recalled the astonished faces of the older couple at the mall in Lethbridge on her way out of the province. Seeing her step out of her Corvette in a wedding dress must have seemed odd to all who had seen her.

She had ignored the gawking saleswomen as she had moved quickly through the department store, grabbing jeans, a denim button down shirt, socks, and sunglasses. She purchased and changed, walking out of the dressing room with her long dark hair free from the confines of pins and a wedding dress stuffed and billowing out from under her arm. Stuffing the thing into a huge, new suitcase had not been easy and the bemused salesman from the second shop had to help her fit it in. Maddy laughed as she recalled him comparing her Alfred Sung gown to a huge uncooperative marshmallow.

She had been apprehensive as she rolled her Corvette up to the Canadian border. An uneasy feeling had settled deep as she handed the border guard her driver's license and wallet-sized birth certificate. She waited as he glanced over her to the battle-weary bouquet of peach and white roses in the seat beside her. Thankfully, he never asked about it and only posed the routine questions before letting her pass into Montana unfettered.

She followed I-15 South through Montana, marveling in the beauty that surrounded her and stopped only for gas, a map to Texas and a bag of cheese puffs. Top down, she blasted the radio and felt the incredible sense of freedom as her tires screamed down the long ribbon south.

Finally, just before the Montana and Wyoming border, she pulled off for the night and checked into a small roadside motel and diner. It sat off of the main highway, giving her a feeling of anonymity to bolster her newfound sense of freedom. She dragged her other suitcase inside, along with her knapsack and a hamburger from the diner.

She looked about the small and sparsely decorated room. A small television sat atop a tall dresser, and an old iron bed covered with a crazy quilt made up the furnishings. The room's rustic warmth reminded her of the times she had spent with her aunt and uncle. Their horse ranch had been a haven to her and she found she still missed those days.

Fatigue tried to gnaw at her shoulders as she slid her backpack onto the bed. It tipped over and she watched as her cell phone tumbled out onto the quilt. Tucking her bottom lip between her teeth, she toyed with the idea of turning it on and seeing if she had any calls.

She laughed aloud at her own thought. "Of course, I'll have calls." She flipped the phone on and sure enough there were seven messages awaiting her.

All from Bethany, no doubt.

"Oh, and Mother."

Her parents were not a first choice but Bethany was. Easing onto the bed she hit Bethany's speed dial and waited, sliding her boots off with her feet. She heard her friend's voice pick up on the second ring. "Madison! Where are you?"

"Hi, Beth. I'm fine, thank you for asking," she answered, kicking her other boot onto the floor and smiling.

"Where are you?"

"I'm in Montana."

"Where?"

"Montana? You know, that U.S. state directly below Alberta?" She gave in to a giggle as that incredible feeling of freedom began to feel more like excitement.

"Madison, they're starting to get worried. God, you should have seen everyone. Your mother became hysterical! And Teddy's mom came totally unglued."

"Wow."

"Your dad actually yelled at Edward Senior about his son's behavior."

"Yea, Dad!"

"He said if he was going to allow his son to be as unfaithful as he was, he should at least teach Teddy to be more discreet."

"More...discreet?"

"Yeah, and stupid Celeste snapped and told your dad the only reason her brother had even stooped low enough to marry new money was because your dad had practically blackmailed her father."

Madison sat back on the bed. "My God. They have come unglued." She tried to laugh, but her father's words would not allow her to feel anything but stunned disbelief. If anyone other than Bethany, her friend since grade school had told her this, she would not have believed them. "My father actually said that? If Teddy was going to be unfaithful to at least be discreet?"

She felt her stomach muscles clench as she said the words out loud. This was what they had planned for her? Her stomach started to hurt and her smile was gone. "He didn't care if Teddy was unfaithful as long as he was discreet about it? What the hell?"

"Oh yeah, and your father then went on to list everyone that not only Teddy had slept with, but Edward Senior as well!"

"Oh, God." Maddy eased back against the pillow and eased her fingers over her stomach.

"The press was going crazy! Mrs. Von Housen told them as soon you get back, there is still going to be a wedding. She has even started making tentative bookings."

"You're kidding?" Madison asked, feeling like this was a scene out of a horror film. Things like this did not happen in normal life. It was saved for that world of make believe that made its way across the Silver Screen. Some things were best left for Hollywood.

Bethany let out a sigh which seemed to echo through the little red phone and across the miles. "There's more."

"What do you mean, there's more?" Madison asked, not sure how much worse things could get.

"I overheard Edward Senior threaten that if you don't marry Teddy, he was not going to merge his natural gas company to your father's oil. From the words that were exchanged, that means your father could lose out big time." Bethany let out another sigh. "Oh-oh."

"Oh-oh? Bethany?" There was a rustle of movement from the other end of the line.

What was going on?

"Madison, this is your mother." Her mother had obviously snatched Bethany's cell phone away. "You get back home immediately! I can't believe you just walked out of the church like that. Do you have any idea what I have had to do to make this all go away? The Von Housens are furious! The press is parked out on the lawn as we speak."

"Mother, I—"

"Oh for God's sake, Madison. It's just a wedding!"

"What?"

"Come home, Madison. Marry Teddy. It's not like you have to have kids with him, or even stay married to him. Darling, your father needs you to marry him. He could lose his business."

"So, it's true. Dad was blackmailing Mr. Von Housen?" Maddy shook her head in stunned shock.

"No! Oh, there was talk of merging the companies for you and Teddy. A deal was made for your future."

"What future? I thought I didn't even need to have children?"

"That is a decision for you and Teddy."

"Mother, Teddy doesn't want children."

"No, darling. Teddy doesn't want his wife to get fat."

"Oh, good Lord! Tell him to marry Celeste, then."

"Now, darling—"

"No! Mother, I have never been fat. But I do want children. Did anyone stop to consider what I might want? Or were Teddy's wishes the only ones considered in this merger?"

Madison could feel the headache from hunger increasing with each word her mother uttered. They left her torn between laughing and crying.

"Darling, you can have them with your next marriage if you and Teddy can't come to some amicable arrangement in the next few years. Now, where are you?" Her mother's voice seemed so different, like that of a stranger.

Madison blinked at the sudden sting in her eyes. Apparently she was going to cry instead of laugh. "This is a joke, right? You really don't want me to come home and marry someone I don't love, do you?"

"Madison, rarely do people with our kind of money marry for love. It's business these days. Now get in your car and get over to the Von Housens. Everyone is here. We certainly can't go home."

"I'm not exactly nearby, Mom."

"Nonsense! Everywhere around Calgary is with in forty-five minutes. You have one hour. I am expecting you to be here."

Madison felt ill and beyond angered. "Well, expect away, Mother! I'm in Montana and I'm not coming back until I'm damned good and ready. Goodbye!"

She hit the little end call button, flicked the cover closed, and tossed the phone on the bed. She let out a loud, painful sigh. If she had her way, she would never go back. There was nothing for her to go back to. Her family were nothing but traitors, bidding her happiness like stocks on the Dow Jones Stock Exchange. Her fiancé was a philandering 'he-ho' who wanted nothing more than a trophy wife. And what a trophy! Apparently, with her came the merger of the two companies.

"Ooh!" Her squeal of frustration was echoed by the vibrating cell phone. She grabbed the phone up to see who could be calling. "Teddy? Teddy wants to talk? Talk to the message!"

She felt better after a hot shower and a bite to eat. Now, settled back against the iron headboard, she sipped lazily on a cold beer and watched as the cell phone began to jump, vibrating along the crazy quilt.

Teddy. Shaking her head, she flipped the phone open, biting back the curse that sprang to her lips.

"What do you want?" she demanded.

"Muffin, come home. This is ridiculous."

"I'll say." She turned up her long neck and waited for his response.

"Tell me where you are, darling. I'll come and get you."

"Well, I don't exactly know where I am."

"Muffin, how could you not know where you are? That's silly."

"Oh, I don't know. I didn't know about a lot of things apparently. You and Sophia, for example."

"She means nothing to me. I swear it."

"You are the most loathsome man on Earth!"

"I slipped, Muffin. Please. Where in Montana are you?"

"How did you know I was in Montana?"

"Your mother told me."

"Then, she also told you that I have no intention of coming back."

"You are behaving like a spoiled child, Madison. The press is swarming all over your spectacle today. Your mother told them the only thing she could think of."

"Which was?"

"That you needed time to reflect. That you went to a spa."

Madison let the sip of cold beer spew as her laughter rose. She didn't know what was funnier, the tremor in his voice or her mother telling the reporters she had gone for a day at the spa.

"The spa?"

"Yes. So you can see how important it is that you return immediately."

"Sounds like you have a real mess on your hands."

"Madison, I'm warning you. There is much more at stake here than just our...future happiness."

"Oh, I know. The merger!"

"What do you know about the merger?"

"More than you think."

"Madison, if your father and godfather renege on their deal and go with that fly-by-night cowboy Kirkland in Laramie, there won't be a safe place for you to hide, do you understand me?"

What? What the hell? Laramie?

Suddenly, her lawyer mind took control of the conversation. None of what he'd just said made any sense. Bethany had said her father was the one who would lose out if this marriage didn't come about. Teddy was telling a very different story. "Surely, they wouldn't do that, Teddy. What does that company have that your father's doesn't?"

"Forget I said that, Muffin. I am just beside myself with worry...for you."

"Teddy, is my father there?"

"Um...no. No...he stepped out for a bit."

She knew he was lying. She also knew that none of this made any sense.

"Goodbye, Teddy."

Flipping the phone closed, she settled back. She had heard of that company, Kirkland Gas. According to her godfather, they hadn't been worth even a look-see. This was getting more and more bizarre. *If they weren't worth the time and trouble, why would Teddy assume they had any chance at striking a deal with Bambardi and Bellini?* Grabbing up her fold-out map, she traced her way to Wyoming and decided a look-see might be in order.

* * * *

The next day greeted her with rain and seemed to follow her as she made her way into Wyoming. The sound of the rain and the rhythm of her wiper blades served to help Madison reflect over not just the past few days, but her whole life. Growing up, she had had everything handed to her on a silver platter, and for a long time she thought that was normal. It hadn't been until she had spent time with her aunt and uncle that she realized how things really were. Living hand to mouth had been a new concept for her. Her aunt and uncle had struggled starting out, but they were rich in one area and that was their love for each other. That was also a new concept for young Maddy.

Memories of their Brag Creek horse ranch brought a smile to her face. She had spent many a summer there. Her uncle taught her all about quarter horses while her aunt spent untold hours teaching Madison how to cook.

Her uncle was very different from her mother. Her mother had always turned up her nose so she could look down on him. She had married up and regarded a horse ranch as paltry and him being a cowboy the closest thing to pig farmer she could imagine. Her aunt and uncle had never been included in birthdays or holidays, yet they never mentioned the slight, even though it was delivered each and every year. There were vast differences in the two families and somewhere between Buford and Laramie, Maddy decided what she needed was to find someone just like her uncle. She missed them and wished she were heading to the shelter of their loving arms. She needed someone she could trust now. Someone who could tell her what to do with the rest of her life. She had certainly mucked it up.

If she ever did get married, she would marry a cowboy.

Gonna marry a cowboy.

Satisfied with her decision, she reached into her bag of cheese puffs and crammed one in her mouth as her cell phone rang, the vibration sending it across the white leather bucket seat. She could see Bethany's name flashing even as it moved across the seat. Leaning over, she chased it.

"Whoa!" She grabbed at it just as it skittered over the edge and onto the floorboard. Flipping it open, she almost shouted, "What up, Beth?"

"What up? What is up with you? You sound happier than I have ever heard you!"

"Oh, I was just making some ridiculous life changes. So, how are the folks?"

"The folks?"

"You know."

"Are you drunk? Maddy, they're really starting to panic here. They're going to send a search party out for you if you don't come back."

Her friend sounded agitated, no doubt from the combined grillings of the century from the mothers of the *slut groom* and *the MIA bride.*

"I'm not coming home, Beth," she told her friend, while trying to see the road ahead through the slashing mud and rain.

"I don't blame you. I wouldn't come back either."

"I think I need new wiper blades. This is almost treacherous. Hang on."

The rain was coming down in torrents and she was forced to pull the car over onto the shoulder. Leaning back, she put the cell phone earpiece in and clipped the microphone to her denim shirt collar.

"Sorry, sweetie. What were you saying?"

"I said I wouldn't blame you if you never came back."

"I knew you would understand. Thank you, Beth."

"Maddy, that's not why I'm calling."

Maddy held her breath, waiting for Beth to finish that ominous lead in. Whatever she was calling about, it wasn't good. "It's about Sophia."

"What about the little tramp?" Madison asked, realizing the rain was coming down harder, faster. She flipped her wipers on high and watched as the drops hit the windshield like clear paint balls.

"She spent the night at the Von Housens last night. I'm sorry, Maddy."

"Don't be," Maddy rushed to assure her, but could feel the sting of betrayal forming a burn behind her eyes. *So much for his declaration that Sophia meant nothing to him. And under the Von Housens' roof. They were also in on this farce wedding!*

"Are you okay?"

"Never better." Maddy wiped her cheek as a tear slipped down.

Damn them all! They would have gladly sent me into a living hell.

"I hope the press loved finding out about that."

"Your mother and Mrs. Von Housen told everyone that you were at a spa to ease your bridal jitters."

Madison felt tears sting her eyes and everything was blurring on the inside of her car as much as the outside. "I've got to go. If they ask, tell them I changed my travel plans and that I'm heading to Washington."

"Which Washington?"

"The state," she lied, wanting to put as much distance as possible between her past and her future. "I'll call you soon." She hit the call end button without another word.

How much worse could this get? She flung the cell phone down and heard it land inside her bag of cheese puffs.

Sophia had spent the night at the Von Housen house? She wasn't sure why this news upset her, but it did. She felt hot tears roll down her cheeks. *It wasn't from a broken heart, only wounded pride. If he had wanted Sophia, then why was he waiting to tie the knot with me? Had it all been a business deal?* She felt her stomach lurch at the hurt and the sick feeling of betrayal. She put her head down onto her steering wheel and let the tears flow.

Damn Teddy and Sophia. Damn the Von Housens and my parents! Damn this Kirkland, too!

Damn them all!

She became aware that her tears had slowed and she was able to lift her head from the steering wheel. She also realized the rain had all but stopped. The sun was trying to break through the clouds.

Maybe this was a sign.

No, that was a sign. She peered up at the wooden sign that stretched high and over the narrow road.

Kirkland Gas, Inc.

For some reason, it reminded her of the sign at the entrance to her aunt and uncle's horse ranch. And that made her angry. Somewhere in the back of her mind, this Kirkland was just as much at fault for her present unhappiness as Teddy was. Hadn't he said Kirkland was the reason he wanted to marry her? She was determined to find out just what kind of hold the man had on her father and her godfather. And Teddy. And herself.

* * * *

Ty Kirkland heard the Corvette's engine roar through the empty parking lot outside of his office. He looked up just in time to see her emerge from the yellow sports car. The rain was pouring again, but she trudged determinedly toward his door.

"What the hell?" He barely had time to get the words out when his office door was flung open. Standing before him, soaking wet, was a vision. Her hair was long and dark, with delicate shades of red. Her clothes, blue denim, were soaked and plastered to her body in a way that made his cock jerk to attention.

So much for standing when a lady enters the room. Or blows in like a tornado.

She spoke and he found he was staring at the pink lips as they formed each word.

"Are you Kirkland?

"I am." He tried to keep his lips from stretching out of the bemused expression he was hoping to give her to the sexually charged grin he knew from past experience worked on most women. It was impossible with this woman. He felt his lips curl up into his patented "render them speechless" smile.

To his astonishment, she dismissed him and began looking around his office, as if sizing him up.

"Did we have an appointment, sweetheart?"

His words brought her back to face him. Her eyes flashed as if in a challenge, a warning.

"No, puddin', we did not."

He fought to keep his mouth still as he leaned back in his chair. "What can I do for you then?"

"Oh, I just wanted to come by and see for myself what all the fuss is about."

"Fuss?"

"Bambardi and Bellini Oil. Ring a bell, puddin'?"

Ty did stand, tossing his pen down. His hands moved to his denim-clad hips. "Bambardi and Bellini sent you?"

"In a manner of speaking, yes, they did."

"I'm sorry. Would you like a cup of coffee? Or a towel, or something?"

She turned back to him. Her slight, curvy frame shivered.

"Here," he said as he came around his desk and snatched up his lamb's wool jacket. "Put this on before you freeze to death. I'll get you some coffee and turn the heat up."

"Oh, so you do have heat in here?"

"Yeah." He laughed suddenly, draping the coat over her shoulders. "I just don't use it. I'm trying to keep costs down." Despite the wet from the rain, her fragrance lingered. The smell kicked up his libido and his cock stirred further.

"I see."

His hands griped her shoulders through the thick coat. "I'll be right back. Make yourself at home." He shot a quick look to her lips. They were lightly glossed and full and designed for kissing. He lifted his eyes and met hers again. She was sexy. He released his hold on her then, before he pulled her into his arms and tasted her. He hurried to the door and didn't look back as he pulled it open.

Ty closed the door to his office and exhaled the breath he had been holding. He was relieved his erection had died down for now and made his way to the small break room, hoping to find a doughnut left over from the day before. He couldn't believe his luck. *Bambardi and Bellini had sent a representative all the way to Laramie. What did it mean? They were interested after all? What the hell? It didn't make sense.* Bambardi had all but laughed at his proposal last month. The old bastard had said Kirkland was too small to be taken seriously. *So, why send a representative?*

"Hey, boss." He barely heard the voice of his bother, Jordan, as he rummaged through the empty doughnut boxes on the table.

"Hey," Ty answered absently.

"What's up?"

"A doughnut. I need a doughnut."

"You hate doughnuts."

"I don't hate doughnuts." Ty tossed up another empty box and gave up on his quest. Coffee would have to do. *Damn.* He needed to make an impression on this lady. He'd overextended with the drilling for oil here and needed that contract. Turning his head to peer back at his brother, his eyes landed on the small plate on the table in front of him. A doughnut.

"Freeze!" Ty commanded as Jordan started to pick it up. Reaching in, he grabbed it from the table.

"Hey, asshole! That was mine!"

"Mine now. What are you doing here, anyway? I thought Doc had you on complete bed rest?"

"Funny. Like getting stepped on by my own horse wasn't bad enough. I can't believe this. I went to the doctor's with a bruised foot. By the time the story got to Mom, I had a broken bone. I tried to tell her it was nothing, but she won't believe me."

"She probably remembers when you told her you slipped in the mud that time you broke your leg. She knew you had been snowboarding."

"I just didn't want her to worry."

"Just a bruise? Wow, the way I heard it, you had several broken bones."

"That's pretty much what Mom heard, too." Jordan pointed to his crutches leaning against the wall and shrugged. "She brought those and insisted I use them."

"Smart boy. You let her have her way. So, you still on vacation?"

"Yep. Some vacation. Mom and Dad are driving me crazy, so I begged them to go to Cheyenne for the day and let me sleep."

"And they fell for that?"

"I think I was driving them crazy, too."

"No doubt." Ty shook his head and almost cursed as he realized he didn't know if the pretty lady took cream or sugar or both. "Damn it." Grabbing up the entire plastic tray, he headed back to his office, stopping at the door just before using his backside to open it. "Get home and get off that foot."

"Ha! Ha!"

"Well, I kind of doubt we're going to need your services as a medic today since you and I are the only ones here."

Ty made his way back into his office, only to find the pretty lady going through the papers on his desk. Personal papers. She seemed to be holding up his financial statement from the bank. "Excuse me?"

Instead of letting the paper go, she had the audacity to hold up her hand as if he were interrupting her. Ty felt his irritation welling up to smother any other thoughts her luscious little body had stirred.

"Um, sweetheart, that's not what I meant by make yourself at home." He waited until she looked up and flashed what he hoped was his best smile, all the while trying to bite back the other comment he had about nosy women. "I, uh, hope you like doughnuts."

Chapter 2

Maddy glanced up from the financial statement she had been caught reading and gave him a thorough once-over. So handsome. So financially unstable. According to the statement, any third quarter profits had been gobbled up by overextending. The bank was probably breathing down his neck. *And what a neck.* She blinked at the gorgeous man who seemed to have moved from bemused stranger to gracious host. She felt a shiver as a cold raindrop slid down her left breast. Maybe the shiver was because he was sexier than hell and the attraction was heating her chilled skin. She watched as his mouth opened. He was speaking to her, but all she could see was how kissable his lips were.

"Sugar?"

"What?"

"Your coffee. Sugar? Cream?"

Maddy swallowed the lump in her suddenly dry throat.

"Um…yes, thank you."

She accepted the cup of steaming coffee as well as the doughnut and even sat where he indicated…away from his chair. The room, as well as the jacket smelled of him, woodsy clean and purely male. Why was she noticing now? Right, all she could do was notice him. His button down shirt hugged his broad shoulders and revealed a hint of the white t-shirt beneath it. Her gaze lowered from those shoulders down to his trim waist. His jeans hugged his hips and defined strong legs beneath the fitted and faded denim.

Purely delicious in denim.

She tried not imagining what kind of body lay beneath his clothes. She sat back and watched as he stood behind his desk. His eyes met hers and he smiled at her again. An easy smile. An honest smile. Nothing like Teddy's slick grin, all too ready. Ready Teddy. She shivered despite herself at the thought of her first and only time with Teddy. She hadn't wanted to think about that horrid evening, but that slick smile of his had led her to his bed and down the aisle. She was never taking that trip again with the Von Housen snake.

He had been just as slick in his lovemaking. If one could call it that. It had been more like an exercise in frustration than a glorious first time. She recalled how Teddy had heaved a tired sigh and merely told her that she would get better at it.

Another slap in the face. Why hadn't she seen it before now? Why hadn't she clued in before now that there had to be another reason for him wanting to marry her? And this handsome Kirkland guy was right in the thick of things. She stared at the tall drink of water that stood before her. *Dark hair, darker eyes, and a body to die for. Why couldn't Teddy have looked like him?*

He blinked and looked slightly unnerved. Good, she wanted him unnerved. Okay he was sexier than hell and built for sex. She wanted him more than unnerved. She wouldn't mind him, period.

"Something wrong, sweetheart?" His voice seemed to touch her with its low husky timbre. However, his choice of names for her left her feeling as if he wanted to put her in her place. *Arrogant cowboy.*

"Sweetheart?" she countered with a practiced lift of her brow.

"Well, you never told me your name."

"Madison."

"Ty," he said and stood again. Leaning his tall frame over his desk, he extended his hand. She stood and slid her fingers against the warmth of his rough palm to touch his fingers. Again, their eyes met and held. Heat shot through her and her breath caught. She hoped to hell that he hadn't noticed.

"I, uh, couldn't help but notice your car." He pulled his hand away and she watched him wiggle his fingers. His eyes darkened. *Had he felt the heat, too?*

Her thong dampened and she struggled for air as well as her voice. "Yes. It was a birthday present from my godfather."

"Wow."

"Yeah, I used to think that way, too."

"Excuse me?"

"Oh, don't get me wrong. It's a great car."

"I'll say. A car like that probably ran him upwards of sixty thou."

"I never asked."

"He must really love you."

"I would rather not discuss him with you, if you don't mind."

"Whoa, sweetheart. Didn't realize I had hit a sore spot."

"Hit a sore spot?"

She placed her half-eaten doughnut and coffee down on his desk. He continued to stare at her as she dragged his lamb's wool jacket from her body. She felt his gaze rest on the swell of her breasts and she watched his Adam's apple slide up and down his throat as he swallowed. The heat in his eyes was turning her on and her nipples hardened from the hungry look on his face.

She was a lawyer. She needed be professional about this visit. It was not like her to think about sex, however, looking at the denim-clad hunk, sex was exactly what she was thinking about.

Maddy draped his jacket on the back of her chair.

"So, Ty, tell me about Kirkland, Incorporated."

Anything to stop me from thinking of you naked.

He shrugged and spread his hands wide. "Not much to tell, really. We, uh, I had the opportunity to speak with Mr. Bambardi and Mr. Bellini a while back about merging some of our assets."

"I see." But she didn't see. *This was the huge conglomerate that Teddy had warned her was going to ruin their lives?* "Tell me, how did you decide on Bambardi and Bellini?"

"How did I decide?" She studied his movements as he thought about her question. He sat back and brought his pen to his firm lips. He slid it across those kissable lips and appeared deep in thought. She watched as he pulled his features into a level expression. He leaned forward. If he was trying to be intimidating, he was only coming off as sexy. "I wanted to expand my company. We serve three facilities here in Wyoming and I felt that Canada would be the perfect place to extend our services. I felt an alliance with Bambardi and Bellini could benefit Kirkland Gas in further exploration in natural resources."

"An alliance? My, doesn't that sound almost like a marriage?"

"Beg your pardon?"

"You know. Marriage. A wedding?" *He's cute but kind of clueless.* "So, whom did you meet with at Bambardi and Bellini?"

"Is this some kind of test? Mr. Bambardi. Why?" His tone was neutral but his body language indicated a sudden uneasiness.

"I see. And did you ever speak to Mr. Bellini?"

"Only in a conference call. Apparently, he was too busy to attend the meeting." Irritation filled his voice as he related this.

"I don't understand," Madison spoke her feelings. She really didn't understand. This Ty Kirkland made it sound as if he stood no chance in doing any business with her father and godfather. *So was he lying?* "I'm not certain I understand your meaning, or your tone for that matter."

"Sorry if I sound a bit perturbed. Let me just say that I was made to feel I was taking up their valuable time and I felt I was being dismissed out of hand. Without even being given a chance to explain my position, I was shown to the door with a 'Thank you for your time, Kirkland. We aren't interested in expanding at the moment. If we change our mind, we'll let you know.'"

This is really fascinating, what the hell is going on? And where did Teddy get his information from? Sudden paranoia maybe? Hearing Kirkland's take on the meeting, coupled with the financial statement, Kirkland Gas looked ready for a takeover, not a merger. Wasn't that how her father and godfather rolled, though? Get a company interested with pretty promises, talk of expanding, and get them to sink all of their liquid assets into some crazy venture, invite them up for a big meeting and drop the bomb on them. Only to push them into a corner, ready to accept anything on any terms. Yep. Kirkland Gas had been set up for a takeover.

"Is that why you are here?"

Oh, now he sounds paranoid. Men! "Call it curiosity."

"That's fair enough." He leaned even closer and his smile carried a "sex her out of her jeans" look. Her heart picked up speed. She was almost tempted to let him have her jeans and any other article of clothing he wanted. "Tell you what, Madison. Why don't I take you on a tour of the plant and then to dinner tonight? It has been awhile since I've been able to show a pretty girl a good time." He even dropped his voice down an octave for added seduction. The effect screamed sexual encounter and she shook off an image of having him take her right there on his cluttered desk. Her pussy twitched and could only imagine what the sexy cowboy was packing in those jeans. However, none of this was making sense. He had to be lying. And more than likely thought he could turn her head with the promise of food and moonlight.

"Dinner? My, you work fast, cowboy. I just want to know one thing."

"Name it. What else can I show you?" He was definitely coming on to her and her body was telling her to answer him in kind. *However...*

"You could start with the truth."

"Excuse me?"

"The truth? All of your pretty talk of merging and expanding…"

"What are you getting at?" Gone was the smile as he rose from his chair.

"It would appear to me that Kirkland Gas is in dire straits. You are overextended and I wonder if you can even make next month's payroll." *Pretty yes, but I'm not stupid, buddy, despite your sex appeal turning my mind to mush.*

He reached up, raking his hand across the back of his neck, in what she guessed was an attempt at maintaining his cool. He apparently failed as the pen went flying down onto his desk. "Is that right?"

"What deal have you worked out with Bambardi and Bellini?"

"Deal? What the hell are you talking about?" He looked confused. He was going to be hell of a lot more than confused when she was done with him.

She was positive that she was as angry with him as she was turned on. This rogue cowboy had caused enough damage to her world. "Come now, Ty. You can tell me."

"Just who are you?"

"I told you. Madison."

"Well, Madison, I'm starting to get the feeling you aren't a representative from Bambardi and Bellini."

"I don't recall ever saying I was."

"Then exactly who are you?" His hands were on his hips and it looked like he was ready to come over the desk.

As tempting as that could be, she banished that image and kicked her temper into gear. "I'm Madison Bellini. The woman whose life you are ruining!"

"You're who?"

"Madison Bellini! Franco Bellini is my father. Joseph Bambardi is my godfather. Yesterday was supposed to be the happiest day of my life. But thanks to you…"

"Whoa, whoa! What the hell are you talking about?"

"My marriage, more like the fatal mistake of almost having one."

She was supposed to be in full and heightened anger, so why was her body reacting to the visible hardening of his? She had never felt her body weeping before when in the throes of her temper. But this man standing before her, his hands on his hips, looking as if he could pounce on her any second made her body hum with hunger and a desire for him to do just that.

He pushed his hand through his hair in frustration. "Run that by me again?"

Don't do it, Maddy. Don't let him get over on you with his sexier-than-hell actions.

"I'm through talking. You can consider any hopes for a contract with Bambardi and Bellini a dismal failure, pretty much like this dump!"

With that, she spun on her cowboy boots and was gone.

As Ty watched her storm out of his office, he tried to make sense of this strange encounter. The way she had flared her nostrils and pursed her lips, Ty wasn't sure if she had been begging to be kissed or pulling a spoiled princess routine that should have landed her across his thighs for a spanking. His cock ached and stiffened at the thought of doing either one or both. The thought of her soft curves pressed against him while his hand caressed and slapped her ass was damn near his undoing.

Turning, he watched her head back out through the parking lot. The sky was clearing and the sunlight bounced off the pavement, making his head hurt to see it.

He raked a hand through his hair again and thought quickly. She had said his hopes for a contract were over. *What hopes? Am I still in the running? And this was Franco Bellini's daughter?* One phone call to daddy would stop him dead in his tracks.

He stared after her as she lowered the top on her flashy yellow Corvette. *Damn her, anyway!* Spoiled little princess in her flashy car, rubbing his nose in his own failure She held all of the cards. One phone call from her and he would never make payroll next month. All of his employees were counting on him. Some of them had worked at Kirkland Gas since his father had started the company. They were counting on him. Their families were counting on him. He hadn't heard from the bank either, making him feel even more desperate. *This could not be happening.*

He had to stop her.

Even as he thought it, he heard her screaming out of the parking lot, tires sliding on the slick pavement. Grabbing up his jacket, he tore out of the office after her. Jumping into his truck, he tore out behind her, trying to catch up with her. He needed to try and explain things to her. Finding out what the hell she had been talking about would help, too. He wasn't about to lose out on this contract over a misunderstanding, no matter how crazy it was.

How had he ruined her life? *The happiest day of her life was probably when someone left the door open to her padded cell.*

She must be some kind of nut.

Beautiful, but a nut.

And she drove like an idiot. The road was slick as hell and she was flying. As he drew closer, he could see her hair whipping back in the breeze. She was probably freezing in that wind. His mind flashed on her as she had stood in his office, nipples straining and calling to him from under her denim shirt. He imagined those nipples were fairly screaming right now in this weather.

Stop it, Ty. She said you were ruining her life? She's damn close to ruining yours! She's not tightly wrapped, ol' buddy. Just stop her from wrecking everything.

Madison looked up again to find the same truck from the parking lot appearing in her rearview mirror.

"That arrogant rogue in denim."

Madison tried again to fish her cell phone from her bag of cheese puffs as she sped down the rain-slicked two-lane road. A quick glance in her rearview told her that maniac was not only following her, he was gaining on her.

"Who the hell does he think he is?" Her emotions were out of control despite all efforts to rein them in. "I'm too smart to be taken in by broad shoulders, a pair of cowboy boots and an ass that beckons to be grabbed. The son of a bitch!"

What does he think? I'm just going to pull over and fall into his arms?

She glanced in her mirror again. Sure enough, he was still in pursuit. What did he think he was going to do? Run her off the road? "Now he thinks he's *Smokey and the Bandit?*"

She couldn't believe any of this. "Oh, B-reaker-1-9. I have an idiot on my ass!"

Anger swamped her as she felt a rebellious tear slide down her face, followed by another and another. She tried to wipe them away, hold onto the steering wheel and fish through cheese puffs again for her phone. To her mounting frustration, each time she thought she had a grip on her little phone, it slid further down into the bag.

She no longer understood any of this. Had she merely been a pawn in everyone else's scheme? Before she could answer, she heard her cell phone ringing.

Damnit! And damn him! God help the person at the other end of the phone!

She reached further into the bag just as she neared the covered bridge. Her tires hit mud and skidded, causing her Corvette to fishtail wildly inside the bridge. The back of her car struck something, jerking her hands from the steering wheel. She was staring at the wooden side of the bridge for a slow split second before it loomed right before her eyes.

"Oh hell!"

Mud spurted up from her wheels and over her windshield. She heard the snapping of wood as her front end hit something. She was suddenly hit in the face and slammed back against her seat. Then nothing. She heard nothing. But she felt as if she were falling. Her face hurt. Grief overtook her as she realized she was falling. She waited for her life to flash before her eyes but it never came. She didn't have a life, only an existence of being everyone's puppet.

* * * *

Ty gripped the steering wheel as his own truck splashed through the mud just at the entrance to the bridge. He stared as he watched the scene before him. Her yellow Corvette disappeared into the wall of the bridge leaving behind a huge hole and a shaft of light behind. He heard the splash as if in slow motion. Tires screeched as he hit the brakes hard.

"Geez!" he muttered as he slammed the truck in reverse. "Geez." He turned back to make sure he had clearance and backed the truck off the road, only to watch the top of her car sliding under the murky river's surface. "What the hell?"

Was she still in the car? He jumped from his truck and tore down the bank, diving into the river and heading for the bubbles that were rising and dancing on the water. Diving under, he fought the current surrounding her car and moved inside with her. She was not moving and still in her seat belt, trapped in her watery tomb.

Digging his hand into his pants pocket, he felt for his pocket knife. Finally, he found it and using one arm to hold her to the back of the seat, he began to saw on the seatbelt that held her trapped. Finally, lungs aching, he hauled her unresponsive body from the driver's seat and headed away from the car with her in tow.

He broke the water's murky surface and hauled her over to the bank. Laying her gently onto the wet ground, he realized his hands were trembling. Taking hold her of her shoulders, he shook her, trying to rouse her.

"Hey. Hey, come on. Sweetheart. Madison!! Shit!" Grasping her turned up nose between his thumb and forefinger, he tilted her head back and lowered his mouth to her lifeless lips.

Blowing his warm breath into her, he counted as he went. Compressions to her body produced nothing. Again, he fused his mouth over her lips and he felt it, pressure from her lips onto his. She had locked her lips to his and was not letting go.

He gave in to her as he felt the tip of her tongue peek through and test the tip of his.

A shock of carnal electricity shot through his brain and down to his jeans as he deepened the kiss, tasting her sweet mouth, river water and all. He heard her choke and released her immediately. Rolling her to her side, he whacked her soundly on the back.

She coughed up more water and lay still, until he rolled her back and lifted her gently to lean up against his chest. He could tell she was shaky and weaving against his thighs. The contact was electrifying. He heard her mumbling, "Gonna marry a cowboy."

"Are you with me, Madison?" He leaned down to see her staring at the water. Looking over he saw no signs of her car anywhere. All he could see was a few pieces of debris and a cluster of cheese puffs floating on the top.

"Ducks!" she murmured.

He let out a loud slow whistle at her alarming state of mind. "Okay, Madison, look at me, sweetheart. Do you remember me?"

He watched as her dark eyes roamed greedily over his face. "Cowboy. Gonna marry a cowboy."

"Come on. Sweetheart, can you tell me your name?"

Madison seemed to nod slowly and made no effort to escape Ty's arms.

"What's your name?"

"Madison, Madison Bellini," she said, gaining a fraction more strength to her voice.

"Okay. That's good. Do you know where you are?"

Madison's eyes grew wide, and Ty was sure they were the darkest brown he had ever seen. "Utah?"

"Not exactly. You're in Wyoming. Do you know where that is?"

"Somewhere south of Alberta."

He grinned at her comeback, despite the seriousness of the situation. Trust a Canadian to respond like that. "You're a long way from home, sweetheart. Do you know why?"

"No."

"You said something about a marrying a cowboy."

"Yep."

"So you're here to get married?"

"I don't know; I can't remember." Her lashes seem to blink and act like a stage curtain lifting to reveal her big brown eyes filling with tears.

If she didn't remember, then she didn't remember him. She didn't remember threatening to drop a dime to dear old daddy on him either. Surely, once she was thinking clearly, saving her life would rate him a stay of execution.

"Madison, do you remember anything other than your name?"

She stared up at him, as if she were searching his face for the answers that eluded her.

"No." Her nose scrunched slightly as tears moved down her cheeks. She gave a small sniff. "I don't remember anything or anyone or..." She narrowed her eyes on Ty. "You, who are you?"

Ty could not believe his luck. His original plan had just been to stop her from calling daddy. Then he had saved her life. Everyone liked a hero. But the way she was looking up at him made his world tilt crazily. Suddenly, he had a better idea. "Why, darlin', don't you remember?"

She shook her head.

"Sure you do, about marrying the cowboy?" he prompted.

His words seemed to register on her pretty face.

"Yes. I'm gonna marry a cowboy."

Those words prompted him into action. He felt as if he were plunging off of that bridge himself, with no way to stop. It was too late. This was a way better idea than the whole 'hero' thing. "Well, darlin', I'm Ty, your cowboy fiancé."

"Okay." Her dark lashes fluttered and her eyes closed as her body went limp.

"Great. I've done it now." Ty tried to feel remorse, but couldn't. There was no way she was dropping that dime on him. Ty smiled, rather happy with his performance. *Hero rescuing Franco Bellini's daughter was good.* "Fiancé is even better."

Chapter 3

Ty stretched his long frame over the sleeping woman in his bed and braced himself as he worked the buttons loose on her damp shirt. So many thoughts were swirling through his brain. He could still hear the splintering of wood and sickening sound of her scream as her Corvette had done the unthinkable, sailing as if in slow motion as it headed nose first into the murky Medicine Bow River.

Had it been unthinkable? She had started to cry as she had stormed out of his office. Had she meant to drive her car off the bridge? Had she meant to try and take her own life?

This was crazy! Was she crazy? She was Bellini's daughter. What had she been doing all the way in Wyoming? Why come all that way just to look me up? As far as he knew, any association with Bambardi and Bellini had ended after that fateful conference call. The one where he had been dismissed so effectively. He swore he would never treat anyone the way he had been treated. No matter how successful he became. Of course, he was never going to be as successful as Bambardi and Bellini.

Returning his thoughts to the woman lying on his quilt, he pushed out a sigh as his knuckles brushed the smooth skin under her damp shirt.

As he slid the shirt gently over her soft shoulders, all thoughts of business fled. His gaze warmed as he took in her skimpy lace bra and the smooth skin swelling above the flimsy cups. All thoughts headed south as he felt his jeans tighten again. Gently, his fingers dipped beneath the clasp tucked safely between her firm round breasts and undid the small plastic hook. He inhaled a deep but ragged breath and allowed the delicate lace to fall to the sides. Her breasts were perfect and the nipples taut from the chill. They lay stiff before him, begging to be touched or sucked. Quickly, he removed the lacy bra, discarding it to the floor with her wet boots and shirt. Staring back down at her, he fought the urge to take one of those taut rosy peaks into his mouth. The thought caused his cock to ache.

He couldn't resist moving his palms down her ribs and he felt her shiver under his touch. A quick glance up found her still sleeping. At least, he hoped she was merely sleeping. Reaching for the fastening of her jeans, he opened the zipper and began tugging the sodden denim down her hips, uncovering her smooth skin and exposing her to his heated gaze. His nostrils flared as he worked them down her legs, finally sending them into the floor. Moving back up, he let his fingers trail up and over her knees, her thighs and hooked them under the waistband of her lacy thong panties. Dragging in a deep breath, he swept them down her thighs and legs, all the while fighting to ignore the gnawing need pushing against his own zipper.

"Geez, you are beautiful, Madison Bellini," he said softly, pushing her hair from her eyes. When her mouth parted slightly, his resolve broke and he lowered his head to hers. His intention just to brush his lips to hers. He couldn't stop there, however and the pressure of the kiss intensified. The full softness fueled his desire and his tongue slipped inside her mouth. He worked gently, exploring her mouth, while at the same time he imagined the throb in his jeans working in and out of her wet walls. He lifted his lips. Still she slept. Her lips were puffy from the kiss. He bit back a groan as he imagined her pretty features and sexy mouth as she climaxed in his arms. Grabbing up the edge of his quilt, he covered her as best he could, tucking in the edges to keep her from freezing or rolling out of his bed.

Reaching for his robe from the hook on the back of his bedroom door, he headed to the mudroom and the dryer. She needed warmth and it was either going to be his heated robe surrounding her or his heated body. Slamming the dryer door closed, he turned it on and fished out his cell phone from his jacket pocket.

He almost laughed as Jordan picked up his phone immediately.

"Get over here," Ty ordered.

"I thought you wanted me to get off my foot?"

"Later. I need your expertise."

"Why? What's up?"

"Get over here. I'll explain then."

* * * *

Ten minutes later found Ty splashing cold water on his face, trying to erase the memory of the beauty in his bed, now wrapped snugly and seductively in his robe. He should never have allowed himself to touch her the way he had. Now he was paying the price for moving his mouth over hers. The taste of her lips still excited the tip of his tongue, sizzling his brain as he imagined her whimper as he tasted her mouth. His tongue had thrust into her mouth as he imagined his cock working her pussy. Even now, it throbbed behind his zipper.

"Ty?" Grabbing up a towel, he looked at his face once again in the mirror, wondering if what he was about to do was best. Shaking his head, he knew he could only hope it was.

"Yeah," he called out as he made his way into the kitchen.

There was Jordan, leaning against the sink, his medical bag on the table. "What happened? You okay?"

"I'm fine. It's um…look, I need for you to swear you won't tell anyone about this. Not Mom or Dad, or any of the volunteer rescue guys, no one!"

He watched as Jordan's eyebrows drew together in concern.

"Tell them what?"

"Jordy, I mean it!"

"All right, geez."

"Come with me and bring your bag."

"I am already hating this." He sounded far from amused as Ty led him to his bedroom and inside. "Who is that?"

"Well, that's why I need your word that you won't tell anyone."

"I don't get it."

"Do you remember earlier when I needed a doughnut?"

"Yeah." Jordan had already moved closer to the woman in the bed and was moving his fingers along the scratches and the bump that rose from her forehead.

"Well, I thought at first that she was a representative from Bambardi and Bellini."

"And?"

"She's not. Well, not exactly. She...um, is Bellini's daughter."

"I don't get it."

"I don't either, but she was clearly upset."

"Why? What did you do to her?"

"Nothing! She was threatening to call Franco Bellini and stop any chances I ever had with getting that contract."

"The contract? I thought they weren't interested?"

"That's what they said."

"Then why was she threatening you?"

"I don't know. I never got the chance to find out."

"Why not?"

"She drove her car off the bridge and straight into Medicine Bow River."

"She should be at the hospital."

"I can't do that."

"Why the hell not? She could have a concussion, Ty."

"If I take her to the hospital, they're going to ask questions. If they find out she tried to kill herself, they'll lock her up."

"For her own good."

"What if it was just road conditions? She has a right to explain herself." He had a lot on his mind and didn't need any questions, especially from his 'do-gooder' brother. The last thing Ty needed was a kick of conscience until he could figure things out. "I need you to fix her up and keep an eye on her until I get back."

"Back from where?"

"I have to go and clean up that mess she left in the river."

"That's illegal. Covering up a crime is just as illegal as not reporting one."

Shoving his hands in his pockets, Ty stared down at the floor. "I'm not about to let her get locked up before I know for sure what happened on that bridge. Besides, she kind of thinks we're engaged."

"She what?"

"She was confused after I fished her out and she thinks we're engaged."

"Now, how did she get that idea?" Jordan's tone held accusation. It matched the look on his face that turned to disbelief.

"I kind of told her we were."

"Are you crazy?"

"Probably. I'm not sure what made me tell her that."

"Oh, I do. You want that contract."

"You didn't see her, Jordan. You didn't see the pain in her eyes."

"It was probably due to this knot on her head. So, she was conscious?"

"Yeah."

"Long enough for you to let her think you two are engaged. What the hell were you thinking?"

"Enough! It's done. Stay here. Keep her quiet. I'll be back."

"You're asking me to break the law."

"I'm asking you to help me. Damn it, just help me."

Ty raked an angry hand through his hair and waited. He watched as Jordan made a face and shrugged tiredly.

"Fine."

He wasn't there. He can't judge me. He would've done the same thing, even if he won't admit it. He walked to the door and hoped he was making the right decision.

* * * *

Madison tried to wake up, but she didn't want to leave the wonderful dream she was having. Her wonderful strong cowboy held her in his arms, removing her fear and placing kisses along her neck and lower. She knew the heat from his touch, his mouth, and felt it surrounding her. She felt protected, safe, and loved. This was what it felt like to be loved. Rolling to her side, she forced her eyes to open. She found herself staring at a bedroom she had never seen before. She tried to sit up and push the covers from her. She felt tired and confused.

"What the hell?"

Swinging her legs over the side of the big bed, she tried to recall her surroundings. The bed and dresser were mismatched, but both were big and similar in that they appeared to be antique. She was definitely in a man's room and not in the motel where she had last awakened. One thing for certain, no motel or hotel had a bed as comfortable as the one she now sat on, not even the high end resorts she frequented.

Sliding off the high mattress, her toes touched the rug and she tested her strength to stand. She felt strange, but not really dizzy. She remembered talking with someone, yelling at him, looking up at him, watching him smile down at her. His dark eyes filled with concern, anger, and even shock. She remembered his strong arms holding her, warm thighs surrounding her, his mouth on hers. The shiver that ran under the robe she wore felt like an electric tingle, warming her even further under the warm thick terry cloth surrounding her naked body.

Yes, he had held her. He had touched her. He had kissed her. And his voice, so deep, so strong. It was if she could hear it from far away. *Who is he?*

Making her way slowly out of the room and into the long hallway, she noticed a shaft of light coming through the window at the end of the hall. It was daytime. She moved down the stairs and neared the sound of his voice, stopping as she heard another male voice. Pressed up against the wall, she listened as the voices became louder.

"Man, you have totally lost your mind over this girl!"

"I know what I'm doing, Jordan."

"Oh, so what's the big plan, Romeo? Get her to fall in love with you? Just so you can get a contract? And that's assuming her memory doesn't come back. How much time do you think your little plans needs?"

"I don't know. I didn't start out to tell her anything. She just laid it right in my lap, you know?"

"Then, where does that leave her?"

"I haven't really thought that far. But you should have heard her. She was gonna call daddy and ruin any chance I ever had of getting the contract with Bambardi and Bellini and I have no idea why. She's like Alicia, man. Born with a silver spoon in her mouth, lording it over everyone. She'll get over it."

"Who are you?"

"Don't start with me, Jordan. Just do what I ask. Take that stuff to your place and don't let Mom and Dad know what's going on."

"You're insane. What if someone saw you?"

"No one saw me."

"And what happens when the sheriff sees that someone has taken out the side of the bridge? You don't think he's not going to drag the river? He's not the sharpest tool in the shed, Ty, but even he is going to notice a huge, gaping hole in a covered bridge."

Bambardi and Bellini. Do I work there? Covered bridge? She remembered a covered bridge. Huddling deeper into her warm robe, she decided it was time to get some answers. Taking a deep breath, she turned the corner and stepped into the kitchen. She saw him immediately, standing there with his back to her, soaking wet, and running his strong hand over the back of his neck.

"Yeah..." he said to the man hidden from her sight. "I just need some time, that's all."

"Oh, you'll get time, and plenty of it. In the slammer."

"Jordan, just do what I say and get that stuff out of here.

"Shit." She jumped at the sudden outburst and gasped as the other man stormed outside, slamming the door behind him. Her gasp drew the soaking wet man's attention. The heat she found in the dark eyes that found her got her attention.

It was as if he was touching her from across the room. She pulled the robe closer together as he took a step toward her.

His dark eyes found hers and he stepped even closer. "Was I interrupting?" Her voice was weak. Maybe it was because he was pure male and sexier than hell.

"No, my brother was just leaving." He was soaking wet and her gaze dropped taking in his large frame. His denim shirt hung open revealing a tanned and well defined chest. His stomach was flat and muscles rippled across his abdomen in carved perfection. His body was a piece of art and her body heated and tingled as she lowered her gaze. The long sleeves of his shirt were unbuttoned at the wrists. His body narrowed at the hips and the faded denim clung to him. His strong legs defined by his wet jeans. She noticed the toes of his worn boots. He was a flesh and blood cowboy. Her pussy twitched; she wanted him. She wanted to know if he tasted as good as he had in her dream. His handsome features morphed into concern. "How are you feeling?"

"Confused, but fine."

His dark eyes took her in from her toes up. When his eyes met hers they were darker, the desire apparent. He darted a look to her lips and her pussy twitched again. Heat flamed her skin and desire pooled between her legs. She watched his Adam's apple rise and fall as he swallowed hard. He was aroused and she intended to use it to her full advantage. She closed the distance between them. "On second thought, why don't you tell me how I feel?"

He grabbed the belt of the robe as she reached for the bulge in his pants. His cock was solid beneath her touch, solid and large. His head bent toward hers and her lashes fluttered closed. His lips came down hungry on hers and her mouth parted for him. The belt of the robe gave way and the soft heavy terry fell open. His hands slid to her waist and over her skin. Every nerve in her body blazed and wanted more.

Her hand tightened around his erection and stroked it through the layer of his wet clothes as his tongue thrust into her mouth. His hands worked up her body and he groaned against their entwined tongues. First caressing, he then cupped her breasts. Her knees weakened and she moved her hand to support herself by placing both hands on his shoulders. He was cold to the touch and wet. His hands and tongue continued to explore her.

She pulled her lips from his and his long dark lashes fluttered open. She struggled for air as his hands circled her waist. "You're cold and wet."

"Help me," he rasped.

The sexy whisper heated her body. She wasn't sure what was happening, but she felt dangerous and daring. She needed him more than air. She pushed the wet denim off his shoulders and allowed the shirt to hit the tile of the kitchen floor.

His eyes darkened with desire. With her heart racing, she placed her hands on his bare chest. His smooth tanned skin was cool to her touch and he let out a slow hiss. He wrapped his arms back around her and claimed her mouth with his in a fierce hunger. Her mouth parted on impact and his tongue slid inside. A moan left her as he deepened the kiss and splayed his hands up her back. She reached for the buckle on his belt and quickly undid it, the button and the zipper. She dipped her hand down across his strong stomach and into the heat that awaited her.

Sliding her fingers down, the tips stroked his rock-hard cock. His hands moved to her shoulders and pulled her lips from his. She opened her eyes and blinked.

"Madison, I'm going to take you right here."

Her lips curved into a smile. She took in his ragged breath and pushed her fingers further down. Wrapping them around his erection she caressed it and teased it. "And what's stopping you?"

He placed his hands beneath the robe and grabbed her hips. He drew her in close to him as she removed her hand from his pants. He pressed her breasts hard against his chest. Her nipples hardened from the coolness of his body and the heat of the moment. As her hands slid to the sides of his jeans, he gently moved her against the wall.

One of his hands trailed down to the wet folds between her legs. She pulled his jeans and boxers down. The action caused his large cock to spring to life. He leaned in and kissed her lips and danced his tongue over them as his fingers teased and eventually one slipped inside her.

"God, you're wet," he groaned, working his finger in and out of her before withdrawing it and bringing his hand again to her hip. He caressed her skin, sliding around to the flesh of her ass. He cupped her tightly and she placed her hands on his shoulders for support. He lifted her in a fluid swoop above his cock. The tip pressed against her pussy then entered. He let out another groan as he held her there. After allowing her a moment to adjust to his size, he began to thrust slowly. "So tight," he choked out before sliding his tongue over her bottom lip. She strengthened her hold on his shoulders and met his tongue with hers. His thrusts picked her up and gently rocked her body against the wall. His cock filled and caressed the walls of her pussy. The pressure continued to build inside of her.

Never had she ever thought sex could be like this. His thrusts became harder and she moaned against his mouth as he picked up even more speed. Her breasts moved against his skin from the motion and teased her nipples to a frenzied state. The pressure finally broke and she pulled her tongue and lips from his, resting against the wall as a shudder overtook her. Her walls tightened around his cock and pulsed as she climaxed. A loud carnal groan left him as he slammed into her hard and squeezed her ass beneath his hands. His cock throbbed as his release squirted into her.

She gasped for breath as, struggling to breathe as well, he rested his forehead against her shoulder. Holy hell, if this was what her life was here, she couldn't imagine wanting to be anywhere else.

Chapter 4

Maddy snuggled deeper under the quilt, dreaming of her aunt and uncle. She sighed and breathed deep. She was there with them on their horse ranch. *Teddy was there. Why was Teddy there? Where was the cowboy?*

A gasp of horror shot her from her idyllic dream and brought her sitting straight up in the bed. She glanced around. Her hands touched and grabbed soft quilt and crisp sheets. She was in a bed. *The cowboy's bed. Ty's bed.*

Holy hell!

She remembered the sex in the kitchen. Her nipples tightened and fluid pooled between her legs at the memory. She was now in his bed and everything was kind of fuzzy from the intense orgasm.

She whimpered as she remembered weakened knees and Ty swooping her up into his arms. He had carried her.

She inhaled deeply. *Hell, the room smelled like him.*

"Oh, my God," she whispered and looked around, frantic now at the thought of what had just happened. He was not her fiancé. She had made love to Ty Kirkland, the man who was not her fiancé, against a wall? He had lied to her? He was lying to her?

Before she could move beyond that thought, he appeared in the doorway, wearing the robe he had taken from her and working a towel over his damp dark hair.

He moved closer, a smile hovering on his firm lips and hunger in his heated gaze.

What is going on?

As he drew nearer, she offered him a shy smile, if for nothing else, to stop the quickening of her heart. He crawled onto the bed and moved her to lie back as he stretched his long frame over her.

She offered her lips up for another taste of him, if for no other reason, to buy her some time.

No sooner had his lips moved over hers, pulling them into the heat of his mouth, than she felt the same heated zing shooting through her, flexing her toes as he untied the belt holding the robe closed over his magnificent body.

"Help me," he told her again and she found her hands moving the heavy terry robe over his shoulders and down his powerful arms with alarming speed.

He reached for her waist and pulled her to him, snaking her leg around his hip as he entered her briefly, giving her another taste of what they had just shared.

Her breath caught in her throat as she recalled with clarity the cries he had wrung from her just moments earlier.

But he's not my fiancé.

He moved deeper inside her, pulling her to him as his lips coursed along her neck, his breath beating hot pelts of excitement against her tingling skin.

Her fingers wrapped around damp strands of his dark hair, pulling him closer still as she met him thrust for thrust. His words of praise resonated within her as he pulled her even closer. Growls of pleasure sounded against her ear as he found a rhythm.

This was nothing like Teddy's attempt at spearing her. He had ridiculed her the whole time he had been inside her. Ty was glorifying her with each movement, letting her know with his words and his body that he worshipped her.

But how is that possible? What could he possibly gain by——

"Oh!" Her outburst stopped Ty and he moved back and peered down at her.

"Did I hurt you?"

"No," she breathed, trying to hold onto him, to feel what she had before. Then she recalled the meeting she had had with him…the contract.

"Easy, easy. I'll get you there."

"I have no doubt," she rasped as his cock moved faster and harder. Pressure slowly crept across her belly and her hips bucked slightly. All thoughts fizzled out and were replaced with wanting him deeper inside her. "Harder." She ground her pussy against him and he growled again.

Lifting her head and wrapping her arms around his neck, she pulled him closer to her. She teased his lips with her tongue and was met by his snaking out and dancing with hers. Her nipples got the full impact of his solid chest as they rubbed up and down against it with each of his thrusts. The ribbon of pleasure built and she met his thrusts harder wanting him even deeper inside her. Finally the ribbon unfurled and she pulled her lips from his. Her body shook harder and her pussy walls squeezed tight around his cock.

A loud primal groan left Ty as he thrust one final time, hard enough to move them slightly up the bed. His cock pulsed and again he felt his red hot release empty inside of her.

Her walls twitched and her shoulders moved sending a ripple of another orgasm through her body.

Ty pressed his chest harder against her as he buried his face in her hair. His chest was damp from his shower or maybe from the sweat of their lovemaking.

What the hell was she thinking? Right, the head on her shoulders had shut down and her pussy had taken over all thought process.

What am I going to do now?

* * * *

The house seemed quiet as Maddy made her way into what appeared to be the living room. She eased onto the sofa and looked about her. The room gave off a warm and friendly atmosphere, reminding her of her aunt and uncle's living room.

Was this Ty Kirkland's house? She was alone in Ty Kirkland's house.

Alone.

She reached for the phone on the end table and hesitated, debating. Quickly, she dialed the number for Beth's cell phone. She tired to figure out what to say and dreaded hearing the update of the wedding fiasco from hell.

Her friend answered on the first ring and Maddy could barely make out anything with all the yelling.

"What?"

"You disappeared? Your parents tracked your cell phone signal and lost you somewhere in Wyoming!"

"They what?" Surely, she had misheard. Her parents weren't that controlling, were they? An image of her successful father came to her mind. *Oh hell yeah they were. Son of a bitch!*

"They are desperate to find you, Maddy. You need to call them. The press is not buying the spa story any longer and they are calling you the runaway bride."

"The press?"

"Oh, my God! Your mother is coming unglued!"

Shaking her head slightly, she tried to clear the cobwebs. She remembered driving through Wyoming, but...

"Kirkland," she whispered and recalled her first meeting with Ty Kirkland. It had just happened, over coffee and a doughnut. Not with flowers and champagne, but over a business deal. Troubled thoughts from earlier resurfaced. He wanted the contract with Bambardi and Bellini and was lying to her in order to get it. *That son-of-a-bitch. He's as bad as my father!*

"What did you say, Maddy?"

"Nothing."

"Sophia is pregnant."

Again, she had to have misheard. "I'm sorry. What?"

"Sophia is pregnant?"

"Teddy's?"

"We can only assume, since she is quite the slut. He's over the moon, but for appearance sake, has broken it off with her on account of your father."

Trust dear old Dad to bulldoze his own way. "Oh, this is getting ridiculous!" *No this is what cheesy movies are made from.*

"You have to come back and set everyone straight. Teddy's losing it."

"Sounds like they have all lost it," she whispered and rubbed her throbbing temple.

"Maddy, I'm serious."

"I can't come back." *I'm debating about killing a hunky cowboy.*

"Where are you? I'll come and get you."

Hell no!

The thought of Beth rescuing her from all of this was tempting, but she knew her friend would try and talk her into going home and facing everyone. That was not the rescue she needed right now. She needed her car, which was in some river.

"I have to go. I'll call you." She hugged herself as hurt and confusion swamped her.

"What are you doing?"

The voice behind her startled her from her troubled thoughts. Turning, she hoped to see Ty. She was disappointed to find his brother there, apparently eavesdropping on her phone conversation.

"How long have you been standing there?"

"Just now. I knocked."

Maddy swiped a tear from her eye as she tried to put on a brave face. She nodded silently and hoped he would go away.

"How are you feeling?" His question caused a bark of harsh laughter to bubble up from deep inside her.

Like a fool.

"Where's Ty?" she asked him instead.

"He needed to take care of a few things and asked me to keep an eye on you until he gets back."

"I'm fine, really." Why was Ty's brother looking at her so strangely? "What?" she finally asked him.

To his credit, he shrugged. "Just wondering how you were feeling, that's all."

"Do you mean physically? I feel as if I've been run over. Are you a doctor?"

"No. A medic."

"Oh." She nodded and recalled him hovering over her at some point. Hovering and arguing with his brother.

"Would you like something to drink or eat?"

She shook her head. She wanted to get out of here. She wanted to know what was going on. Not that she could see that happening any time soon. She wanted her car and that too seemed like an impossibility. "Did Ty say when he would be—"

A screen door slammed somewhere, causing her to jump.

"Jordan?" a voice called out from the direction of the kitchen.

She watched as his face grew pale at the sound of the woman's voice. Clearing his throat, he turned as her voice drew nearer. "In here, Mom."

Mom? Maddy pulled the robe closer as the woman appeared.

"What are you doing, Jordan? You shouldn't be—" She stopped suddenly as her gaze found Maddy by the phone table.

This is their mother?

"Hello." The woman slid a glance to Jordan.

"Um, Mom, this is Madison."

"Madison." She rolled the name on her tongue as she moved closer to Maddy and smiled. It was as if she knew the confusion swirling in her head.

"Honey?" A man's voice trailed through the hall until he, too, joined them in the living room. The screen door could be heard slamming again.

"Harold," the woman said. "Meet Madison."

"Madison." He nodded in her direction. "Jordan, what's going on here?"

"Um, Dad, Madison is, um…"

Suddenly, Ty appeared behind his dad and relief washed over Maddy at seeing him move toward her, even if the look on his face made her feel anything but relieved. Something was troubling him, she could see it. His arm stole around her waist and he drew her to him.

"Um, Mom, Dad. Madison is my fiancée."

* * * *

"Your what?" His father glared at Ty.

He felt Madison pull away from his embrace. "I'm his fiancée."

Puzzlement etched itself on his dad's face. *Oh hell! He's going to lose it.*

"You're engaged and didn't even tell your own mother?" His mother turned and glared at him as well. "Ever since you took over the plant for your father, you've drifted further and further away from us. Harold, I want you to look. You have worked our son to death."

"Well, he's obviously had time to find himself a wife." His father looked at his mom.

"Madison, is it?" his mom asked. "I'm so happy to meet you!" His mother's voice sounded watery, as if any moment she would dissolve into tears of joy.

Oh, shit! This was not supposed to happen.

"I feel like we're going to be a family again." He stared at the scene before him as his mom reached out and hugged Madison.

"Um…Mom? Madison was in such a hurry to get down here, she forgot to pack any clothes. Do you think you could find her something?"

If his mother smelled a rat, her expression was not giving it away.

"Sure, honey. You come on upstairs with me and we can talk." His mother linked her arm through Madison's and began to pull her away. Madison's gaze held his as she was being led away.

Ty didn't have to look at his father to know the man was staring a hole through him. He kept his gaze on Madison and his mother until they disappeared from sight. Only after they had headed up the stairs did he look at his dad. "Let's talk in the kitchen."

Shooting him a skeptical look, Jordan led the way. Ty followed.

"Are you kidding me?" Ty's father shouted as he trailed them into the kitchen.

This is going to be bad.

How the hell am I going to explain this one? With lies, what else? He seemed to be the king of lies now, especially over the last few hours. Okay, lies and bedding a spoiled oil heiress from Alberta, Canada. Not good. Even though the sex had been incredible, it had been a stupid move on his part. What had he been thinking? *Oh, right.* He had stopped thinking about the same time he had put her in his robe. All blood had left his brain and headed south. His groin had stiffened and with his cock happily trying to claw out of his jeans, he had been left to fend for himself with nothing to help him but his dick. "Dad, please. She'll hear you."

"Sorry, Ty. I'm just…shocked as hell. Where did you two meet and when?"

Geez, I hadn't thought that far ahead. "Um, it's a long story."

"No it's not," Jordan interjected, smirking at his brother.

Ty cleared his throat and hoped Jordan would realize it was a warning. "Dad, I know this is kind of a shock." *That's the understatement of the year. What the hell have I done?*

"I'll say. You've been practically living at the plant ever since Alicia…"

Jordan's snicker reached him and he turned to burn a menacing glare in his direction. *I must not kill my brother.*

"Sorry," Jordan offered. "It's just funny how we refer to what happened by just using her name, like she was a hurricane or something."

"I'd rather not refer to her at all, if you don't mind." Ty sat down at the kitchen table and ran his hand through his hair, raking his bangs back. "Look, just don't ask me any questions about this, okay?"

"You've got to be kidding me." His dad was far from amused. The last thing he needed was his father pissed. That would be bad for everyone. Telling him the truth would not only piss him off, it would cause lots of damage. His father's gaze narrowed on him.

Hell, damn, hell!

"Don't you know that your mother is upstairs right now finding out everything? If I don't hear it from you, she holds all the cards. That is not going to happen."

"Dad, it's just…you know."

"She's a mighty pretty young lady there, son. Jordan, what do you think of your brother's soon-to-be wife?"

Jordan smiled at his dad and then turned to Ty who waited for his brother to spill the beans. "I think she's real pretty and Ty has outdone himself this time. I can tell he's very attracted to her."

Ty wanted to punch his brother for reveling in this. Jordan was right though. He was *very* attracted to Madison. And he had outdone himself.

"So what is Madison's last name? I didn't quite catch it," his dad pressed on.

"Bellini," Ty said, looking back at his dad and wondering how long it would take him to put it together. He started to count the seconds in his head.

"Alberta, Bellini…as in Franco Bellini?"

Six seconds, not bad, Dad. "That would be the one."

Setting his jaw, his dad narrowed his gaze. "Why don't you start from the beginning?"

* * * *

Maddy sat on the plush bed in the Kirkland's master bedroom. It was bright and decorated in a lovely floral. Everything matched and accentuated the hardwood furniture. It looked lush and without a doubt expensive. All around the room there were pictures of Ty and Jordan at various ages. On the wall by the white bedroom door were recent ones that had been professionally done. She sighed, got off the bed and walked over to take a closer look.

"Those were just done. Such handsome men. I've always wanted a girl but the good lord blessed me with the pair of them." Mrs. Kirkland sounded so proud.

Turning, she looked at Mrs. Kirkland. "They're very handsome, Mrs. Kirkland."

The blonde-haired woman gave a laugh and waved perfectly manicured nails. "Oh please, you are going to be my daughter-in-law. Call me Jill. Mrs. Kirkland is my husband's mother."

Maddy looked back at the pictures. Describing Ty Kirkland as handsome was an understatement. His eyes were dark brown as was his hair. It was a little longer in the back and had a bit of a wave to it. He was clean-shaven in the picture, unlike today. He seemed to have a week's growth on his face. His jaw was square and even from the picture, she could tell he was broad shouldered. It had felt good to be in those strong arms. Again, good being another understatement.

"You're quite taken with Ty, I can tell," Jill offered, causing Madison to look back at her. She was standing by her closet studying her.

Taken with him, interesting phrase. Best not to tell his mother the sex is incredible.

"He's a great guy. He must be, since we're engaged," Madison replied with a small shrug.

Maddy could make out Ty's voice clearly, as well as his father's shouting back. Their mother smiled, nervously almost, as she went about finding some clothes for Madison to put on.

"You'll have to forgive Harold. He's not upset, he's just…well, this is such a shock."

"It is?" *Boy is it ever.*

"Well, yes. We've been over taking care of Jordan for a few days and…here, try these on." She handed Madison a pair of jeans and a sweater.

Shocked at the sweet hospitality of the woman, Madison said, "Thank you, Jill."

She watched as Jill brushed a blonde gray strand of hair back. "No, Madison, thank you. Ever since Ty took over the gas plant for Harold, all he does is work. We see less of him than we do of Jordan and he doesn't even live here. It's just that, well, I'm sure Ty told you about Alicia."

Maddy froze. *Alicia. Nope. He hasn't told me about Alicia. Who the hell is Alicia? Now, how am I to answer?*

She was saved from having to as she heard her last name all but shouted through the house.

"Oh, dear." Madison looked on as Jill moved to the open door. She turned back with an apologetic smile on her face. "I don't know what they are talking about now, but anytime that name is mentioned, Ty just sees red and loses his temper. I'll be right back."

Maddy waited until Jill closed the door before throwing Ty's robe open and shedding it to put on the clothes his mom had offered her. The jeans were a little loose in the waist, but her hips held them up and the sweater covered her to her thighs. Moving from the mirror, she stared down at the pictures of Ty and Jordan scattered across the dresser. Her gaze warmed as she found more portraits of them on the wall. Ty as a young boy, laughing, holding a ball, his dark eyes alight with mischief. She caught herself smiling in the mirror just as more voices rose from downstairs.

"So you're the sexy fiancé." She gritted her teeth. "The fake sexy fiancé. The sexy fake fiancé who can't stand to hear my last name." She studied the picture closer and sighed. "What am I going to do with you that I haven't already done?"

Chapter 5

Ty groaned as his mother came into the kitchen, craning his neck to look behind her to see if Madison was in her wake.

"Where's Madison?"

"I left her upstairs. Now, what is all the yelling about?"

"Yelling?" Ty's dad snaked his hand across his neck as he tried to evade the question. "No yelling, sweetheart. We were, uh—"

"Laughing," Jordan added quickly.

"Laughing?"

"Yeah, we were laughing about how sneaky Ty was. Getting engaged and not telling anyone."

Ty watched as his mother crossed her arms over her chest, a clear signal that she was not accepting this as being anywhere close to the truth.

After she held his father's gaze for a minute, she blinked slowly. "Okay." She sounded as if she would accept their explanation, for now at least. "So, I guess my next question would be, why were you keeping it a secret? Why didn't you tell us that you were engaged?"

"What?"

Ty turned at the sound of Madison's voice, only to find her standing just inside the doorway, wearing jeans, a sweater, and the most hurt expression he had ever seen.

"Madison." He stood, moving toward her, only to find her eyes pooling with huge tears. *Aw, no. Not tears. Anything but tears.*

"I can't believe I'm engaged to a man that didn't even tell his parents about us. Are you embarrassed by me?"

Oh hell! Don't cry, please don't cry.

"Of course not, sweetheart, I'm not embarrassed by you," Ty tried to soothe the woman whose big brown eyes were wide with tears.

Madison inhaled sharply then let it out in a sob and tears rolled down her smooth, flawless cheeks. "Then why didn't you tell them?"

Ty couldn't believe that she even looked pretty when she cried. Trust his luck. Thank heavens he was used to beautiful women.

"It's because I'm fat!" She buried her face in her hands and cried out more tears. "You think I'm fat!"

Fat? What the hell? What the hell kind of nonsense is this? He shrugged. Since he was now supposed to be the loving fiancé, it was just as good a time as any to be comforting, sweet, and God have mercy on him, charming. "No, baby, of course I don't think you're fat. Hell no, I'm not embarrassed. I think you're the prettiest little thing I've ever seen." Ty honestly thought so, and even though her sobs had stopped, she now stared at him with a tear-stained, unhappy face. He hated to know he was the cause of it. She obviously needed more reassurance. She sniffled and he took her in his arms. Her soft curves rested against his body and her head on his shoulder. Ty had to guess she stood about five ten and no more than a hundred and fifty pounds, which was nothing to his six five, two hundred and forty pound frame. She wrapped her arms around his neck then stretched up to look at him.

His body was aware of everything about her from the curves, to the rise and fall of her breasts against his chest. She fit against him perfectly and it turned him on knowing what smooth perfection was beneath the sweater and jeans. His cock stirred as blood pumped toward it. He had already had her twice and now wanted her again. He shifted his thoughts away from anything that would give him a full-fledged erection.

"I'm sorry I never told my parents. I've just been so busy with you making the trip down here to see me, the business and all."

"Trip?" his mother asked, sounding strained.

"Madison is from Alberta," Jordan answered for him.

Madison turned in Ty's arms and looked at Jordan. "As in Canada?"

"Don't you know where you're from?" his father asked.

"It seems that when Madison crashed her car, she lost her memory," Ty explained and felt the soft curves start to tremble again and a small sob escape her. "Maddy was in such a hurry to get to me, she—uh, wrecked her car and she's a little addlepated. "

"Addlepated?" His father lifted his brows.

"I am?"

"Yes, sweetheart," he whispered against her ear.

"Okay, was she asking?" His father bounced his gaze between he and Madison.

Ah hell, here we go!

"She's pretty certain she hit her head." He glanced at his brother. "Jordan?"

"Amnesia," Jordan supplied smoothly.

"Really?" His mother sounded sarcastic at best.

Ty gently reached up and brushed Maddy's bangs away from her forehead and showed the purple bruise and scratches beneath.

"Oh! You poor baby," his mother cooed, like she was talking to a helpless child and moved closer to them.

Turning slightly, Maddy looked at his mother. The turn brushed her body against every part of his body. It was intoxicating. His body warmed and his cock grew harder.

"I'm so sorry," she apologized to his mother.

"Oh, honey, you're with family now. I'm sure if my boy loves you enough to marry you, we're just going to eat you up like apple pie." His mother was being…well…his mother.

"Really?" Madison pulled out of his arms and moved closer to his mother.

"We're family and we'll work through this ordeal as a family," his mother assured the sexy but very clueless Madison, taking her hands. Ty's gaze roamed over the delicate fingers in his mom's grasp. He noticed it at the same instant his mom did, the faint tan line where an engagement ring should be. *What the hell?*

"Oh, sweetheart." His mom turned a horrified glare to him as she held up Madison's left hand. "You lost your engagement ring!"

Madison looked at her hand and then up to Ty. He watched as complete horror washed over her face. She lifted her hand and brought it closer to her face, as if she were trying to locate the ring. "I lost my ring!" She started to breathe funny and looked as if she was about to start crying again. Ty felt as if the earth had just dropped about ten feet under him.

"Oh, don't you worry, honey. My boy will get you another one," his mother volunteered.

Oh, shit. Sure, I never got her a first one. What the hell, people?

"The most important thing is we didn't lose you." His mother took Madison for what seemed like the umpteenth time in a hug.

"Ty," his father interjected, pulling him aside. "Was she in a yellow Corvette?"

Ty felt the floor drop again.

"Yeah." Ty pushed a heavy sigh out, waiting.

His father turned Ty to face the kitchen window above the sink. Ty felt dizzy as he watched the procession of law enforcement leading a tow truck with her yellow Corvette riding along on top. "Shit!"

"Oh, shit," Jordan echoed, watching as the sheriff made his way up the back steps.

The knock brought Madison's head up from his mother's shoulder. Ty could have sworn he heard her whisper, "Oh, shit."

Ty stared as Sheriff Dinkins made his way into the kitchen. Madison stepped back from his mother and he reached out, taking hold of her upper arm and pulling her close to him. He could feel her body trembling.

"Shh," he whispered, pulling her closer. "I've got you."

"Afternoon, Sheriff," His dad and mom stood side by side, creating a barrier between the sheriff and Madison. Ty's arms moved around her and he held her closer to him. As she put her arms around his waist, she snuggled tightly against his frame.

"Afternoon, folks." Ty found the sheriff was staring intently at him from over his mom's shoulder. "Found a few things in the Medicine Bow River," he announced, setting a soaked knapsack onto the kitchen table. "Missy, does this belong to you?"

Ty felt her jerk at the sound of the wet knapsack landing on the table and held her closer still.

Jordan moved closer to the knapsack, creating a full wall between the sheriff and Madison. "Sheriff," Jordan explained. "She isn't feeling very well right now."

"Oh, I'd say not. Should I come back for the answers I'm looking for?"

Ty felt Madison straighten suddenly, trying to move from his protective hold. His arm tightened around her.

"It's okay, Ty," she said, peering up at him.

"Is that your car, Missy?"

"Yes."

"We were just going to call you," Ty offered.

"Yes!" his mother and father chimed in together, joined by Jordan.

"We just wanted to make certain that Madison here was all right first. We figured her car wasn't going anywhere." Jordan actually laughed and to Ty's relief, so did the sheriff.

"Well, what happened?" the sheriff asked. "I found no skid marks to indicate that she even tried to apply the brakes. So I'm sorry, but I have to ask this…"

Ty pulled her to his side again.

"It was my fault," Ty blurted out. "We, uh, had an argument and she was upset."

"Oh, Ty!" his mother voiced her utter shock.

"Lover's spat?" the sheriff asked, grinning.

"Yeah. We're engaged." He was amazed how easily the lie rolled off his tongue.

"Well, under the circumstances, I reckon there's only one thing I can do here."

He stepped forward. Ty pushed Madison behind him to protect her, his body tightening at the thought of the sheriff hauling her away. He watched as the sheriff's hand came toward him. "Congratulations, Ty."

As he reached around Madison and pumped the sheriff's hand, his breath left his body in a loud whoosh.

"Missy, you need to slow down. Looks like those expensive wheels of yours hit that mud at a high rate of speed. You must have been pretty ticked off at him. It's a damn wonder you didn't take out the entire bridge. Tell you what. I'll let you get whatever you need out of the trunk and then I'll have the car dropped off at the garage in town. How's that?"

"Um…" Ty could barely find his voice.

"Thank you, Sheriff," Madison said as she moved from behind him. Looking down, he found her smiling at the older man with appreciation in her sparkling dark eyes.

As she started to move past him, he realized he couldn't very well let her discover her trunk had been emptied. "Um, sweetie?" He took hold of her shoulders and turned her toward him. "Why don't we let the sheriff take the car and we can go over later and get your stuff?"

"But it's right out there."

"Yeah, but I wanted to talk to you," he whispered, toying with a strand of her dark hair. To let her know what he wanted to talk about, he brushed his thumb slowly across her lips.

"Okay."

"You two lovebirds need to decide on this now. That sky is ready to open up any minute."

Ty lifted his head. "Okay, Sheriff, go ahead and take the car into town. Jordan can go over later and get her things out, can't you, Jordan?"

"I'm supposed to be on bed rest."

"Nonsense," Ty's mother interjected again, making the hairs on Ty's neck stand on end. "You can help your new sister-in-law out, Jordan Kirkland. My God! Her car plunged into the Medicine Bow. She could have killed herself."

Ty felt his body tighten again at her words. He stared down into Madison's face, trying to see beyond the confusion. *Had she tried to intentionally take her own life?* Or had she been so hell-bent on dropping that dime on him that she somehow lost control of her car? He lowered his face toward her, slowly, hesitantly, until his mouth fused over her lips.

"Ty?" she whispered.

He hummed a response as he kissed her forehead.

"What did you want to talk about?"

"Hmm?"

"Oh," Jordan leaned in and offered. "He probably wants to know if you want a ring just like the last one he bought you."

"What?" Ty's question came out more like a threat of bodily harm.

"Just helping out my new sister-in-law. Wasn't that a two carat diamond?"

Madison gasped at the words. "Was it?" she asked.

"Oh yeah," Jordan continued. "I remember little brother showing it off, proud as a peacock."

"You did?"

"Yeah, I believe his words were, 'Nothing but the best for my Madison.'"

Ty braced himself as Madison slid her arms around his neck and pulled him down for a kiss that scorched more than his lips.

He would kill Jordan later. She teased his mouth with the tip of her tongue, making his cock hard against her. He moved to pull her closer when suddenly, she broke the kiss and lowered herself from his embrace. Before he could voice any objection, she had moved away from him and began to prowl inside her knapsack.

Is she remembering? Would she turn toward him at any moment and realize what a liar he was?

"Um, sweetheart?" he asked, moving up behind her. She seemed to stop momentarily as his cock cradled her from behind.

"Yes?"

"Don't you want to go and finish talking?"

"Um." She seemed uncertain, even as she leaned against him.

He pulled her up even tighter as he put his hands around her, one moving lower to slide the sweater up. He pushed his face into her hair and nuzzled it to find the soft skin of her neck. Just as he found what he was looking for, he watched as she upended the knapsack onto the table, all of her wet belongings spilling out. He peered down over her shoulder as she began to fish through her items. She located her wallet, and opened it, checking inside. He stared down in amazement as she flipped through at least two dozen credit cards. Again, she fished through the mess on the table and he heard her swear softly under her breath.

"What's wrong, sweetheart?"

"Um, everything is ruined."

"Not everything," he whispered again, planting a heated kiss onto the skin of her neck.

"Oh, I just meant everything is wet."

His hand snaked lower between her thighs, working his fingers along her channel. "Now, you're getting it."

"Hey, you two."

Ty could not believe he had forgotten that his mother and father were still in the room. Looking up, he turned his head to find his mom, hands on her hips, leaning against the sink.

"Yes?" he asked her, feeling rather reckless.

"I hate to break this up, but your dad is outside trying to calm the mares."

"Aw, hell!" Ty reluctantly let go of Madison and grabbed up his hat.

"Ty Kirkland, do you not see that sky out there?" his mother admonished. "Put your slicker on, boy."

* * * *

Ty made his way back to the house as the rain continued to pour down in stinging sheets.

He felt wet, even under his slicker and hat, and couldn't wait to get back in to where he could get dry and warm...and feel Maddy again. Stepping into the mudroom, he lost all thoughts of snuggling with his fake fiancé as he peered through the window into the kitchen to see Jordan teasing Maddy with something he held in his hand.

He couldn't help notice how she laughed freely with Jordan. He had never seen her laugh before. He had never caused her laughter, only tears. He felt slighted. He felt angry. He felt jealous?

"Jordan!" he barked, breaking up their little game of cat and mouse.

"What?"

"Come here. Please," he added, leveling a stare at Madison that told her he was not pleased.

He watched as Jordan made a face before making his way over the threshold.

"Shut the door," Ty said, keeping his voice low. Jordan did as he was ordered.

"Okay." Ty watched as Jordan leaned back, folding his arms.

"What are you doing?"

"Nothing."

"Nothing? What are you even doing here?"

"Mom invited me over for dinner."

"Shit."

"Thanks a lot, little brother. What's up your ass?"

"Nothing. Look, I need Mom and Dad to go back home with you."

"Yeah, I don't think they want to."

"You have to convince them otherwise."

"Why?"

"Because, a two carat diamond costs a lot of money. Unless you want it coming out of your paycheck…"

"Fine. God, loosen up, would you?"

"What are you two whispering about out here?" He looked beyond Jordan to see Madison stepping out into the mudroom.

"Come here," he coaxed, giving her what he hoped was his most alluring smile. She came nearer and when she stepped close enough, he lowered his head, allowing the water trapped in his Stetson to funnel out and spill like a spout into her upturned face.

Her shocked gasp filled the room just before she screamed. Ty started laughing at his joke as she continued to sputter.

"I-I can't believe you…just did that," she gasped as she tried to step away from him.

"Well, I can play, too, Maddy." He laughed again at her expression of shock.

"Oh, Maddy, what happened to you?" his mother asked as she stepped into the room.

"He-he…"

"Ty Kirkland, you ought to be ashamed of yourself!"

At first, he thought she was joking, but her tone was serious. "It was a joke."

"Maddy, honey, run upstairs and get a towel from the closet in the hall. And if you wouldn't mind, bring one for funny boy here."

Ty felt a twinge of guilt as he watched Maddy walk stiffly away from him. He felt tension surround him.

"Way to go, Romeo," Jordan added, making Ty feel even worse.

"I didn't mean anything. It was a joke."

"A joke?" His mom was really pissed at him. "That poor child nearly drowned and you hit her in the face with water? Hell, Ty, she doesn't have any clothes to call her own and you soak the only thing she has on!"

His mother's words hit him hard. He hadn't thought about it that way. Hell, the way she put it, he was the worst kind of asshole. He was just trying to show them all that he could loosen up. Weren't they always telling him to lighten his load a bit? Loosen up? Join the rest of the world? Laugh once in awhile?

"Now, you stand right there and think about what you did." With that she turned and left him.

Ty reached a hand out and snagged Jordan's arm as he too made to leave. "Get Mom and Dad outta here."

"Yeah, I'll try."

"I'm serious, Jordan."

"Uh, Ty? Have you forgotten something? Like the small fact that you aren't really Maddy's fiancé?"

"Maddy? Why is everyone calling her Maddy all of a sudden?"

"Mom heard you call her that."

"Yeah, but that's different. That's..."

"Your pet name for your fiancée?"

"Yeah."

"Ty, man you are starting to believe your own lies. She isn't really your fiancée. This is no more than a Bellini takeover."

"What did you say?"

"Come on, man! She isn't even your type."

"My type?"

"Yeah. You know, like Alicia, tall, blonde. Face it, Madison is no blonde."

"Neither is Alicia." Ty grinned mockingly as he spied Maddy returning with his towel. As she tossed the towel to Ty, Jordan moved past her. Ty grabbed her arm and pulled her gently toward him.

"Don't you dare!" she warned, struggling a bit.

"Aw, come here. Look, I'm sorry, sweetheart. I wasn't thinking. I was just playing."

"Somehow the words Ty and playing don't seem to fit in the same sentence."

"Oh, really?"

Her next words stopped all thoughts of playing. "Who is Alicia?"

He stared down into her upturned face and tried to find the words to tell her about Alicia. "Well, Alicia was my…um, we were going…"

"To get married?"

"She broke it off and married Tom Walsh."

"Did you love her?"

Ty pushed a labored breath from his lungs. "Tell you what. Let's talk about this later. I'm still soaking wet." He stepped back from her and peeled the rain-soaked slicker from his shoulders.

"Okay."

Ty noticed the uncertainty in her eyes and he stepped closer to her. He wanted to tell Maddy that he loved only her. It seemed like the right thing to say at this moment, but the trust he saw pooling in her dark eyes held his tongue.

He squeezed his eyes shut and kissed her quickly before heading in and upstairs to clean up for dinner.

* * * *

Maddy stood at the stove and stirred the carrots absently, her mind sorting through what she had just seen in Ty's face and had heard in his voice. He had been hurt by this Alicia, of that she was certain.

"Maddy?"

Hearing Jill's voice brought her thoughts back to her stirring.

"Are you okay? You want to sit down? I can finish those up for you."

"Oh," Maddy answered quickly, offering a quick smile. "No, I'm fine. I want to help."

She heard her own words and thought how strange they sounded. She really did want to help and not just with the dinner. This was crazy. He was pretending to be her fiancé, no doubt out of his need for a lucrative contract with Bambardi and Bellini. He was no different than Teddy. Yet, as she closed her eyes, all she could smell was his earthy scent; all she could feel was his arms pulling her closer, his lips on hers. And all she could hear was his voice, calming and exciting her with his words of love. He was very different from Teddy. The memory of how he felt when he was moving between her legs made her stomach coil with pure need.

"Maddy?"

"What?"

"Are you sure you're okay? You're making little noises."

Maddy felt her face flame. *Oh, my gosh. Standing here, next to his mother and I'm thinking about finding him and the nearest bed.*

"Um, Jill?"

"Yes, dear."

"Do you live here?"

"We sure do. We've been staying over at Jordan's helping him since his accident."

"What happened to him?"

"He was trying to break that horse of his and it stomped on his foot. He's supposed to be off his feet for at least two weeks, but you can't tell him anything. He thinks he knows better than the doctor."

"Mom, are you busting on me again?" Jordan called as he entered the room.

"Yes, I am busting on you. Look at you. Not even using one of the crutches I brought you. I swear, Maddy, my two boys are just as stubborn as the day is long."

"Ah." Jordan leaned in and tired to kiss his mom's cheek. "Tell you what. I could still use some bed rest. Why don't you and Dad stay with me for the next couple of days?"

"What?"

"What? Don't look so shocked, Mom. I'm never going to get healed up properly if I don't do as the doctor says, right? Besides, I'd miss your cooking."

Maddy watched as Jill crossed her arms over her chest, obviously not buying a word of it. For some reason, Maddy couldn't help the giddiness that welled up at the thought of having the house and Ty all to herself.

"Go and find your father and your brother. We're almost ready to eat."

Maddy began to move the plates to the table, her mind conjuring her cowboy naked in his bed with her.

What was she doing? He wasn't her cowboy. He wasn't her anything, not really. He was just using her.

"Okay, that's it. Sit."

"What?" Maddy shook her head. "I was just wondering about Alicia." Maddy felt bad about lying, but it beat telling the woman that she had been having mental sex with her son.

"Oh, that one." Jill snorted. "I don't know what is wrong with that girl. I watched her grow up into the haughtiest little trick this town has ever seen. And poor Ty. I guess he just couldn't see her for the deceitful little liar she was."

Maddy felt a lump in her throat.

"Has he told you what she did to him? How she tore his heart out?"

"Um…"

"No, of course he hasn't. He's too much of a gentleman for his own good, I swear! Even when she made a fool of him, he never publicly acknowledged the fact that she had cheated on him. Not even when she married that silly Tom Walsh."

This was the same man who was lying to her in order to gain a contract?

"Maddy, honey. You don't know how happy I am that he found you."

Maddy swallowed hard as that lump seemed to grow, choking off her air.

"Maddy?"

It was no use. Her thoughts were troubled and swirled in her head.

"Ty, make her sit down, would you?"

Maddy jerked her gaze to find him standing in the doorway with a look she could not identify.

"What's going on?" he asked, moving toward her.

"She insists on helping, and I appreciate the help, but…"

Maddy needed to get away from those eyes. "Nothing is going on. I'm just…I need some air. Excuse me."

Turning, she headed out into the early evening air. Thank God the rain had stopped. Breathing in the sweet smells after the rain, she moved away from the house and looked up at the sky.

The way he stood there with that inscrutable expression had caused her heart to lurch. She saw the man who had been so hurt by betrayal, instead of the one who was lying to her. She was lying to him. To all of them. She couldn't do it. She could not look them in the eye and continue with this. She had to go back in that house and tell them—

"Maddy?" Ty's voice sounded low next to her ear and caused her to nearly jump out of her skin. "Are you all right?"

All she could do was shake her head.

"Look, sweetheart," he said soothingly as he pulled her back against the warmth of his body. "Mom told me what you to were talking about."

"I brought it up. I'm…"

"I know. Are you okay?"

"Um…"

"Maddy?" He tried to turn her to face him, but she didn't want to see his face again. She knew if he looked into her eyes right now, she would lose her resolve. "Maddy? You aren't still mad at me, are you?"

She shook her head.

"Are you remembering?"

She almost nodded, but stilled at the last second. *Do I want to confess? Would that mean never looking into his eyes again?* Slowly, she lifted her gaze to his. He was too handsome and too near. She would never be able to get to the truth with him standing so close. So handsome. *Did he really have the honor his mother suggested? Could he tell the truth?*

"Ty? What were we arguing about before?"

"I don't even remember."

His lie slammed into her. Pushing her lips together, she faced him. As she stared up into those sexy, dark eyes, she wondered just how far he was willing to go in order to get that contract. Another thought frightened her. How far she would go to see that he got it?

Reaching up, she toyed playfully with a snap on his shirt. "Was it about Alicia?"

"What? No!" There it was again, the same look she had not been able to identify. *What did it mean?*

"I'm just trying to figure out what you could have done that would make me so mad I would drive my car off of the bridge. Did I try to kill myself?"

"No. Maddy! Where would you get an idea like that?"

Oh, probably from eavesdropping on you and Jordan.

There it was again, more than concern. The worry creasing his dark brows only made the heat in his eyes burn hotter. He could have scorched her with this look. Heat rose up her neck and burned her earlobes.

Why was he looking at her as if he wanted to be her fiancé? Was he that good of a liar? Or was she that much a fool?

"You okay, Maddy?" The voice from the back door belonged to Jill.

"I think that means supper is ready." His mouth lowered to her lips and her knees weakened in anticipation.

At that moment, she wanted him right there in the backyard. He smelled as earthy as the air around her. She knew that look in his eyes.

"Come on, you two. I want to taste Maddy's carrots and potatoes! They sure do smell good."

She watched as Ty's expression grew to one of amazement. All movement that resembled an impending kiss stopped. "You can cook?"

"What? You mean I can't cook?"

"Um, no! I just..." He worked a gulp past his Adam's apple. "Come on." He took her hand and walked to the house.

Chapter 6

Ty held Maddy's chair for her before moving to sit beside her, effectively crowding the two of them together, which she didn't mind at all. His mother brought the roast beef to the table and Maddy lifted her nose to catch the delicious aroma.

"Oh, Maddy," Jill paused and hesitated. "Honey, I should have asked before now. You aren't one of those people who don't eat meat, are you?"

"You mean a vegan, Mom," Jordan supplied from the other side of the table.

"Don't correct your mother, son," their father chimed in, leaning in to carve the roast.

"I wasn't, Dad. I was only trying to help."

"Don't back talk, Jordan."

Maddy looked from Harold to Jill, feeling as if she were watching a tennis match. She suppressed a grin, thinking of how much love she felt at this table. She had never had that at home. Her family rarely, if ever, shared a meal together, much less so much love, even when fussing back and forth. At her house, her father ruled, her mother planned, and she tried to get out of the way.

Her smile tugged at her mouth as she glanced up. She witnessed the eyeballing word play between Ty and Jordan. They were having a silent argument. Finally, she felt Ty's body jerk and heard Jordan yelp in pain.

"What in the world?" Jill exclaimed.

She watched Jordan's face screw up into a pained grimace. "Oh, Mom," he said through clenched teeth. "I think you and Dad need to stay with me a few more days. My foot is really acting up."

"You shouldn't have been clomping around on it," Ty offered, spearing a slab of roast and placing it onto her plate.

"We'll see, son."

"Uh, Mom," Ty was quick to throw in. "I can take care of things around here a few more days."

"You? Mr. Workaholic?"

"I'm not a workaholic!"

"Harold, tell him."

Harold sighed. "You're a workaholic, Ty. Pass those potatoes over here."

"Are you?" Maddy lifted her brows and looked back to Ty.

He scooped out a second spoonful of her carrots onto his plate, set the bowl down and grinned. Leaning in, he touched her nose with his. "No!"

"Oh, please. Maddy, you are going to end up just like I was for fourteen years. A Kirkland Island. All to myself!"

"Jill, you were never an island."

"These potatoes are fantastic," Jordan exclaimed.

Madison looked up and smiled. "Just a little fresh garlic and some pepper with the butter." She looked down at her plate again.

"So how did you and Madison meet?" The question from Ty's father brought her head up suddenly, as her fork fell loudly into her plate.

Remembering that she didn't have to provide an answer almost made her smile. She would get to see firsthand how Ty would spin his lies. Turning, she fixed him with a look of wonder. "How did we meet?"

He swallowed the mouthful of carrots before returning her smile. "We met in the Cheyenne chat room, through the computer. We got to talking and before long I was heading up to talk to Leo Bambardi and we decided to meet. It just kind of went from there."

"Love at first sight, how romantic," his mother exclaimed.

"Something like that." Ty reached for his water as he slid his other hand across Maddy's thigh under the table.

"Well, at least something good came from that visit."

Ty choked on his drink. "Um, not now, okay, Dad? So, Jordan, how's the foot?"

"Hurts like hell, thank you. So, what happened when you two met? Was it love at first sight?" Challenge reflected in Jordan's eyes as he slid his chair back from the table.

Ty's fingers climbed their way to nestle between her legs. "It was...amazing," he finally answered and slid his fingers against her crotch.

"All I'm just saying is it's a miracle you two found love the way you did. When you came back from Alberta, you were so stressed, I thought your mother was going to sign you up for one of her days at the spa."

Maddy choked on hearing these words.

Ty was there. He took her glass from her and whacked her on the back soundly.

"Harold, enough."

"Well? I'm sorry. With the interest outstanding on the loan at the bank, there is no way that we are going to get another one," Ty's father said coolly.

"Dad!"

"Fine. We've faced bigger obstacles before and we have always overcome."

"That's true," his mother chirped in yet again. "Oh, Maddy, it's comical now that I look back. Harold and I put everything we had into the gas plant. We were poor as could be the first few years of marriage, like two struggling church mice. We were happy, though. It was those trials that strengthened our marriage."

She looked at his mother thoughtfully. "Well, I'm sure that Ty and I will have our share of trials. Maybe not financial ones, but every marriage has little hiccups. I think that as long as both people understand how important it is to work through them together, anything can be overcome." She turned to Ty. "Isn't that right, honey?"

Ty looked at her as if he had never seen her before.

"Ty?"

"Oh, right! I'm just, it's just still hard to believe that my high society princess has such an attitude toward marriage," he finally spit out and started cutting the slice of roast on his plate.

"I just hope he doesn't continue to be the workaholic you said he was. I hope he will let me help where I can." Maddy tried to sound sweet as well as sincere.

"Oh, that boy of mine is so stubborn and takes things on all on his own," his mother volunteered, as if Ty was not sitting there.

The stubborn boy looked from his mother, to his plate, and then to Maddy. She studied him.

Finally, he stopped chewing and asked, "What's wrong, sweetheart?"

"I was just thinking that since we're going to be married and all, I would like to learn what it is you do. Maybe I could help you."

"Well, sweetheart, I try to keep my business and personal life separate." His answer surprised her.

Puckering her lips, she gave him a little frown. "Well since this business is so important to you and you put so much into it, then it really has everything to do with our personal life. Besides, it would at least help to know where the plant is so I can bring you dinners."

Ty froze and jerked his face toward her. "Bring me dinners?"

"Why yes, you have to eat, don't you? I'm sure the lunches I pack won't get you through to whenever you decide to come home."

"Damn, little brother. Did you hear that? She'll make your lunches, and bring you dinners?" Jordan sounded more than just a little amused. Ty looked at his brother who was grinning like a fool. "I tell you, Ty. You really lucked out."

"That's very sweet, Madison." Harold smiled at her. "I think your learning a little about the company would be good. I have no doubt you are going to make Ty a good wife. If those potatoes and carrots were any indication of your cooking abilities, my son is sure going to put on weight."

"I'll help with dishes then. That way, Ty, you can take Maddy on into town," Jordan offered. "Give you a chance to check things out,"

"That would be great, Jordan. If you don't mind, Ty?" She fluttered her lashes in his direction. "I'm sure the drive will give me a chance to become more familiar with you. Again."

Ty smiled. "I think it will be great. Positively perfect."

* * * *

The fifteen-minute ride into Laramie was uneventful. With every glance her way, he noted something different. The red in her hair seemed more vibrant than he remembered. Her profile seemed a bit more delicate, refined. Her hands, resting on her thighs, were soft and inviting and he wanted to reach over and take hold of her left hand.

He had time to think about all that had transpired since he had met her. Jordan's words came back to haunt him. *A Bellini takeover?* Ty had to admit, he had gone after her in the first place over the contract, but she was going to ruin everything. He had people counting on him. Kirkland Gas employed a lot of people and they people had families who were counting on him. And she had reminded him of Alicia, with the way she threw a tantrum. He had to see this through.

Ty now knew he had a bigger problem on his hands. Damn it, he liked Maddy. Yes, the sex was incredible, but he really liked her. She was nothing like the spoiled princess he had first taken her for. He cast a quick look toward her, while she went through her wallet. He noticed again that she had a lot of credit cards. Still, she was a princess. The thing was, her attitude at the table about marriage wasn't what he was expecting. He loved the carrots as well the potatoes. *The woman could cook. That was another thing that just didn't fit. Hell, Alicia couldn't make toast on a good day.* He wondered if her down to earth attitude would disappear as her memory returned. If the return of her memory meant she would turn back into the screaming shrew he had first met in his office, he hoped it never came back.

The town was still awake and there were people on the street. He decided to park in front of the ice cream shop. "You don't mind the walk, do you?"

"No, don't be silly."

As they got out of the truck, something caught Madison's attention. He turned to see it was the jewelry store next door to the ice cream shop. He grimaced at first, then realized now was as good a time as any to seal this deal and turn on the charm. *So what if Mrs. Baxter who owned it was also the biggest gossip in town?* If he bought her a ring here, it wouldn't be long before everyone in town knew of the engagement. That was not necessarily a bad plan since he needed to be convincing. It would certainly cut down on his seeing other women, but they all seemed to blur together in his mind at any rate.

A wicked image of Maddy sprawled naked on his bed and one of her perky breasts in his mouth flashed through his mind. This was no blurred memory. He had to focus on the moment and not on sexual escapades. His cock stiffened at the memory of how tight and wet she had been for him. He wanted her again, there was no denying it.

What am I doing? Was this just strictly a shrewd business move? She was beautiful, sweet and her desire for him was in every move she made. Maybe she wasn't strictly business after all. She certainly was pleasure. Maybe she was a shrewd business deal with perks.

"See? Garage is closed. Do you want to go in to the jewelry store? Maybe there's something in there close to your other ring."

Madison sighed. "I'm not sure what my old one looked like."

Of course not; she never had an 'old one'. She didn't have one at all. Then again, she did have a tan line where a ring had once been. Instinct told him there was more to Madison's past than met the eye. He shook his head and thought he must be totally insane by taking a girl like Madison into a jewelry store. Then again, none of this seemed sane. Fate had delivered her to him and she was the answer to all of his problems, like it or not. It didn't make him feel very heroic, but he had saved her life. The least she could do was save his business. And two karat or three, it was a low price to pay for the reward.

"Well, let's see if there is one you like then," he offered as she walked over to the sidewalk where he was standing. "Come on, it will be fun." He held out his hand for her to take and remembered how warm and soft her skin was and how it heated his own just by the slightest touch. She took it and he realized that for her height she had small hands with long slim fingers and perfectly manicured nails. He held the door for her and walked in behind her. If nothing else, this was going to be interesting.

"Well if it isn't Ty Kirkland," Mrs. Baxter greeted then shot a curious look over to Madison. Her grip tightened on his hand. "What brings you in, dear?"

"Actually, Mrs. Baxter, I would like to introduce you to my fiancée, Madison. She would be the reason we're here," Ty lied to the woman, feeling a slight hesitation come over him as he spoke.

"Oh?" Mrs. Baxter looked more than her usual inquisitive self. "You said fiancée?"

"Yes, I did." He didn't need the town gossip blowing this. He didn't care for the look of skepticism on her face. Not good if she didn't even believe they were engaged. "Madison, this is Mrs. Baxter. She owns the jewelry store and makes one of the best pecan pies in the county." He figured a little flattery would go a long way.

Madison reached with her free right hand to shake Mrs. Baxter's. Ty was quick to notice she never let go of his hand. "It's a pleasure."

Mrs. Baxter smiled and shook her hand and then gave her the once-over. "So, what did you have in mind?"

"We would like to look at engagement rings. Madison has lost hers, so I was hoping to buy another one for her." He gave the elderly woman a wink and smiled. "Maybe it was fate. I should have bought her first one here."

Mrs. Baxter grinned. "What kind did you have in mind?" she asked Ty, sounding very pleased.

Ty smiled graciously, and decided this was the most fun he had had in awhile. "A solitaire, I think. Let's have a look at your high end ones." He had bought an engagement ring from Mrs. Baxter before, the most expensive ring in the store. It had been a pear-shaped solitaire that was a full three karats for a woman who would eventually leave him for the new guy in town with more money than his family had. This ring only had to be two karats technically, however he was willing to spend whatever he needed to. He needed to keep Madison Bellini happy. He wanted Maddy happy.

What the hell? He chased that thought. Of course, a contract with Madison's father's company was worth millions.

"Well, let me show you what I have." Mrs. Baxter walked over to a display case.

Ty turned to Madison. "Come on, sweetheart. Let's take a look."

He was astonished at how much more stock the jewelry store had gotten in over the last two and a half years since he had bought Alicia her ring. Mrs. Baxter was quick to point out the largest ring she had currently. Ty tried to hide his irritation with Mrs. Baxter's exuberant salespitch, as she cooed over the largest array of jewelry he had ever seen. No doubt, she would point out the most expensive. She probably felt that the break up with Alicia was his fault, too. No doubt, she would make him pay through the nose.

To add to his irritation, Madison was fairly bouncing in anticipation as Mrs. Baxter fished out the biggest stones first.

He listened as Mrs. Baxter cooed and Madison oohed and ah-hed over each one. Ty frowned at the gaudy rings and reached back to rub his neck as Madison held up yet another for him to approve. He growled in exasperation as Mrs. Baxter fished out a three-karat ring that he swore was identical to the one he had bought for Alicia.

Not that one. Please. His breath left his body in a whoosh as he felt suddenly sick. He waited for Madison to announce that this one was the perfect ring.

"Hmm," Madison murmured, as she held her slender hand out, inspecting what to him represented the most ostentatious bauble he had ever seen. Taking a deep breath, he waited for her decision.

Madison scrunched her nose. "It's a little big," she told Mrs. Baxter quite sincerely, "and I don't care for the shape."

"What?" The word left his body in a rush of disbelief.

She leaned in and stretched up toward Ty's ear. "It's also incredibly ostentatious." Her voice was so low he barely heard it. Her breath teased his skin and turned him on.

He couldn't stop the grin he felt stretching his mouth.

"What's the problem, dear?"

"Since I refuse to have a wedding band to fit around it, it just won't do."

"Oh and what type of wedding band did you have in mind, dear?" Mrs. Baxter sounded surprised, and very disappointed.

"Just a plain gold band, nothing fancy." Had he heard her correctly? "I like that though," she said and pointed a perfectly long, polished nail on the display case.

Mrs. Baxter smiled and pulled out a slightly raised square cut diamond. Ty had to admit it was quite stunning. It was not overly large, maybe a karat and a half, but very classy.

Madison slipped it on and in Ty's opinion, it looked to be a perfect fit. It was a ring she could wear a plain gold band with and suited her long slender fingers impressively. He had to give Madison credit. The color and clarity was undoubtedly next to flawless. Madison eyed it lovingly on her finger and turned to him. "I like this one."

Ty was stunned, the lady came from more money than he could only imagine having and she wanted that one. "Are you sure you don't want something bigger?"

"What would I do with it, honey? Cut glass?" She blinked long lashes at him. There was something sexy about her wide-eyed innocence. He could have swooped her up right then and there.

He heard the bell above the door jingle, but never bothered to look. He was too busy watching Madison and how perfectly happy and beautiful she looked. She was breathtaking. "Are you sure?"

"Yes, I like this one," she assured him.

"It's one of my best quality rings. It's unique," Mrs. Baxter intervened and moved in for the sell. "Though it's a little pricey." He was not up for Mrs. Baxter's antics. Ty turned to the shop owner. "If that's what the lady wants, that's what she gets." He forced a smile. "We are talking about Madison, so cost is of little consequence."

"You've lucked out, Madison. Our Ty is from one of the wealthiest families in the area." Mrs. Baxter smiled and slipped the ring off Madison's finger to remove the tag. "It seems to fit your finger perfectly."

Madison smiled sweetly at the woman. "Yes, in fact I'd like to wear it out." She then turned to him. "If you don't mind?"

"Of course not." He smiled at how happy she was.

"Thank you." She reached up and quickly kissed his lips. "You're amazing," she told him with the warmest smile he had ever seen. His body hummed in desire.

"So are you," he told her with a wink. It was not a lie. The ring she wanted was not what he had expected from her. "Why don't you look around and I'll pay for the ring."

She nodded. "Sure, I want to find something for your mom."

Ty could not believe she had just said that. None of his girlfriends had liked his mother. 'Meddlesome' is how they had always described her. On the other hand, his mom had never liked them either, that is until Maddy.

Feeling the tap on his shoulder, he turned around, coming face to face with the last people in the world he thought he would run into. His heart came to a stop. *Talk about bad timing.*

"Hi, Ty. Fancy meeting you here," Alicia greeted him, while hanging on the arm of her husband Tom.

"Alicia. What a surprise, I hope you're both well." He tried to remain as polite and sincere as possible.

"That we are." Alicia raked her gaze over Ty and snuggled in closer to her husband's side.

"Honey! I think I found a gift for your mom," Madison exclaimed as she walked over and slipped her arm casually around Ty's back as if she had done it a hundred times before. The simple gesture stirred his libido. She left her arm there just along the waistband of his low-riding jeans. He couldn't remember the last time a woman had done that. There was something intimate in her casual touch. His body heated at her nearness.

He watched as Alicia studied the way Maddy slid around him. She looked...jealous. "And you are?"

Looking at her, Maddy slightly lifted her nose. He wanted to laugh. She was actually looking down her nose at Alicia.

Alicia had once been his everything, including a gold digging woman who loved the Kirkland money more than she did him. He watched as Alicia took in every detail of Maddy. She scowled at Maddy's turned up nose. In fact, if Ty didn't miss his guess, Alicia was pretty miffed.

"I'm his fiancée," Maddy dismissed her and turned to him.

Ty wanted to laugh out loud. He smiled broadly at her. "What did you find, sweetheart?"

"I found a gold chain with a locket for your mom and I wanted your opinion."

He ignored Alicia and Tom. It was rather easy to do with the look of excitement on Maddy's face. The look brought her large dark eyes to life. "A chain and a locket?" He found it a little unusual. Then again everything about this moment was unusual. Just like his new fiancée.

Fiancée. He liked the sound of that as much as he was liking Maddy. He allowed himself to enjoy the feel of her fingers tucked into his waistband, the look in her eyes, the excited smile dancing on her lips.

Maddy's smile reached deep inside him. "Well, I thought the locket would be a good idea since your mom has lovingly opened her heart to me. So, I found one that's a heart shape and big enough to actually hold pictures." *Hell.* She had to bring up the fact that his mom had taken her into her heart. The whole family had. His mom was probably planning their wedding at this very moment. Guilt swamped him and it felt like a lead balloon in his gut. He hadn't started out to get a contract, but to stop her from ruining any chance he still had at getting one. Now, he was beginning to feel like the worst heel, letting her think they were engaged.

"Come on. You need to see it. It's my way of showing your mom some of the love she has given me."

Looking up, he was met with an expression on Alicia's face that drove all thoughts of contracts from his mind. She looked mad enough to chew glass. He was a little surprised at Maddy's reply, but it seemed to be the perfect thing to say to get a rise out of Alicia.

"Well if you'll excuse me, I believe I am being paged," he joked and slipped his arm protectively around Maddy. In truth, he wanted to scoop her off the ground and thank her with kisses. He caught Alicia's reaction to his touching Maddy. Her eyes flickered and he thought he saw her nostrils flare. "It was good seeing you both," he said over his shoulder as he walked away with Maddy.

Alicia and Madison may have both been born to privilege, but they were total opposites. It dawned on him that he felt nothing for Alicia. He was truly over Alicia. *When had that happened?* "So, what am I buying now?" he joked as he slipped his other arm around her and turned her so they were facing each other. Their eyes locked and his body seemed to pick up on the attraction that flickered for just a second in her dark eyes.

After she laughed, she announced, "You're not buying anything. I'm getting this for my future mother-in-law."

She slipped out of his arms and pointed to the largest heart locket in the case. He was sure it was also the most expensive. He knew as soon as he saw it that his mother would love it.

"Sweetheart, are you sure?" He was still in a bit of shock over everything that had just happened.

Her dark eyes were wide and suddenly she looked a little hesitant. Then, she smiled. "Absolutely," she said with a nod. Turning to Mrs. Baxter, she opened her wallet. "I hope you accept this card?"

"Why of course, and with tax, it will be just over three hundred dollars. I'll just run the card."

Ty watched as her hand froze, refusing to let go of it. Now, this was more of what he'd expected.

"Maxed out?" Ty asked, grinning as he reached for his wallet again.

The look he saw on her face was not one of embarrassment, it looked more like real worry, she looked afraid.

"No actually." She slipped her credit card back into her wallet and she pulled out a stack of American bills. "I'll pay cash instead. Oh, and Mrs. Baxter, what designer watches do you carry? *My Ty* could use one."

As Mrs. Baxter lifted her eyebrows, Ty was forced to look away in order to hide his smirk. He caught a glimpse of Tom staring down into one of the display cases, but Alicia was staring at him, or them, taking in every move and every word. The look on her face was priceless and Ty couldn't hide his smirk.

"We have some nice Gucci watches." Mrs. Baxter's words brought Ty turning back to the two ladies.

"What?" he asked, almost breathless.

"Gucci will do nicely, thank you."

He bit back any words of refusal as he took in the stubborn set of Maddy's little jaw. He had to hand it to her, she had certainly made an impression on everyone tonight. Especially him.

* * * *

Maddy loved the ring. She kept looking at it on her finger in the truck on the way home. It was perfect, unlike the one from Teddy that had damn near overpowered her hand.

Thinking about everything that had transpired since arriving, her thoughts rested on Alicia. She was perfect, a life-size Barbie doll. Big blue eyes and butter yellow hair. She was bigger in the chest than Madison, but not by much. She was pretty and perfect and for some odd reason, it bothered her. She knew that Alicia had been far from impressed to see Ty with her, and even less over the fact that Madison and his mother got along. She smiled when she realized Alicia seemed like a female version of Teddy, always after the better deal and the bigger account.

"What's the smile for?" Ty turned into the long dirt road that led up to the Kirkland home. The rain had stopped, but everything was still wet. It smelled so fresh and green. Madison loved it, she loved being away from the city and all its pretensions.

"Just thinking about that couple in the jewelry store. I don't think Alicia liked me."

Ty's laugh caused Madison to look over at him. He looked really good when he smiled and his laughter was even sexier with a warm rumble purely male. "I don't think she did, either, but that's okay. She doesn't have to like you." His added chuckle flamed her body and her pussy twitched.

She wanted him.

Again.

His parents would still be at the house.

"Ty, can you pull over for a second?"

He frowned. "Sure, are you okay? Is something wrong?" He sounded so concerned and she inhaled. She couldn't believe what she was about to do.

"I'm fine."

Ty pulled over to the side and brought the truck to a stop. She debated. Yep this was the time, she had to do this now before they went any further. "Can you turn off the lights and the engine for a second?"

He looked really worried now. He did as she asked then turned in his seat and looked at her. "Maddy, what's wrong?"

She blinked, inhaled deeply, and then undid her seatbelt.

Chapter 7

Ty had no idea what to think. A sharp stab of worry pene-trated him. *Did she know this was fake?* Was she going to tell him now that she remembered and she wanted her dad? What the hell would he say?

Reaching over, she undid his seatbelt. He moved it out of the way and looked at her, waiting.

"I just wanted a minute alone with you." Her voice was low and sultry. It heated his body. "Everyone is going to be there when we get back and…"

Ty relaxed a little. "Maddy, whatever it is—"

"Actually, just this." She moved across the seat and brought her hand up to his cheek. Her palm was warm and soft against the face he hadn't shaved in the last couple days. His libido kicked up a notch and he made out her lashes as they fluttered closed. Her lips came against his and he was a goner. All thought left and he brought a hand up to her back. The velvety smoothness of her tongue slid across his lower lip. He opened his mouth and was pleasantly pleased when her tongue slid in.

Shifting in his seat, he was able to move his other arm to her as she deepened the kiss. His cock sprang to life behind the zipper of his jeans and started to ache. Her other hand reached down and ca-ressed the growing bulge over the denim. He groaned against her tongue. He pulled his mouth from hers as she continued to work her hand over the bulge beneath her touch. "Maddy." His voice was hoarse. "If you keep this up, I will take you right here."

She giggled. "I was hoping you would."

He let out a hiss and moved closer to her. She started working the belt of his pants. He slowly undid her jeans. Slipping his hand down over her skin, he teased and caressed her beneath the open denim. He grew harder over the fact she wasn't wearing any panties. He trailed his fingers lower and reached her wet folds. She bucked slightly against his touch and quickly removed her hands from his erection. She brushed her lips against his.

"Allow me." Her voice was even sultrier than it had been before.

This was unbelievable. She was unbelievable...and incredible. She gently pulled his hand away and Ty became more than curious. She kicked off her boots and then slipped her jeans off. She was half-naked in his truck. *Now this is a guy's dream.* She giggled again and moved toward him. His hands ran up her thighs and reveled in the silky smoothness of her skin. She straddled him and placed a knee on either side of him. Then she undid the button and zipper on his jeans and Ty's cock throbbed. She teased her tongue against his lips as he reached for a hip and the other went between her parted legs. He caressed the wet folds and teased a finger inside her. She moaned softly as she struggled to pull his jeans down. Helping her, he lifted his hips slightly off the seat.

He was more turned on than he ever had been in his life as the fabric brushed over his exposed erection. He lowered his hips and she adjusted her knees on the seat. Her hands gently rested on his shoulders and he moved his hand from between her legs to her hip.

"I want you inside me," she whispered and lowered herself over him. Ty squeezed her hips as the tip of his cock pressed against her then entered her with a thrust. He groaned only to have her mouth cover his and absorb it. She gently moved up and down on him and he met her thrusts with his own.

He removed his lips from hers. "God, you feel good." He thrust into her harder and reclaimed her lips. She slowly picked up speed and Ty's thrusts increased, becoming harder and more deliberate. Her soft wails of pleasure fueled his desire and he wasn't sure if he could hold back much longer.

Her pussy tightened around him and she pulled her lips from his. She threw her head back and tightened her hands on his shoulders. Her wet walls squeezed his cock as he shot his release into her. He groaned as he pulsed in climax within her. Her breath was ragged, as was his and he held her tightly to him as she lowered her head to his shoulder. She rested on his lap a second. He slipped his arms around her and held her. It was official. He was completely taken with her and in way over his head.

* * * *

Maddy couldn't believe she'd just had sex in a truck. Amazing sex in a truck. When they pulled up in front of the house, she noticed the other vehicle and knew his parents were still inside with Jordan. She was dressed again, though in dire need of a shower. Jumping out of the truck, she inhaled deeply, filling her lungs with the freshness of the evening air. She shut the truck door and surveyed her surroundings. Looking up at the sky, she noticed that the rain clouds had pulled away to reveal a clear black blanket filled with millions of stars. She inhaled again, loving the way the air smelled fresh and green. This was her idea of heaven. She was amazed that the sky she was looking at was the same one over Calgary, blackened by the pollution and bright city lights.

"You okay?"

Maddy looked over the hood of the truck to Ty and realized he looked amazing with the moonlight highlighting his hair and giving a sparkle to his eyes. "Fine. I'm just enjoying the air."

"I'll be right back."

She nodded and watched him disappear up the front steps and into the house. She moved over to the steps and sat down. She thought of her mother and how horrified the woman would be if she knew that Madison was sitting on a front porch stoop in a pair of jeans.

A gentle breeze blew and she pulled Ty's jacket around her and took in the faint smell of him again.

What am I doing? This was not exactly sane. Then again, neither was pawning your only child off to a cheat of a man who didn't love her. Ty didn't love her either, but at least she had picked him herself, sort of. Besides, he was the exact opposite of Teddy. Teddy was slick, suited and very snobby.

On the other hand, Ty was down to earth, worked for a living and had a certain charm. He was the kind of man that made a woman feel feminine. Not to mention the sex was better than she could ever have imagined. The thought caused desire to tease her pussy. She didn't want to think about sex.

She wondered how things were back in Calgary and if they had sent the cavalry to Washington yet. She had almost blown everything tonight at the jewelry store. If her parents had tracked her by her cell phone, they would be watching her credit cards as well. She wasn't looking to be found. Knowing her father, he had probably taken the company plane to Seattle himself. She smiled, thinking of him on a wild goose chase.

She heard the door open and then close again behind her. She didn't even look, she just stared at the water off to the left and the big blanket of stars above.

"You realize my mother is dying to see this ring, since she didn't get to see the first one. And she liked my watch." Ty sat down next to her on the step.

"Do you like it, though?" She turned to look at him and wondered if maybe it had been too much. He had bought her the ring because he needed a fiancée. She had bought him the watch because she needed a friend. She suddenly missed Bethany very much. Not that Bethany would be able to help her now. In fact, Maddy had entrenched herself with the proverbial enemy.

"I do. It was very sweet." His eyes studied every detail of her face.

"I can't get over how nice it is here." She inhaled deeply again. "I love the way it smells after a rain. The sky is so amazing with all those stars." She looked up again at the twinkling lights as the gentle cool breeze whispered again, causing her to shiver.

Ty moved closer and put his arm around her. He shifted her slightly so she could lean up against him. As he held her, she rested her hands gently in her lap. "You seem pretty happy here."

"I am." She wanted to tell him that this was like nothing she had ever seen or experienced. She didn't want to come across as sheltered. Then again, she was supposed to be suffering from amnesia.

Ty laughed and hugged her. "Me too. I don't remember the last time I just sat out here and looked at the sky."

His voice sounded different, more relaxed. Being held by her new fiancé seemed natural; it didn't feel like they had just met that day. She had never felt so safe in her life. Her heart seemed to beat a little faster and she had to admit that Ty Kirkland affected her. He made her feel good inside. He touched her and treated her as a woman should be, not like a pretty breakable doll.

"Will you need to get up early in the morning?"

"I have to be at the plant by seven, so I have to leave about six thirty."

Madison turned in his arms so she could look at him. "I would be happy to make you breakfast."

Ty smiled and looked a little surprised. "That's pretty early and you've had quite a day. If you're up though, that would be great."

Madison smiled and nodded. "Ah yes, the call of food. I'll make sure I'm up. And ask your mom if it's okay that I take over her kitchen. You should probably go in and get some sleep." His eyes locked with hers.

Butterflies tickled her stomach and her nerves were suddenly unsettled. "Thank you for the ring." She stretched up to give him a quick kiss and felt her boot heel slip.

Ty's arms came around her and pulled her close. Her lips came down harder on his than she had originally planned, but they were met by his most eagerly. The kiss was not as heated, but long and lingering, causing a slow burn to ignite in every nerve of her body. The smell of Ty's cologne and manly scent thrust her body into full alert as he slowly moved his tongue into her mouth. She felt his hands slide up her back and press her closer to him.

The effect she was having on him was obvious by the sudden hard bulge behind the zipper of his jeans. Interesting, since they had just indulged themselves sexually moments earlier. Finally, she lifted her face back and looked at him.

They just looked at each other for a moment. "If your parents are still up, we should show them the ring." She softly placed her hand on his chest.

"I would say that would be a safe move. My mom will never let us hear the end of it if we don't."

Madison nodded. "Shall we?"

"I'll be there in a minute."

She turned and walked into the house. *What the hell am I doing?*

As he heard the door close behind her, Ty sighed. He was still a little stunned from the kiss that hadn't started out to be so passionate. He had intentionally tried to keep the kiss from becoming something sexual, but somehow, it had started to heat up and a flame of desire seared him. Women were his specialty and he had kissed his fair share, but none had ever been so sweet and innocent in intent and caused such a reaction. Madison was bright, funny and seemed to put other people first; nothing like the spoiled rich girl he figured she would be. He had tried to keep that last kiss low-key. He had failed miserably. He didn't want to lead her on but his body craved her. He wanted her, there was no disputing it.

He thought that her coming from high society to ranch life in southern Wyoming would have thrown a wrench in her world. Even with her not remembering her high society lifestyle, he had been awed by the ease in which she seemed to fit right in here. He had been wrong; she seemed perfectly happy.

He had seen her wallet and knew she had money, yet she was happy sitting on the front steps and staring at the sky. Madison Bellini was nothing like any person Ty had ever met. Another thing he had been wrong about, but as he looked up at the night sky, he felt strange as he realized that he really didn't mind being wrong. He sighed and decided that now would be a good time to rescue Maddy from his overly thrilled and zealous parents.

He stepped into the house to find them both standing around Maddy, fawning over the ring on her finger. When he had bought Alicia hers, his mother had later referred to it as 'large and overbearing, much like the mouth on her.' Her reaction to Maddy's ring was much different, but then, so was Maddy.

He watched as Maddy lifted her gaze to him and he smiled at how she looked a little unsure. Ty would have taken her for someone with a little more confidence. *Where did her insecurity come from?*

"They like the ring," she said, sounding nervous.

Ty glanced at her lips and remembered the kiss. He wanted to kiss her again. "Well it's a nice ring." He looked at his parents. "I think Maddy has had enough excitement for one day."

"Well, don't you stress about a thing. Have you set the date yet?" his mother asked with a grin.

Ty's heart came to a stop and watched Maddy's head snap around to look at his mother. She carefully withdrew her hand and took a step back, turned and looked at Ty blinking her long lashes at him. "I don't remember." She was getting that look like she was about to cry.

Think fast, or she's going to turn on the waterworks.

"Actually, sweetheart, we hadn't."

Madison's features seemed to relax and brighten again. "Oh, well I guess now is as good a time as any." She cast him a smile as Ty's brain registered the meaning of her words.

"Now?" he asked a little shocked. Once again, he needed to think fast. "Well, you did tell me it would take you at least six…months to plan it."

"Well Lord love a duck. Six months?" his mother sputtered, causing Ty to wince.

An odd expression lit Madison's eyes and he watched her tongue peek from behind those lips that held him captive. "Six months?" she countered. He stared at her as her lips twitched with what he could only call amusement. Before he could guess what was coming next, she began to move toward him. No, she wasn't just moving, she was a wet dream walking toward him. He could not breathe, even as she drew nearer and slid her hands up his chest. She peered up at him, making him keenly aware of every movement she made.

Stretching up, she grinned, teasing his cock to a full standing ovation. "I guess that was before I knew what a bad boy you were."

Ty almost choked as she moved her lips to his jaw, reminding him of their unbelievably hot tryst in his truck. He groaned, wanting nothing more than to lay her down on the kitchen table and fill her again. "Okay." He barely got the word out as he fought to gain control in front of his parents.

"Okay?"

Ty nodded. lowering his frame to accommodate her teasing. He couldn't think. All he could do was feel the blood rushing through his veins and every curve pressed so intimately against him. "When were you thinking? Three, maybe four months from now?"

Madison gave him a broad grin and drew her tongue along his jaw line, causing him to almost lose all control. She was definitely a looker, one with a fantastic body that he wanted to explore further.

"Actually, Ty, honey. I was thinking three weeks from now."

Ty swore he had misheard. "Excuse me? I didn't quite hear that?"

"Three weeks from this Saturday," Maddy repeated with a smile and a flick of her tongue near his ear.

"Three weeks?"

"Is there a problem?"

He had just over three weeks to get her to fall for him, convince her family they were an item, get a contract and break up? Was it going to be a challenge? Yes, absolutely, but not impossible. "If you think you can plan the wedding in that time, it works for me."

Madison's smile broadened.

"Marvelous!" he heard his mother exclaim.

"Yes, isn't it?" Maddy agreed. He thought he heard more amusement in her voice as she lowered herself from him again. He watched as she turned to face his mother.

"Would you help?"

Ty was beyond stunned. Most brides dreaded their mother-in-law having any say in their wedding. All the stars in the heavens knew that Alicia hadn't let his mother even mention it. Now, the pretty brunette who he was becoming crazy about wanted his mom to help.

What do they teach women up in Alberta?

"I would be thrilled! Now we can talk about that tomorrow." his mom assured her then hugged her. "Harold and I are going to spend another day or two at Jordan's." She leveled a warning look to Ty and frowned. "Is that okay, Maddy? I mean would you prefer if we were here?"

Please don't say yes; please don't say yes!

"I would rather know that Jordan is off his foot and healing." Her smile was sweet. Ty was almost as convinced as he was relieved.

His brother smiled and Ty knew he owed him huge. No fear, Jordan would remind him about it until he had settled the debt. He could only imagine what he would have to do in return. Right now that wasn't his immediate concern. Getting his family out the door was.

"Are you okay, Maddy?" Jordan's voice cut through his thoughts.

"Yes, I'm fine, thank you." Ty watched as she stepped back away from his mom and closer to his chest. He couldn't fight the urge and rested his hands on her hips from behind. "I think I'm just tired. It's been a long day."

Crashing your expensive car into a river, losing your memory and meeting your fiancé's family would do that. Only to one day, or worse, any minute get your memory back and realize your life is a lie. Oh hell, this is bad.

"Oh, honey," his mom said, "you just need a good night's sleep." She turned to his dad and waved him over. "Let's get Jordan home and let our future daughter-in-law get some rest."

She looked back to Maddy. "That reminds me. I washed your wet clothes for you. They are in the dryer. I have no clue why Ty didn't do that for you. Usually he's really good at doing laundry."

"Well, Mom, we should let her get some rest." Jordan limped convincingly toward the door. Another debt he would have to pay his brother.

His father placed his hand on his mom's lower back and nudged her forward. If he had known they were leaving, he might have convinced Maddy to wait until they had gotten home before shedding their clothes like a couple of high school kids. However, he had wanted her as much as she had wanted him.

He paused on that thought. She wanted him. She desired him and not his money. He tightened his hands on her hips as that thought sank in deeper. A sudden and fierce possessiveness rested over him and Jordan's earlier words came back to haunt him.

You really lucked out. Jordan had been right. Ty had. "Good night, everyone," he called as his father got the door.

"Bye," Maddy called and waved.

His eyes followed the door as his family left. The sounds of them getting into a vehicle was a wonderful sound. He let go of Maddy and walked over to the door and locked it. He turned and leaned against it. She smiled and stepped closer to him. His heart picked up speed. He sure could get used to being alone with her.

"So." She closed the distance between them and desire sparked in her eyes. "Is there a guest room or am I sharing your bed?"

Oh yeah, real used to being alone with her.

Chapter 8

Ty lifted his head and let the steaming hot shower hit him full in the face. Eyes closed, his thoughts were on the woman he had just tried to awaken with lustful kisses. She had stirred and had even moaned as his fingers found her under the covers.

She had even mumbled something, but for the life of him, he still couldn't make any sense of it. *No, Teddy? She had to have been dreaming.*

Turning, he flipped the showerhead onto pulse and let the water beat a tattoo across his shoulders…shoulders he had worked last night lifting and holding Maddy against him in ways that had surprised her.

Ty chuckled as he recalled her words then. Her fingers had wrapped in his hair and she had pretty much shouted to the world how he was making her feel.

Her words had urged him to take her even higher, until she had broken apart in his arms. Like a bright, starry shower, she had soared and he suddenly found himself wondering if he had been the first to ever take her there. *Or had she had been with a man before?* His laughter died as the thought settled around him. He couldn't imagine her with another man. He certainly couldn't imagine her giving herself to another man the way she had given herself to him last night. She had held nothing back from him. It felt as if they had been created just to set last night on fire.

He felt the pounding roll across his lower back as he pictured her twisting in his grasp as she let go. Her limbs had held him close, the muscles bunched in her thighs as he lifted them higher still. Her cries of ecstasy brought him to a full-fledged hunger once again. He knew what he would do. He would sneak back into his room, slip under the covers and take her even higher, this time take them both.

Ty quickly stepped from the shower and slung a towel across his wet hips, barely tucking the ends together as he stepped from the bathroom and into the hall.

Bacon?

Did he smell bacon? The aroma of frying bacon and fresh coffee battled his libido for attention. Ty felt the corners of his mouth slide upwards as a vision of Maddy lying across the kitchen table fired his imagination.

Making his way toward the kitchen, he found he couldn't wipe the smile from his face. He was feeling reckless and playful this morning. Face it, he was randy as hell.

"Maddy. Sweetheart," he called out in almost a sing-song fashion. "It's your lovin' cowboy come to stake his claim. Whew, girl. I hope you haven't set the table yet, 'cuz I'm hungry, but it ain't for food!"

Ty stepped into the kitchen and froze, finding the room filled with not just Maddy, but his parents and Jordan. His fingers went immediately for his towel as he locked eyes with Maddy. He wondered if his eyes were as wide as hers. *And was that a smile she was biting back? And biting back hard.*

His mother's voice broke into his confusion. "Well, we certainly won't be using the good china."

"What...what..."

"Are we doing here?" Jordan supplied, trying to stop the laughter that had him all but doubled over. "What the hell was that? Your cowboy Tarzan call? Smooth, Ty."

"They brought my things over." Maddy beamed.

Ty jerked his gaze to Jordan who was in the process of lifting a cup of coffee. Or hiding behind it. Jordan lifted his shoulders in a shrug.

His attention was brought back to Maddy as she turned again to face him. "So, of course, I insisted on making them breakfast."

"I'll just go and…"

"Get over here, Tarzan," Maddy teased, crooking her finger at him. He kept his eyes trained on his parents as he made his way over to her.

He let her pull his face closer and waited as she whispered, "Remind me to buy some paper plates today."

"I will," he whispered back, snaking his mouth across her lips quickly. Stepping away, he tasted her on his lips. "Mmmm. Cherry?"

"It's lip balm."

He leaned in again. "Yeah, if you say so."

Gasping, Maddy hit him in the shoulder as he made to dodge her attack, laughing as he made his way back down the hall.

"You two," he heard his mom accuse behind him.

"Who *was* that?" he heard his Dad retort.

"Funny, Dad," he called out as he went to throw some clothes on. *Damn.*

The smell of eggs joined the coffee and the bacon and Ty realized he was starving. He tucked his denim shirt into fitted jeans and buckled his belt as he started down the stairs.

Stopping just inside the door, he took in the sight before him, this time seeing a scene of warm domesticity.

He noticed Maddy had her hair pulled back in a braid that fell down her back and allowed little ringlets to escape and frame her face. She had on a burgundy, button-down, flannel shirt over a black turtleneck sweater. They were tucked neatly into the small waist of a pair of snugly fitted black jeans. She was holding the coffeepot and smiling at whatever Jordan had said. Turning at the sound of his step, she gave him 'that' look again, causing him to wish the house were empty.

Ty felt like he had been punched in the stomach. She looked so beautiful and perfectly at home in *his* family's kitchen.

"We thought we'd be safe in setting the table, if that's okay," his mom said, digging at him.

"Morning, Mom," he greeted. Glancing at the table, he found the toast and bacon. He also noticed the table was set for five. He watched as Jordan placed scrambled eggs on his plate.

Moving toward Maddy again, he leaned in to pour coffee and whispered, "What time did you get up? It's not even six in the morning." He knew he sounded surprised.

Madison's smile wavered a little and she bit her lower lip. "Well, you said you had to leave by six-thirty."

Ty couldn't get over how sexy she looked with that slightly uncertain look and her lip between her teeth. The same lip he had had the pleasure of nibbling last night. A small fire started building inside him and grew as he debated whether to kiss her again. "I'm just surprised, sweetheart," he said, bending slightly toward her and was gratified when she tilted her face up. He gently brushed her lips. "Cherry," he whispered.

"You don't like cherry?"

"Love it actually. Let me taste it again," he teased.

Hell!

She was supposedly his fiancée. He had every right to kiss and taste that lip balm, not to mention her soft lips again.

He watched as she moved the coffeepot to the side so he could move in closer. He stepped into the inviting space she had created and slipped his hands over her hips. The taste of her was just as intoxicating as last night, especially when he felt her mouth open slightly. Ty definitely wanted to experience that kiss again, but could tell by the look on Jordan's face that he should probably calm down, at least until he got rid of everyone again.

He pulled away and watched her smile impishly just before she gave him an understanding wink and slipped around him toward the table.

That wink seemed to hit him like a speeding car hitting a cement wall. She was getting to him. Sure, he'd been attracted to women before, but nothing like this. This woman was like a bad habit. A bad habit, and he couldn't get enough of her. He watched her pour the coffee, leaning slightly as she poured Jordan's. Ty could not help but notice her firm and perfectly rounded ass in those long, snug jeans.

He caught Jordan's questioning look. Ty gave his head a shake. Okay, her being a hot babe was a challenge, but nothing he couldn't handle.

"I hope you're hungry," she stated with her million-dollar smile. Actually, it was worth a hell of a lot more than that, but he didn't even want to think about that. He had to get through breakfast first without acting out his urge to kiss her. Or pull her into his chair and take her as if Jordan and his parents weren't sitting there leering at him.

Oh, he was hungry all right, but it had nothing to do with the food on the table; more like what he wouldn't mind doing to her on that table. "Oh, I could eat."

He glanced over at Jordan who was trying to swallow the sip of coffee he had just taken and the laugh he was fighting to control.

"Good, I made lots," she replied as Ty sat down at the table where he usually sat. "I'm glad you guys came by. I didn't know how much bacon to cook, so I ended up making the whole package."

Ty could not believe they were all having breakfast together. It had been almost two years since they had all gathered at the table before starting the day.

"I think, seeing this wonderful breakfast you've made, means you're feeling a little more like yourself?" His dad practically drooled at the heaping plate of bacon.

"Apparently, I like to cook." Madison smiled at her future father-in-law.

"And she's really good at it," his brother noted.

Ty thought of Alicia and how she hated the thought of cooking, in fact she had once managed to set the stove on fire just boiling water. "So, why are you guys up so early?" he asked his parents as Madison finally sat down at the table to join them.

"Well, I thought I would come into the plant for a bit and your mother has the charity bake sale at the church to plan," his father said, heaping scrambled eggs on his plate. "The spring festival is only a week away."

"Bake sale?" Madison looked up from stirring her coffee

"Over at the church, we do up a bake table for the county fair and the proceeds go to food baskets for the needy families in the area." Her enthusiasm for her community service was almost overwhelming.

"Oh that sounds like fun," Madison said as Ty picked up his coffee mug. "Maybe I could go. I would love to help in anyway I can."

"I was hoping you would say that. Because we'll need to go ahead and book it for your wedding."

Instantly Ty felt the assault from the coffee as it entered his windpipe in pure defiance. *Church fundraisers? Church booking? What next?* He coughed to gain air.

"Oh, Maddy, the church is so lovely. We can introduce you to the ladies at the church and spend some time together," his mother exclaimed with enthusiasm. "Are you okay, Ty?" his mother finally asked.

"Fine," he replied hoarsely, while he took the glass of water held in front of him. He followed the manicured nails with their white tips up long slender fingers, past the ring he had paid for last night, quickly along the burgundy sleeve, up to the brownest and prettiest eyes in Wyoming. "Thank you," he managed to choke out as he reached for the glass of water.

"What a beautiful bracelet," his mother squealed and grabbed Maddy's hand just as he was about to take the water.

Maddy looked a little surprised and Ty looked twice as surprised as her hand turned, lost its hold and dumped the cold water down the front of him. The glass safely landed in his lap as he pushed away from the table to dodge it.

"Oops. Ty, I'm so sorry," his mom apologized as she released Maddy's hand.

Jumping up, Maddy ran to the counter, quickly grabbed a towel and rushed over to help. Ty moved the glass from his lap and stood up. Madison patted his shirt dry and looked up at him. "I'm really sorry," she whispered, her eyes sparkling with amusement.

Ty felt himself smile. Her smile was contagious. "I'll bet," he grumbled playfully. "I needed cooling off anyway."

He heard his mother stifle a giggle and watched Madison's eyes widen. "Really now?" She sounded surprised.

It was a good thing the water had been cold because he could not help watching her mouth form the letter 'R' in really and the 'W' in now. "Yes, really and now, I better get changed and get to work."

He moved around her and headed to the stairs.

"What about your breakfast?" she asked in surprise.

Ty turned and looked at his family as they watched them curiously. He saw the look on Maddy's face and felt frustrated that she was clueless about the effect she was having on him. "It's okay, sweetheart, it's not breakfast I'm hungry for." He waited just long enough to see her full, pretty mouth drop open, then turned and walked up the stairs to change. It was going to take a lot more than a glass of cold water to keep him cool around that woman.

* * * *

Madison had changed out of her jeans and into a long, blue denim skirt. She had replaced her black turtleneck for a white one, but still wore her boots.

She waited until they were parked at the church before she gave her future mother-in-law the locket and chain. Jill was so happy she shed a few tears of joy and asked Madison's help to put it on right away. She told Madison it was one of the nicest gifts she had ever received. Jill also said it was just wonderful that she had a future daughter-in-law that she could love and respect.

As they entered the little gathering hall in the basement of the church, Madison felt her nerves flutter. The last time she had been in a church, she had discovered her entire family had betrayed her for a business deal.

Not unlike now. She stepped past Jill to peer into the chapel. Still, her life was suddenly so different from anything she had ever experienced and she could not believe how much happier she was. The only real problem she could see was that she was not only really attracted to Ty; she was starting to genuinely care for him, and his family. *Am I starting to love him?* Kissing him and making love to him had become her favorite things. *Who would ever have thought?* Certainly not her. She had always been a 'proper lady' where men were concerned. She couldn't even call what she had done with Teddy being intimate, or pleasurable. Ty had a way of making her feel as if she were the only woman on earth. When he looked at her, she felt her stomach coil tightly and her knees begging to buckle.

"There she is!" Maddy's thoughts were interrupted by a familiar voice. "Our little Miss Future-Kirkland." Mrs. Baxter rushed forward to greet Maddy as she followed Jill into a room where other ladies, varying in age, were gathered.

"Hi, Mrs. Baxter," Madison greeted and noticed that the woman was eyeing Jill's neck.

"Jill, that locket is simply beautiful," she exclaimed, right proud of her merchandise. "Your little Madison has quite good taste. She insisted on that one for you."

"That's our Maddy," Jill replied, sounding pleased.

Madison smiled and wanted to laugh, but the blonde in the short red skirt and matching suit jacket caught her attention. It was the blonde Barbie from the jewelry store and she was glaring at Madison.

Ah yes! Alicia. If her skirt got any shorter it would be classified as advertising.

She gave Alicia a smile and tilted her chin slightly. It was apparent that Alicia was not impressed by Madison's slight air of snobbery. The cool glare turned into an instant frown.

Madison gloated and took a seat next to her supposed future mother-in-law.

"I get the impression Alicia doesn't like me," Madison whispered truthfully.

Jill lifted a dark blonde brow and actually snorted softly. "You have what half the women in town want." She giggled. "Married or not."

Madison nodded as the older woman with Alicia approached. Alicia trotted reluctantly behind her.

"Well, Jill. Bonnie Baxter was telling us all about the little gift your future daughter-in-law bought you. I must say, the locket is quite something." The older woman then turned to Madison. "I'm Maureen Weathers. Alicia's mother."

Madison stood as proper etiquette demanded and shook the older woman's hand, maintaining eye contact until she released it. Turning, she caught Alicia raking her from head to toe, apparently taking in everything Madison had on. "Alicia…"

"Yes, Madison, isn't it?" Alicia asked and extended her hand.

"That's right; I take it the man you were with last night was your husband?"

"That's right, he's an attorney. I must say we were all very surprised to hear that Ty was engaged. Wonder why he was trying to keep everyone from finding out?" Alicia's gaze turned icy with her obvious taunt. Madison withdrew her hand from one of the weakest handshakes she had ever felt.

"Ty wanted to wait until Madison got here before telling anyone," Jill told her flatly. Madison caught the look that passed between Maureen and Jill. *Frosty.*

"Well, it's been so nice to meet you both and especially at a church fundraising project," Madison remarked as she turned to Alicia, "I just love service work, don't you?"

"It's charming." Alicia's response sounded like it had been said through gritted teeth. "Come on, Mother, we should sit," Alicia added crisply, while she physically pulled on her mother's arm.

Madison gave Jill a wide-eyed look. "I can't imagine Ty with someone like that."

"Well, let's just say you're a welcome relief from the girlfriends in his past," Jill told her, smiling. She placed her hand on Madison's knee. "Don't worry, dear. Remember that the Lord doesn't give us anything we can't handle. And I thank Him every day for not asking me to handle them as in-laws. Oh, don't look so worried. I have no doubt that you can handle Alicia."

"Her mother seems just as charming," Madison whispered softly.

"Charming?" Jill huffed. "Just add a little more sarcasm and that would be the best way to describe her. She flaunts Alicia's advantageous marriage. At first, she was very mad at Alicia for dumping Ty. Until she found out just how much money Tom had." Jill sighed and Madison noted a sadness in her face. "Alicia and her mother sure rubbed Tom in Ty's face."

"I see," Madison commented quietly, as she took mental note. She glanced back over at Alicia and Maureen. She knew people like that. Hell, she had been raised by people like that and had almost married someone like that.

If anything good came out of this fake memory loss and pretend engagement, maybe Madison could see to it that Ty not only got over Alicia for good, but that Alicia stayed in her corner. She had seen the way the blonde had practically undressed Ty with her cold, aloof eyes at the jewelry store.

Alicia shot her a scowling look. Madison felt her stomach tighten. She had the feeling that Alicia didn't like losing. She also had the feeling she and Alicia were going to have more than one run in. Madison sighed. After the last twenty-four hours, she was ready for just about anything.

Chapter 9

Ty sat at his desk, trying to go over the books. His gaze strayed once more to the clock, only to find the minute hand had only inched its way closer to one o'clock. *Had the clock stopped?* He pushed out a sigh as he realized it had not. Time was just dragging by.

He was having a really hard time concentrating. Part of it was hunger, the rest was the worst, because he could not stop thinking about Maddy. She had crashed into his life in a flash of yellow and water and in less than twenty-four hours, she had turned his family's home and his personal world upside down.

He let out a slow breath and stared at the ledger on the laptop. It stared back. This morning had made him realize that he had not spent a lot of time with his family since he and Alicia had broken up. He had thrown himself into work at the plant and with plans for the gem mine in Sheridan County. He had the land; he just needed to come up with enough capital to get to those gems. His grandfather had bought it years ago and had never done anything with it. Eventually, his memory failed, and he forgot about the property taxes along with everything else. Ty had hoped drilling for oil would pave the way for more excavation. Of course that was looking like another pipe dream. He tried not to laugh at his own play on words. His father and his grandfather had sworn there was oil on the land just outside the office. Ty had always felt compelled to keep the drill going, searching deeper. Of course, that too was eating into the profits. He needed that contract before he lost everything.

He thought of how much money Madison Bellini came from and though he knew many rich girls, they were nothing like her. Yes, she could spend money like the best of them. Last night at the jewelry store had been proof of that. However, most rich girls he knew were not exactly thoughtful creatures. They were just the opposite and behaved more like spoiled brats. He thought of Maddy's lip balm, tasting like cherries and how kissing her was becoming addictive. She seemed to fit against him perfectly, like some one had designed her just for him.

That was insane, since the only reason Madison was there was because of one little white lie on his part. And, he reminded himself, he didn't believe in fate, destiny, or soul mates and all that other romantic crap. That was more Jordan's department. Jordan was the romantic, not Ty. Ty was the love 'em and leave 'em type.

And Maddy was sweet and his parents liked her. *Hell, even Jordan liked her.*

Suddenly, there was a knock on his office door.

Now what the hell?

"Come in," he yelled, grateful for the distraction from his thoughts about Maddy.

His office door opened and long legs in a short skirt appeared. His eyes moved up the long legs to the short skirt and up to the face of a Barbie doll, one that looked like she had been crying. "Alicia?" The surprise was overwhelming and far from hidden.

What in the hell is she doing here?

"Oh, Ty. I can't take it anymore," she whimpered, moving toward him with a slow, sultry swagger in her hips. As she moved closer, he could see her make up was smudged. He had never noticed just how much she actually wore.

"Can't take what?" he asked, still unsure why she had driven out to the plant. In all the time they were together, she had only been to the plant a handful of times. Usually, it had been for money or to ask him something he didn't want to do, like attend a dinner at the nearby country club.

Alicia slid a long limb over the corner of his desk and crossed her legs so they were very close to him. "I can't take Tom anymore. I thought that I loved him but I just don't." She gave a sniffle and scooted her barely covered ass closer to him.

An alarm went off in his head and Ty pushed his chair away from the desk and stood up, putting some distance between them. "I'm sorry to hear that," he told her, only half meaning it. If her skirt were half an inch shorter, he would be able to make out the color of her thong. Of course, that was only if she was even wearing one. Alicia had been notorious in the past for short skirts and no panties.

"I had to come and see you, to tell you how I feel," she said, bringing on more tears. Ty hated it when women cried, and two years ago, if Alicia had been sitting on his desk crying, he would have been all over her.

He felt bad for her sitting there now, but for the most part, he was unmoved by her little display. "And just how do you feel?"

She uncrossed her legs to recross them the other way. Apparently, she was wearing red panties today. The fact she had stay ups on with that short skirt amazed him. Then she dropped the bomb.

"I had to lose you to realize that I still love you."

"Lose me? As I recall, you dumped me cold over signing a prenup agreement and took off out of town to get married to the wealthy new attorney who drew it up." The tone of his was flat, which surprised him. He thought his tone would have held some bitterness. It didn't and he realized he was no longer bitter. He was just stating the facts.

Alicia's blue eyes widened and she slid off the desk, revealing more than any married woman should. "Ty darling, it tore me up to see you with that brunette last night. It helped me to realize the mistake I made in marrying Tom." She took a seductive step closer to him. "I don't want you to make the same mistake with that brunette."

Ty realized just how jealous Alicia was over Madison. "That brunette happens to be my fiancée. Her name is Madison."

"Whatever! Like it really matters to me what her name is?" Alicia gave a disgusted snort and continued to move closer to him.

Ty could not believe this. Out of every low thing Alicia had done to him, this was by far the lowest. "Well, it kind of matters to me," Ty told her in a firm tone.

"What about us and all the good memories?" She moved closer still. Her movements caused Ty to move back even further.

"You made your decision the day you married Tom," Ty told her firmly. "Now since you're married to him, why don't you get out of my office?"

"She can't love you like I do." Alicia closed the distance between them and put a hand on his chest. "You know that, don't you?" she whispered and moved her lips to his.

"You're absolutely right. I'm more into the man than the wallet," a crisp, female voice replied from the office door.

Ty turned to stare in surprise at Madison, standing just inside his office door.

"Maddy!" he cried, thinking this had to be the worst timing in the world. He could only imagine what she was thinking.

Alicia moved her hand from Ty and wheeled toward Madison. "What exactly is that supposed to mean?" Alicia was mad; Ty could not believe Madison had chosen now to walk in with his ex-fiancée touching him and seconds away from trying to kiss him.

"It just means that I know there is a lot more to Ty then his wallet. Now if you don't mind, I came to have lunch with my future husband. Maybe you should go see your own husband," Madison suggested coolly.

"Ty and I were talking, if you don't mind," Alicia hissed, moving a little further away from Ty.

He waited for the explosion of anger. He just knew Maddy would be angry. Instead, she lifted her eyebrows in amusement. "Oh, that's what you call it?"

"Actually, I would say we were done," Ty interjected, causing Alicia to turn to look at him in surprise. "We were done over two years ago."

"We are going to finish this conversation, Ty," Alicia hissed as she headed to the door. She stopped and looked at Madison. "You know there is no way he could love you. Look at me, I'm perfect, and you," she continued with contempt "*you* are boring."

Ty suddenly felt bad for Maddy. Alicia was doing her best witch without her broom act. She was trying to upstage and upset Maddy and that bothered Ty for some strange reason.

Madison didn't take her eyes from Alicia nor did she look fazed by her words. "Maybe, but at least I was raised with enough class to cover my ass when I walk into a church," she commented, almost conversationally. "The door is over there. Please use it." She pointed to the threshold behind her, dismissing Alicia as if she was a rather unimportant servant.

Alicia scowled and stormed out the door, slamming it behind her. The slam caused Maddy to cringe a little. Ty braced for the explosion of anger he was sure would erupt. If not an explosion, some kind of rebuke. Instead, she walked over to his desk, carrying what he could now make out as a take-out bag from his favorite deli in town. Swinging from her wrist was a larger bag, a shiny one with rope handles.

"I brought lunch for you and Jordan, and some cream puffs from the bakery. And," she continued, while swinging the larger bag in front of him, "I brought a few things from the wedding boutique and I wanted your opinion on them."

"Maddy, I can only imagine what you thought...what this looked like when you walked in," Ty stated, hoping she was not going to think the worst.

"It looked like Alicia was about to kiss you," Madison answered, setting the bag from the deli on his desk and the other on the floor in front of it. "You don't need to explain yourself."

Ty let out a sigh and moved around his desk to her. "I want to explain." He took her hands in each of his. "It's over between Alicia and me, despite what she may think."

"I know," Madison replied quietly, looking up at him with those dark brown eyes framed with her thick, long, black lashes. "I trust you."

"It's just—" Ty could not believe her words. "Really?" He could feel his own amazement etch itself into his features.

"Of course. I hope lunch is okay. Your mother and I ran late at the church and then went shopping, so I thought I would just pick you up something since I didn't have time to make you anything this morning."

"How did you get here?" he asked, suddenly wondering if she had remembered the way to the plant. *Is her memory returning?*

"Your dad." She beamed. "Your mom and I ran into him in town. He told me how to get here and let me take his truck. He went home with your mom." Her smile warmed him from the inside out.

"My dad let you drive his brand new truck?" He was shocked, actually. If truth be known, he was stunned. Ty pulled on her hands, gently bringing her closer to him. "I'm sorry about Alicia."

"Don't be," she replied softly, so softly that Ty just about didn't hear her.

Ty couldn't believe that Alicia had described Madison Bellini as boring. The more Ty got to know her, the more interesting she became. Her long denim skirt and cowboy boots were a contrast to Alicia's little red suit, as was the very little make up she wore. Ty could not fight the urge.

"Come here," he whispered as he let go of her hands, wrapped his arms around her waist and pulled her to him. He saw her eyes close and he bent his head for the taste he had been thinking about all day. Her lips again tasted like cherries and greeted his. He felt her arms go around his neck as her mouth opened slightly and he gently moved his tongue over her sweet, full lips.

Her tongue greeted his just after a small sigh escaped her. She tasted heavenly and he pulled her closer to him, wanting to feel more of her body against his. The mere touch of the swells and valleys of her slender form sparked a desire in him that he only knew with her. He had had women turn him on before, but never with this much intensity.

He deepened the kiss and felt her body melting into his, increasing the heat between them. Her fingers played with the waves of hair at the back of his neck, sending erotic tickles down his spine. His desire grew and pushed his cock hard against the zipper of his jeans. He knew he would lose control if this continued and gently pulled away from her.

"I think you should stop by like this more often," he told her, regaining his breath.

She gave him a smile that hinted at a devilish thought. "Only if you promise to kiss me like that when I do."

Ty knew it was kisses like the one they just shared that would assure her of a lot more than a kiss. He had already been kicking himself for his most ungentlemanly behavior where she was concerned, considering the false pretense in which they were together. "Careful, sweetheart, kisses like that push chivalry to the side."

Madison gave a flirty smile and lifted one of her perfectly arched brows. "I'll take my chances."

Ty grinned and brought his lips back down on hers. This time the kiss was a little more primal, more carnal. His tongue explored her mouth tasting all she had to offer. And she was offering. His hands moved over the small of her back down over the fitted denim of her skirt covering her soft but firm flesh. Somewhere in the depths of the kiss, however, he saw again the trust in her eyes as she had peered up at him. He heard her words again concerning Alicia's visit. She trusted him. He was lying to her and she trusted him. Could she really be in love with him or was she only acting as a fiancée would, giving up her kisses, her body, her heart?

He felt his passion flare as new emotions zinged through him. He fought to hold himself in check before he took her right there on his desk. However, she was not willing to end the kiss, enticing his mouth with her tongue. Finally, he pried her loose and set her from him.

"Whew!" He grinned as she licked her lips hungrily, playfully. His gaze slid past her to the bag on the floor, thankful for something to distract her. He didn't understand what had just passed between them, but he needed to get a handle on it before it happened again. Maddy stepped out of Ty's embrace and he noticed her cheeks tinted with pink. She was definitely a lady. He could not help thinking what a tramp Alicia was next to her. "So what's in the bag?"

"Wedding stuff." She rolled her eyes with excitement. "Before we went to the deli, your mom took me into the quaintest bridal shop."

Ty raked his hand across the back of his neck. *Ah yes. The bridal shop. Well, I guess if I were getting married, there would be wedding planning and shopping. Thank heavens this will be over soon.*

"I hope that's okay?" Madison asked, sounding worried.

"Sweetheart, it's perfect," Ty replied, sitting back in his chair. He watched her as she spread his lunch before him and once again knew an odd flutter in his gut. "Tell me that my sandwich is turkey breast and I would say you are perfection."

She leaned up and kissed his cheek. "Actually you'll have to find out on your own." She reached into the shiny bag on the floor and pulled out a stack of papers. Ty examined them closer and realized they weren't papers, they were wedding invitations. "These are the ones your mom and I liked. But I wanted to get your opinion."

She held them up, and he heard her laughter bubble up as he reached out to take them. He could do this, they were only invitations and it wasn't like they were actually going to be sent out. And it made her happy.

While he tried to discern the difference in the invitations, Maddy reached into the bag again.

"Next," she said as she pulled out fabric swatches. "These are the colors that I think would look best for the best man and groomsmen's vests. I thought that once you chose which one you preferred, we could plan the rest of the wedding colors around it." She set them on top of the invitations.

Ty reached a hand to rub the tightening cords in his neck. She seemed so happy, flitting around, talking about colors and what not and he felt like a complete heel. If the feisty woman who had stormed into his office yesterday had any idea he was only pretending to be her fiancé, she would do more than call her daddy. She would more than likely kill him.

His gaze found hers, alight with…mischief? She was enjoying this too much for him to let her suspect anything now. He tried to concentrate on his new wedding duties.

This is crazy! Alicia had excluded him from their plans and told him she would just 'keep him posted' as she went. He watched Maddy bend back over into the bag as he continued to weigh the two color swatches.

"Then of course, last but not least." Maddy straightened, holding a hanger in each hand. Ty felt his jaw drop in shock. "Which style do you prefer?" she asked, glancing from the white merry widow with the real tiny g-string and garters to the white almost see through baby doll with fluffy soft looking trim.

Ty inhaled sharply, making a hissing sound. He could picture her in both and the thoughts that followed were beating on his libido. He was supposed to decide on one? He focused on Maddy, not the skimpy lingerie. He tried not to think of them on her, or what they would look like crumpled on the floor, as his body covered hers, while his cock moved deep inside her making her moan in pleasure. "I like them both," he replied honestly, surprised that his dry throat and mouth had allowed him to speak.

"Excellent," she replied in delight and thankfully put them back in the bag. She looked back up at him and smiled. "Well, I will leave you with your wedding homework and hopefully you can let me know tonight what your thoughts are."

My thoughts are to have you put on the lingerie and let me take my sweet time taking it off you before I lick every inch of your body. "You're not staying?" Ty asked, trying to clear his head of the lustful images of his hands running down Madison's naked curves while her back arched in climax.

"I'm actually going to go help your mom with the garden. I'll see you later."

Ty leaned in for one more cherry flavored kiss before he let her go.

There was a sound of throat clearing from the door. Ty couldn't remember hearing it open.

"Sorry to interrupt," Jordan said without an ounce of apology in his voice. "But Mom called my cell and told me Maddy was bringing lunch."

He bit his tongue and turned to Jordan. "Yes, Maddy picked up sandwiches from the deli and cream puffs from the bakery." He glanced at the bag on the floor and looked back over to his brother lifting his brows. "And wedding stuff."

Jordan gave him a revealing snicker and then turned to Maddy. "He's kidding, right?"

Maddy looked puzzled and glanced at Ty with a question in her eyes. Then she looked back at Jordan and said, "No, I didn't make lunches this morning and your mother raved about this little deli, so I thought I would grab some sandwiches and some pastry and come down to see you guys. But I need to get back now, so you can keep him company." Sliding onto Ty's desk, she leaned in for another kiss, dragging him closer with a handful of shirt front.

Ty kept his eye trained on Jordan as he kissed his fiancée again. It wasn't lost on him that she had perched on his desk the way Alicia had. Only this time, he felt a reaction he hadn't known with the blonde Barbie doll. Too soon, the kiss was ended. With a whispered, "Hurry home," she slid from his grasp.

"I'll leave you to your wedding homework," she said as she breezed out of the door. Ty watched as she moved across the parking lot.

Oh, I'll hurry home.

Dragging his hungry gaze from the window, he watched as Jordan reached for the deli bag. He seemed troubled. Before Ty could ask, his brother asked, "Was that Alicia I saw leaving here earlier?"

Ty let out a sigh. "Yeah, she came by to cause problems and tell me she's willing to leave Tom for me."

Jordan snorted. "What did you say to her?"

"I told her that we were done."

Jordan blinked a couple times. "You turned her down flat?"

Ty smiled at his brother's disbelief. "Hell, yes! She didn't want to hear it, and tried to come on to me...and that would be about the time Maddy walked in."

"Oh, shit. Was she hurt?"

"No! She uh...helped me throw Alicia out and told me she trusted me."

"Oh, geez. So, you've already got Maddy wrapped around your little finger."

"Maybe. Maybe she's got me wrapped."

"Yes, I noticed you two have the kissing part down pat," Jordan teased. Ty bit into his sandwich and knew immediately that Maddy had brought him his favorite, turkey breast. A slow warmth spread through him. She must have gone to the trouble to ask someone, either his mom or the deli owner. That she would go to that extra trouble made him smile.

"Let me guess, turkey breast?"

Ty met Jordan's inquisitive expression with a toothy grin. His gaze lowered to the invitations and pieces of fabric on his desk.

Wedding homework, does she not realize I'm working? Of course she does, that's why she brought them to you.

"What is it?" he asked, wondering what Jordan was thinking as he stared down at his sandwich.

"So, she's perfect?"

"Perfect? Close enough. And she certainly has my attention."

"Bologna."

"What?"

"What are you doing, Ty?"

"Don't start."

"Ty, she's not really your fiancée."

"Do you want to tell her that?"

"Do you think I'm an idiot? I saw how things are this morning, Tarzan."

"How things are, big brother, are none of your business!"

"Bullshit! You're lying to her in order to get a contract."

"Just leave it alone."

"What? Are you telling me that you actually feel something for Madison Bellini? Because, frankly I am a little surprised at how comfortable you two are around each other."

"All right. No, she's not really my fiancée. I never met her before the other day when she blew through here accusing me of ruining her life."

"So you thought you'd just take her up on it?"

"I'm curious about her."

"Um, you're lusting after her. There's a difference."

"Look, she showed up here out of the blue. I still don't know why. I'd like to find out."

"Is this before or after you break her heart?"

"I'm not going to do anything."

Jordan's jaw dropped in surprise. "Tell me you're kidding? You could very well end up hurting her."

Ty shook his head. "Hurt her? I wouldn't do that, ever."

Jordan's eyes widened in surprise at Ty's words. "Why do I have the feeling you're serious?"

Ty thought about Madison and the way she had handled Alicia. "Because I think I am."

* * * *

Madison was glad to be outside in the fresh air. The rain had stopped and though things were wet, Jill had been determined to get some work done in her garden. Madison pushed her jeans into her boots and joined Jill as they worked to loosen the soil. Of course, gardening was a new experience and though it was wet and messy, Maddy somehow didn't mind. She thought of her mother again and almost laughed out loud at the thought of her horror-stricken reaction if she knew Madison was not only getting dirty, but enjoying working in the dirt.

Oh, the Bellini home had a massive garden, but it also had a staff of three to take care of it. At first, she couldn't understand why, if the Kirklands had money, they didn't just hire people to tend to the horses and garden.

She was outside not even fifteen minutes when she realized why. Jill seemed to love her garden. Madison had never seen anyone get so excited over planting vegetables. She found Jill's enthusiasm contagious and started asking questions. Jill was happy to answer them and they were laughing when the black Ford F350 pulled up in the back of the house about a foot away from where the garden started.

Madison felt a tingle of excitement as she knew immediately it was Ty. Within seconds of the driver's door slamming, the large-shouldered, sexy man moved around the front of the truck and toward her.

"What are you doing home?" Jill asked as Ty walked toward them. "Is everything okay?"

Ty gave his mother a smile and held out a hand for Madison to take. "Everything is fine. I just thought I would come home and get some things around here done."

Madison took his hand and pulled herself up from the wet ground where she had been helping weed. She slipped her hands out of the gardening gloves and smiled up at him. "How was lunch?" she asked, feeling her smile widen.

"I would say it was as about as perfect as you." He scooped her up in a hug that lifted her off the ground.

"Careful, I'm dirty," she warned him.

"I'll live," he replied as he put her down.

Madison noticed that his mother was watching them with a smile. She looked back at Ty, "We're gardening," she related cheerfully.

Ty chuckled and adjusted his Stetson. "I noticed. Have you done this before?"

Madison shook her head. "No, I don't think so."

Ty gave a chuckle. "So, a new experience. Mom, I could have done this for you."

"Yeah, right! In the first place, I almost fell over seeing you away from that plant in the middle of the day. And in the second place, with Jordan fully recovered, I needed something to do."

"What do you mean, Jordan's fully recovered?"

"I called Dr. Phillips today and he told me that Jordan had only bruised his foot. The little stinker was fishing for some attention, I guess. He thought he was going to have a full-time cook and maid. I guess I showed him!"

Maddy watched as Ty closed his eyes and breathed in deeply.

"So I figured I would teach Maddy here how to prepare a garden. Won't be long before she has her own garden to care for. I think with a little practice and a little help from me, she'll be fine. Especially since that section of land of yours is prime soil for a garden. All you have to do is finish building that house."

Maddy turned to give him a questioning look. "What land?"

"When the boys were young, they were each given a section of land. We knew that one day they would move away and start their own families, so we decided they should stay close," Jill answered, causing Madison to turn her attention back to Ty's mother. "When Ty was engaged to Alicia, he had the foundation started. Only she didn't want to live so close to us. She wanted to live in Laramie, close to her parents." Jill sounded less than pleasant, even a little huffy. Madison had come to learn that Alicia had that effect on Jill.

Madison turned to Ty. "Just how close is it?"

Ty looked at her and quietly answered. "About two miles back, just on the other side of the tree line."

Madison nodded. "Two miles back doesn't sound too close."

Jill gave her a loving smile that warmed Madison to her soul. Suddenly she wished all this was real; the mother-in-law who adored her and the sexy cowboy fiancé. She didn't belong in the pearl perfection of high society. She belonged in a place like this. Sadness seemed to pour over her like a bleak rain.

"Sweetheart, are you okay?" Ty asked, pulling her from her thoughts.

She turned and looked at him, but could not gain the power to smile. "I'm fine. I was just thinking."

"Not about Alicia, I hope," he said, placing his hands on his hips.

"Why would she be thinking about Alicia?" Jill now sounded strained as well as displeased. She was actually hacking at the mud with her gardening tool.

"Alicia came by the plant today and Madison walked in while she was there," Ty told his mother dryly. "Nothing happened, Mom. So don't give me that look. In fact, I made it very clear to her that it was over."

Jill let out a sigh. "So now she thinks you have a chance at being happy, and she wants to ruin it for you?"

"Something like that," Ty replied.

Madison could feel his large solid frame just behind her. Just knowing he was close seemed to erase the sadness.

As she took off her gardening gloves and stood, Jill looked ill. "You've been different ever since Maddy got here. I like it, Ty. She has a positive effect on you. I know things must be a little awkward right now, but if you give it time, I just have that feeling that you two will get through this."

Madison had never wanted to blurt out the truth so badly in her life. She couldn't though, not without ruining everything. She walked over to Jill and gave her the best smile she could.

"Jill, Alicia isn't going to come between us." She wanted to tell Jill that she loved Ty and they would live happily ever after. Since that was not going to happen, there was no need to add to her disappointment with more lies. She wasn't in love with Ty, however she was consumed with lust for his body. "I won't let her hurt him again. And you're right. I think if we have time to work on it, there is nothing that can break us apart."

Jill managed to nod and relax a bit. "I know you'll do what's best for my boy, Maddy. You already have."

Madison let out the breath she didn't realize she'd been holding. Everything was fine, for now. She had a sinking feeling, though, that where Ty's parents were concerned, this could get complicated.

"Do you want to see it?" she heard Ty ask quietly behind her.

Madison swung back to find him with his hands partly tucked into the side pockets of his jeans, suddenly looking a little unsure of himself. Madison knew that was not a common look for him. "See what?"

"The land, where I have the house foundation," he answered, with a little stammer.

Madison suddenly felt her heart beat a little faster at the sight of how vulnerable he appeared. There was something very sexy about it. She felt the sadness break away a little more and her smile broadened. "I would love to."

Ty gave her a lopsided grin that stopped her breath. He was so drop-dead gorgeous. Madison wished she could keep this moment in her memory forever. The way he looked and his almost shy smile. "Do you remember if you've ever been on a horse?"

Madison wanted to laugh out loud. Her uncle bred quarter horses and palominos. She had done more than her share of riding and occasionally some stunt riding when no one was looking. Stunt riding was considered far from ladylike, therefore not acceptable. Something else her mother would be horrified if she were to ever find out about. "I think so."

"We could take the horses over if you wanted."

"Yes, I want to." She longed to tell him that, until she got here, the only time she had ever felt free was on the back of a horse.

Ty seemed to relax a little himself over her enthusiasm and turned to his mom. "You don't mind if I steal Madison away for a bit, do you?"

"Steal away."

Ty grinned and held out his hand to her. "Come on, I'll teach you how to saddle a horse."

She put her hand in his and followed him toward the stable. She wanted to laugh and was pretty sure she could teach him a thing or two about horses, but she bit her tongue. She loved the way her hand felt in his and thought about what she had said to Jill about keeping him from being hurt. How was she supposed to do that? Other than make certain he got the contract he so desperately needed.

Chapter 10

As they guided their mounts around another bend, Ty glanced over at Maddy once again. He felt the corners of his mouth lift at the pride he felt just riding beside her. She sat her saddle like a girl who had been around horses. He let his gaze roam down her straight back to the perfect positioning of her legs. Even her heels were down in the stirrups. He imagined that she had learned dressage as a girl, or something equally hoity-toity.

Still, her position and seat were something to behold. He guessed even amnesia couldn't wipe out her knowledge of riding horses, that once a person taught their body how to respond to a horse's movements, the rhythm just didn't go away. It just came naturally. Sort of like the way she moved with him.

His gaze roamed back up her thighs and he imagined her movements in the saddle matching his, moving against her.

He watched her as if transfixed as she turned to ask him a question. Again, he stared at those lips and watched her in slow motion. He watched her expression turn to surprise at what he knew had to be a look of pure desire on his part. He watched the color appear on her cheeks as she blushed.

Lips pursed, he winked at her boldly, moving his horse to a trot, leaving her to catch up. He led her through his property and noticed she rode the quicker pace with ease. He slowed to point out the dirt road that was put in when Ty had started to build the house, as well as the blooming crabapple and wild honeysuckle.

He led her up to where the foundation still stood with the frame. He had forgotten that he had even put front steps up to the front door, which he hadn't gotten around to installing. After Alicia, he had wanted to forget about this place. Now he was taken aback at the beauty that surrounded him.

He watched her dismount and gently guide the horse over to the foundation for a closer look.

"You can wrap her reins around the saddle horn. She won't go anywhere," he told her as he watched a gentle spring breeze move the curly wisps of hair around her face. She turned and nodded, doing just that before moving closer to the foundation.

He dismounted and watched her take in everything around her. He did the same, thinking back to the time he had brought Alicia here to show her. She had assumed he was building the house merely to enhance the price of the property. She had assumed he was only going to sell it, make a big profit from his parents' gift. When he had laughed and told her that he was building a home for them, she had laughed back and told him he had to be dreaming if he thought she was going to hide away like some prairie farm wife. No wonder he had been toying with the idea of putting the land up against a loan.

"So," he commented. "This is it, just over two acres."

"You stopped building on it," she said quietly.

"Yeah."

"She really hurt you, didn't she?"

He shrugged it off as had become his habit anytime that part of his life was brought up.

"You tried to build something, Ty. Something strong."

He nodded. "I almost finished building the house after Alicia and I broke up, but there was always something to do at Mom and

Dad's or at the plant. I forgot I had the steps and the framing done."

Madison looked at him and then back at the trees and the land in front of her. She didn't say a word. She just looked on in wonder. Leaning against one of the beams, she just stared out. She had a sad look about her, and for the life of him, Ty couldn't figure out why. A slow tear moved down her smooth, tanned cheek. He didn't understand where that had come from. He mounted the steps and walked over to her.

She gave him a guilty look and wiped her tear away.

"Sorry." Her voice was barely a whisper as she gave him a weak smile.

Ty had several emotions running through him, but the only one he could identify was curiosity. "Don't be. Are you okay?"

Maddy dried her eyes and wiped her hands on her jeans. She left them on her thighs and stared down at the ring on her finger. "It's so beautiful out here." She sighed heavily and looked up at him. "Some people live in their little part of the world and never look past what they know. If they did, they would see there is so much to life, more than they could ever have dreamed. They take for granted what they have."

Ty could not believe how much sense she made, so introspective and honest with her opinions. Opinions so true, he wondered how she could feel so strongly when she couldn't answer without her memory in place.

"I look at this, at you and your family and it amazes me that Alicia could not be happy. I don't get it."

How many times had he been tormented with the same questions? He had never understood how Alicia could have taken everything he was trying to offer her and toss it away as if it were garbage, as if he was garbage. He had even begun to feel like garbage, too. Especially recently, when he lost the contract with Bambardi and Bellini. No, not losing. He'd never even got up to bat. He had wondered what had possessed him to even try dealing with Bambardi and Bellini. And now he wasn't even sure if he could meet payroll without taking out a mortgage on the very land they were standing on.

"All of this is a lot of work." Ty took in every detail of her face, as if he was looking at her for the first time. In some ways, he was. Hearing her words and seeing her in fitted jeans leaning on a secured four-by-four of his incomplete house almost seemed symbolic in some way. She and Alicia had both grown up with a silver spoon in their mouths, yet they were as different as night and day. Alicia had stood still, refusing to get near the house for fear she would soil her clothes. Maddy had been playing in the dirt, rode a horse and was now leaning against a dusty post.

"A little hard work never killed anyone," she said. "Anything worth having in life takes work."

Damn. She's right. If he wanted the plant to succeed, he was going to have to work hard. Even if it meant…

"Alicia is a fool." She had whispered it, but he'd heard and couldn't stop his smile as she moved away from him.

Again, he found himself comparing her to Alicia and once again, Alicia came out wanting. Maddy was amazing. There was not one boring thing about her. She was wise beyond her immediate limitations. She was so different from Princess Alicia. He wondered if that would change once she remembered who she was, who her family was, what she had come from. He also wondered if her family was even looking for her.

"What are you thinking?" he finally asked, hoping it would break the spell she had no idea she was weaving over him.

"I was just trying to picture the layout of the house." She gave him a grin.

Ty felt her smile touch him and cause his lips to twitch into one of his own. "We're standing in the living room."

"Why would you not put a big window in here, so you could look out at the yard?"

He chuckled. "I suppose I never really thought about it. The trees out here do turn different colors in the fall. Each one is spectacular."

"I would love to see that." She inhaled a deep breath. Something caught her attention again at the back. "What are those?" she asked, pointing toward some tall, bushy trees with white leaves.

Ty waked over to stand just behind her and laughed. "Those are chokecherry trees. Those white flowers will turn to berries and my mom will make her jams."

Maddy turned and looked at him surprised, "Your mom makes jam?"

He noticed they were standing less than a foot apart. He stared down into her face as her eyes seemed to come alive at the mention of making jam.

"Yes, to the point she has won ribbons with them."

He watched as her cheeks tinted with color again. "Why are you looking at me like that?"

Ty shook his head. He didn't know what to say. He looked down at his worn brown cowboy boots then up at her again. He couldn't just come out and tell her it was eating him up inside to lead her on this way by letting her think they were engaged. He sure as hell couldn't tell her he was really beginning to like being engaged to her. Not just because of the perks. Hell, he could have any woman in town he wanted. He needed more time with Maddy to try and figure things out. "Did you mean what you said to my mom about us just needing time to sort things out?"

Madison let out a sigh and moved past him to the front where they had started. He followed her and came to a stop. Moving toward the beam she had been leaning against, she turned back and looked at him with solemn eyes. "Please, try to understand. We're like strangers, Ty."

More than you realize, sweetheart.

"Yeah, I guess we are."

"But I don't want to be strangers. I…want to sit with you, holding me like you did last night on the steps. I want your mom to teach me how to make jam and find out how she gets her towels to smell like they do, all green and…flowery, and…" Her voice seemed to trail off and she turned her back to him.

Ty felt something inside him tug and he realized it was his heart. Everything was new to her; so different, he was sure, from the life she had led. Here, she just wanted to be part of his world and experience it.

Every second he was around her, he found himself wanting her to be part of his life. How backwards had he made things between them? He hadn't been counting on this. Then again, he hadn't been counting on her. He gave a twig that had blown in from the trees a slight nudge with his boot tip as he stared down at it.

Finally, he looked up and watched as another tear rolled down her cheek. "Ty, please say something." Her voice was as tear-stained as her face.

Why did he find himself wanting more than anything to make her happy? "A clothes line."

"Excuse me?"

"She hangs the towels outside to dry to get the smell of nature in them. That's why they smell green and flowery. Winter poses a problem."

He moved toward her, lightly taking her arm. He didn't know why he was going to do this, but he gently turned her to the left side of the house. "I had been thinking of putting one in over there." He pointed to an open space.

Madison turned slightly and looked up at him. "I meant every word I said to your mom." Her voice was a whisper and there was a look of uncertainty in her dark brown eyes.

Ty still gently held her arm. With his free hand, he brushed the hair from her face and then gently wiped the remains of the tear on her cheek. "I thought so, but I wanted to make sure."

He let both hands fall away from her and just stared into her eyes. "Things will be different when your memory comes back. Life will go back to the way it was," he said honestly.

She shook her head and he could see more tears welling in her eyes.

"Maybe I don't want it to."

Ty was overwhelmed with disbelief. She couldn't know what she was saying. *Why wouldn't she want her life back?* The tears spilled from her eyes and rolled steadily down her cheeks. "No tears, Maddy. Come on, please." He quickly, but gently wiped them from her face.

"I'm sorry. I just feel like I'm very close to losing everything."

Ty took hold of her face in his palms, peering down into her upturned face.

A new fear assailed him. *Would the return of her memory drive her off another bridge?* What did he know about her anyway? Nothing of her life before she blew through his office and into his world. Nothing before she dropped into the Medicine Bow River. Nothing. He felt the same way he had when the sheriff was trying to question her. He hadn't understood why he'd felt compelled to shield her. It hadn't been anything he'd actually thought about doing. He'd just done it. He'd reacted. But, now, as that same feeling swamped his very gut, he knew what it was. He wanted to protect her.

"Trust me, Maddy. You'll gain more than you lose."

She looked up at him. God, he wanted to reassure her, let her know that what ever it was that had chased her off of that bridge, that he would be the man who would bring her back. He shook his head as he realized he was in worse shape than she was. What did he have to offer her?

Wait. What was he even thinking? They weren't really engaged. He couldn't even offer her that.

Lord, if you have ever heard my prayers, please hear this one. "I don't want us to be strangers either."

She brushed his hands from her face and stepped toward him, grabbing each side of his jean jacket in her hands. She rested her head against him and he felt the gentle breeze come again. He enjoyed the heat her closeness sent through his body. He gently put his arms on her shoulders and pushed her back so he could see her face, but her head remained bent. "So much has happened to bring us to this point."

Ty let out a slow, heavy sigh as he stared at her pretty, sad eyes. He thought at one time he would never recover from Alicia, shutting everyone out in the process. Now he was standing in a half built house with this incredible woman. "If you think time is all we need, then I'll give it as much as it takes."

Her dark eyes got a sparkle. "Me, too."

Ty knew as soon as he heard those words that he had just started to fall. He leaned his head toward hers, watching as her eyes closed. Slipping his arms around her waist, he pulled her to him as his lips came down on hers. He felt her hands leave his jacket and slowly move up over his chest. Her lips were sweet and full, and he felt his body melt at their warmth. Her touch awoke every nerve in his body. As he felt her tongue gently brush his lips, he slipped his out to meet hers. That was all it took for his body to ignite, and he found himself pulling her closer. He deepened the kiss and let his hands slide up her back. Her arms locked around his neck as a small moan escaped her.

Suddenly, it was if he could not get close enough to her. He had never felt so connected with another soul in all his life. He allowed his hands to roam down her back and over her bottom. He took the firm flesh in his hands. Her tongue teased his desire to a scorching, primal need. He pressed her against his hard cock that now ached for more of her, just like every other time Ty touched her. His hand moved up and around to the front of her shirt, cupping a large firm breast in his hand and searching for the nipple through the fabric with a teasing movement. Another soft moan escaped Maddy as his hunger raged, the sound almost his undoing.

He wanted her more than breath, but he couldn't get his troubled thoughts to leave him. Ty feared that once she remembered who she was and why she had sought him out, she would believe he had used her and take everything she had brought into his life away.

He gently lifted his head. Pulling his lips from hers, he felt the sudden coolness of the spring breeze on them. Her long lashes fluttered open and she looked into his eyes.

"Maddy, sweetheart, we had better put a stop to this," he told her, then drew in a ragged breath. Removing his hand from her bottom, he hesitated. He could feel her nipple erect under his fingers.

She took her lower lip, now puffy from their kiss, between her teeth.

"Ty?" The worry on her face and in her tone spoke volumes. "What are you not telling me?"

Ty couldn't believe she had asked that.

"What?" He shrugged.

She lifted her dark, slender brows indicating she was not buying it. Heaving a heavy sigh, he posed a question to her. "How much do you think all of this is worth?" He spread his arm out indicating the land surrounding them.

"Worth? Ty, you can't put a price tag on something you love. You can't buy it or sell it, or even use it as a bargaining chip."

"I was thinking more along the lines of a mortgage."

"Why?"

"I'm in a bind. I don't even know how I'm going to meet payroll next month."

He watched as something resembling real pain and loss clouded her eyes again. "No. Use it like that and you will lose it."

His hands gripped her shoulders as she made to move away from him.

"Hey! Come here. Come here. I didn't say I was going to. I was just thinking about it." Pulling her closer, he felt her tremble. "Easy, easy."

"Promise me you won't."

"I promise."

"No matter what."

"I promise." He squeezed his eyes closed, resting his chin on the top of her head and continued to hold her. "Besides, seeing all of this through your eyes has made me realize just what it really means to me."

He felt relief wash over her. Pushing back, he peered down at her. She sniffed, reminding him of a little girl. Ty gave a chuckle and let his hands slide to her waist so he could pull her back into his arms. He looked around the house that was still only a frame. "So, what do you think of the place?"

"I think it will be unbelievable with a little work. Kind of like us."

Ty smiled. He couldn't agree more.

Chapter 11

Riding back, Madison tried to put her feelings into words. As always, being on a horse seemed to help her think clearer. Only this time, she was having to work through her feelings as well.

What is happening to me? She was a lawyer, with a sharp mind. Yet, lately she was behaving more like a lovesick ninny. When she had first met Ty, she had felt there was something more to this man than all of the others put together. He had been charming and even playful. Even after she had threatened to put the cabosh on his precious contract, he had saved her life. He could have just let her drown.

She had overheard his dad talking about their financial straits. She had come to know Ty and knew he was stressed over the contract, the money, the payroll. She could see the worry in his eyes, though he was quick to hide it from her. The fact he had finally confided in her just made her even more determined to help him. So many people were counting on him. His family, half the town, and instead of being the workaholic they had described, he was taking time to be with her. Still, a part of her still shouted that he was only doing this in order to get what he wanted, and what he wanted was the contract.

But wasn't she doing the same thing?

She knew she should come clean and tell him the truth. She worried at her lower lip at the thought of revealing to him that she never had hit her head hard enough to lose her memory. At first, she had remained "clueless" in an attempt to disappear from her family. But waking up in his arms had been the turning point. So what if he only wanted a contract? He had saved her life and given her a glimpse of happiness. She would never settle for anything less than that. And for that, she owed him. She would get him that contract. It was the least she could do.

Looking over, she watched the man as he rode beside her. Somewhere along the way, her fake fiancé was turning out to be sweeter and sexier than any man had a right to be. The worst part was he was really likable. He was driving her insane. She almost laughed out loud at the thought of actually getting him to the altar. Ty struck her as the 'once burned, twice learned' type.

She rode along a few feet behind him, drinking in the beautiful scenery and enjoying the peaceful feeling that riding in the woods always brought to her. In spite of the situation, and the uncertainty, she didn't care if she never left.

As Ty led her back into his parents' back corral area, she saw Jordan on the back of a very large black horse with a red mane and tail. The horse was a beast, pretty to be sure, but a beast just the same. Madison jumped down off the palomino and looked at Ty. "He doesn't waste any time, does he? Nice horse," she commented.

Ty nodded and turned a worried glance her way. "He's been running wild on this land for a while. Jordan has been itching to break him. His name is Demon."

Madison watched Ty shake his head and dismount. "You know, this means Mom and Dad are probably going to cramp our style."

Maddy laughed. "We better get that house built then. As much as I love your truck…"

Hearing Jordan curse, she turned back. A cool wind came up and a crack of thunder rattled the sky.

She watched as Demon reared up on his hind legs and let out a loud whinny. In an instant he dropped back to his four legs and bucked violently, throwing Jordan off his back. Jordan's boot heel got hung up in the stirrup, which just seemed to annoy Demon more. Jill screamed and Ty cussed. From the corner of her eye, Maddy saw Harold running toward his hysterical wife.

Maddy had been around horses her whole life, and especially remembered some foul-tempered quarter horses her uncle had owned. This Demon reminded her of them. She dropped the palomino's reins and made her way to the coral where Demon was throwing a full-fledged fit, whinnying, rearing and pawing the air with lethal hooves. She jumped up on the fence and spoke softly and calmly to the horse.

"Come on, Demon. Settle down," she soothed as she jumped down into the coral. The horse put up a protest and snorted at her.

Oh yeah, he was mad. Demon reared and she dodged. She needed to get the reins that were secured tightly to the horn on the saddle.

"Come on, Demon, be a good boy," she crooned, quickly glancing at Jordan. He was being dragged along with each hop the horse took, but he was still struggling, which was good. The horse stopped suddenly, snorted, pinned his ears back and stared at Maddy. That was not a good sign, but at least she had his attention. "Please, Demon, come on, baby," she murmured and moved a slow step closer to the horse. She could hear Ty cussing in the background, but she ignored him.

"Good, Demon, good horse, so pretty," she continued, trying to calm the very hostile animal like she would an upset child. She took another step closer. The horse reared again, but with less force and Maddy stood her ground firmly. She was worried about Jordan being seriously injured by the horse, which was about seventeen hands. "Come on, baby, be a good boy; no one's going to hurt you."

The horse whinnied and snorted and twitched his ears as Madison slowly took another step. He was a lot of horse and there was a lot less of Madison to deal with it.

"Good, Demon. Come on, sweetie, let me pet you and tell how pretty you are."

She swallowed hard at the lump in her throat, knowing her next two steps would get her to the reins, but also put her under his churning front legs if he reared. She tried not to be nervous, for the last thing both she and Jordan needed was for Demon to lose control. She swallowed hard again and took another step.

"Look at you, such a good boy, such a good Demon," she soothed ever so gently. "I just want to pet you; you're so pretty, such a very pretty boy." She knew she had to keep talking while she took just one more step. She had to get to the reins without startling him and putting Jordan and herself in any more danger.

She sent a silent prayer and inhaled a slow, deep breath.

"Good, Demon, that's it." Her heart was beating in her head and throat, yet her voice remained cool and calm. "Okay, Demon, stay good, sweetie."

She took the last step and reached for his bridle. He started to rear but Maddy had a firm hold on him.

"Oh no, you don't," she warned a little firmer as she held him. She reached slowly up and with a shaky hand, stroked his nose. The horse seemed to settle at the affection, even while his big brown eyes rolled with uncertainty. Madison looked down to Jordan, who was lying on his back with his foot in the stirrup. He turned his head and nodded. She looked over to Harold and motioned him in to the corral. Turning toward Ty might have been too much movement for the horse.

"Demon's so good," she continued to soothe as Harold moved toward Jordan and gently freed his boot. Then he helped Jordan to his feet and dusted him off. Jordan stepped back a little stiffly as Harold stepped close to Maddy and undid the reins. Once he had them firmly in his hand, he took the bridle from Maddy and led Demon toward the barn. Maddy moved over to Jordan to ask if he was okay. Ty was already standing next to him. He wheeled around and looked at her like she had sprouted a second head.

"What on God's green earth possessed you to do that?"

Okay, the strange look is directly related to his temper.

"I was helping your brother."

"You were not using your head!" he snapped in fury.

His words hit her the wrong way.

"Oh, really now?" She tilted her chin in defiance. She turned to Jordan and with a worried look said, "Let me get the corral door for you."

"Madison! We're talking!" Ty yelled after her.

She didn't bother to turn around as she answered. She just kept walking. "No! You're yelling and I'm walking away."

"Fucking unbelievable, Jesus Christ, you should have thought about what you were doing."

"Ty, watch your mouth in front of the lady," his father scolded from somewhere behind her.

Madison opened the corral door and headed toward the house.

"A lady does not hurdle a corral and get in with a temperamental Arabian. Madison, get back here! I'm not done with you!" he called as she reached for the front door.

Madison, not Maddy.

Turning, she found him hands on his hips, fuming. "As long as you insist on throwing a tantrum like a child, I'm forced to treat you like one." With that, she spun on her boot heel, swung open the front door and walked into the house. Her fury mounted as did the sounds of Ty's boots as he came in behind her.

"Are you calling me a child, there, princess?" His voice carried a dangerous edge along with a challenge.

He was spoiling for a fight, and if there was one word Madison hated being called worse than muffin, it was princess. She came to a stop and spun just as Harold and Jill helped Jordan in the door. "What did you call me?" she demanded, rising to his challenge.

He pushed his face closer to hers, noses almost touching. "Princess!"

"You are calling me a princess? Mr. Rough-and-tumble-look-at-me-I'm-a-cowboy, is calling me a princess?"

"Yeah!"

"Well, if that's the way you feel, then what are we doing?"

"Oh dear," was all Jill said as she shut the door.

Ty gave her a dirty look, then turned from his mother back to Maddy. "I ought to turn you over my knee, you know that?" His tone sounded ruthless and hit all the wrong buttons on Maddy.

Her good breeding was gone and her temper raged into full swing. "You'd get more than you bargained for if you tried."

Ty scowled and his nostrils flared, rather like Demon's. He took a deep breath and Maddy braced for a blast. "I hate to break this to you, *princess,* but what you did was downright stupid!"

"You did not just call me stupid!"

"I know well trained cowboys that wouldn't have jumped into that corral. God, girl! You should have let my dad or me handle it."

She could feel the heat radiating from his body as his scolding continued.

"You chauvinistic pig! I'm sorry if I broke the sacred Wyoming macho codes, but you get this through your stubborn head right now, Ty Kirkland! Just because I don't pee standing up does not mean that I'm less then your so-called superior sex!"

"Stubborn?" he roared at her with his temper rearing in a way similar to a bucking, disgruntled horse. "How can you call *me* stubborn?"

"Well letters make words and when you put those words together, that makes something called a sentence," she told him, knowing her voice and volume were far from ladylike.

"How dare you become condescending with me."

"Well the tone fits a spoiled child having a tantrum!" she yelled back at him.

He looked dumbfounded, but only for an instant. "Well, *you* are the expert on spoiled."

"Says the man with wounded pride because his bride-to-be took action in a life or death situation. Do you want a band-aid for that hurt ego?"

"You sharp tongued little girl!"

"You have no idea!" she yelled back.

"What was I thinking?"

"When?"

"That's it!" he exploded, suddenly grabbing her arms. "Either get that temper in check, or I'll do it for you!"

"And you're an egotistical ass who needs to learn a few things on how to be a gentleman."

"Well little Miss High and Mighty, out here a gentleman gets run over. Why don't you take that wad of cash and buy something useful, like a reality check!"

"I'm not Alicia!"

"You got that right!"

For an instant, Maddy hated him. Then again, she once read that there was a fine line between love and hate. She wanted to cry.

"What, no comeback? Good!" He let her go and stepped away. "I'm outta here. I have to get away from that spoiled temper of yours."

Maddy felt her soul split at the tone and harshness of his words. Tears came to her eyes and as much as she wanted not to cry, Ty's words hurt.

"Still silent? What a refreshing change from that foul temper!" He must have seen the tears in her eyes because he looked away too quickly. "I can't take this." Turning, he headed for the door.

"Where are you going?" she asked, her voice sounded pitiful and she resented her emotions coming into play.

"Well, *darlin'*, that's for me to know and none of your business." His voice matched the sneer on his face, and Maddy felt the wound go deeper than she expected.

A tear escaped and rolled down her cheek. Ty flared his nostrils and walked out the door, slamming it behind him. She listened as his truck tore out of the drive like an angered demon from hell.

She looked up, meeting the shocked and saddened expressions of his family. "I only tried to help."

Jordan moved slowly toward her. "Ty is stubborn. I've never known him to back down. It's a failing," he told her, giving her a hug. Maddy felt more tears spill down her cheeks and soak into the soft, worn denim of Jordan's shirt.

"Neither do I." She pulled away from Jordan and looked at Harold and Jill. "I'm so sorry," she sobbed as she turned and ran upstairs to the room they had shared.

She shut the door and fell on the bed crying. "Is this how it's going to feel when I tell him the truth?" She sobbed into the pillow and let all the hurt inside her flow into wounded tears upon the pillow.

* * * *

Ty could hardly see the road he was so mad.

What the hell went through that pretty head? He slammed his fist against the dashboard. He had never been so scared in his life. He had been almost paralyzed with fear, staring dumbfounded as she had jumped the corral and sweet-talked a horse about two hands too high for her and tempered like the devil himself. *Where the hell would the Bellini princess learn to do that? It was apparent that she'd done it before.* She had scared the shit out of him. He had never felt a knot fill his entire stomach like the one that wouldn't leave him now.

Demon was just that, a demon. That damn horse could have killed Jordan nine different ways to Sunday. She had saved his brother's life. Still, it didn't change the fact that what she had done was stupid.

"Stupid!" He let out a frustrated growl.

He saw the town lights come into view. There was no denying he liked Maddy. Hell he didn't know what physically attracted him more, her eyes or her smile. The curls in her long dark hair that formed natural ringlets were as beautiful as the lady herself. There was so much more to the rich princess then he had imagined she could be. *She was real and sweet and...*

"Oh hell!" *This is crazy.* He was crazy about her and he should never have reacted the way he did. She had truly looked heartbroken when he'd stormed out. And he had slammed the front door behind him for effect.

He had been torn between thrashing her and holding her so tightly that she would never scare him like that again. The knot in his stomach grew painful as he recalled her tear-filled face. Scanning ahead, he saw the neon lights of Roper's Bar calling him down the street. Just up ahead, he saw the pay phone. He angle parked in the stall and stared at the phone. He readjusted his Stetson and let out a sigh.

"Maddy, what have you done to me?" he asked the empty cab of the truck. He knew the answer. She had, without meaning to, turned his life upside down. He was falling in love with her. As crazy as it was, it was no more crazy than him not making it to Roper's Bar at the other end of town. His fights with Alicia would have had him on his third beer already. Maddy was right about one thing. She was not Alicia. He knew Maddy would never back down the way Alicia had after a dust up. Not Maddy. He got out of the truck and shut the door. He reached in his pocket and grabbed change for the phone.

* * * *

Maddy lay in his bed, holding his pillow to her nose. She couldn't figure out why she was crying over her exchange with Ty. It was past insane and bordering on idiocy. It wasn't like she and Ty had a real relationship. She had begun just trying to find out just what Ty Kirkland had to do with her almost marriage to Teddy. She was also hiding out here. Hiding out and falling head over heels in love. He needed the contract with her father's company and she needed out of her marriage contract to Teddy.

It was supposed to be a short arrangement, yet here she was crying over Ty like they had been together since the beginning of time. *How, in such a short time, could I come to care so much about a total stranger?* She knew how. Ty didn't feel like a stranger. Everything about him was familiar. She knew he was probably just after the contract, but he had saved her life. Maybe he was feeling something for her as well.

No, that was insane. She had to pull herself together. She had a law degree from Harvard. She was not some flighty teenager, she was a grown woman. There was no way he was falling in love with her. That was too fanciful.

Sitting up, she wiped at her tears as a knock sounded on the bedroom door.

Looking up, she found Jordan leaning in.

"Are you okay?"

"Yeah, just feeling silly."

"Feel like taking a phone call?"

Suddenly, her blood chilled within her veins. *Her parents? Bethany?* "Who would call me here?"

"Some cowboy."

"Ty?" she asked as she scrambled off of his bed.

"You think you're surprised. We're his family and we're all stunned. Used to be he'd call at three in the morning wanting us to come pick him up at the bar, at least that was the rule with Alicia. Apparently, something has changed him. My guess is that something is you."

Maddy didn't know what to say. She was stunned. The man who had left her earlier would not be calling her. She made her way to the receiver waiting for her by the phone.

"Hello?" She felt apprehensive as she spoke. She really didn't want to cry again.

"Maddy, I'm so sorry, sweetheart." Ty's voice sounded strained and downright miserable. "Are you okay?"

She felt tears sting her eyes, but fought to keep them at bay. "No."

A long, heavy sigh came through the receiver. "I didn't think so. I'm not either. I overreacted and I am so sorry."

"I'm sorry too." She heard her voice go watery.

There was a long silence, and Madison felt her heart reach her throat. She couldn't even hear him breathing. Finally, she heard a small breath.

"Maddy, I left with the intent on going to Ropers. It's a bar but..." The silence seemed to stretch forever. "Never mind. I'm coming home."

"Okay," she managed to get out without the tears choking off the sound.

"I need to see you right now and talk this out."

His words were so soaked with turmoil that a tear rolled down her cheek.

"Me too," she said in a whisper. "I'll watch for you."

"Okay," he replied hoarsely and she heard him hang up the phone.

She placed the phone on the base and looked up at the perfectly white ceiling.

Oh, what have I done? He sounded miserable. How could he be just as miserable as me?

She turned around to face the Kirklands. They all looked worried and surprised at the same time. She didn't know what to say.

"So he's coming back?" Harold asked over his newspaper.

Madison wiped the rebel tear and nodded. "Yes."

"Whatever it is you've been doing to that son of mine, don't stop, Maddy. You're the best he'll ever find," Harold told her firmly. He turned to his wife. "I never thought that boy would meet his match."

Jill nodded and turned to Madison. "Maddy, honey, I know Ty can be a bit stubborn and a little hot-headed, but don't give up on him."

Madison felt Jill's words touch her heart. "I don't think I could even if I wanted to."

Jill laughed. "Spoken like a woman in love."

Love? Ty? Oh, Jill, if only I could tell you the truth.

"If you don't mind, I told Ty I would watch for him."

"You know, Maddy," Jill said, stepping closer for a quick hug. "That son of mine may wear the pants, but you just remind him who holds the rope."

"Okay," she answered, heading for the front porch. She stopped, seeing Ty's lamb's wool coat, the one he put on her the first time they had met. Taking it down from the coat rack, she slid her arms in and wrapped it close about her, snuggling in its warmth.

* * * *

Ty brought his truck to stop on the wet drive. Maddy was sitting on the front porch in a wooden deck chair she had pulled up to the railing, resting her chin on her hands and staring out at the night. Her hair was loose and hanging in ringlets down past her shoulders and she was wearing his big jacket. She seemed lost in thought and didn't even seem to notice the truck.

All Ty noticed was her. He jumped out of the truck and shut the door. The sound seemed to startle her out of her reverie. She looked at him and stood, her sad expression reaching out to him.

"Don't make me come up there, Madison Bellini," he teased, with a smile.

A smile began to transform her face. By the time he moved a step, she had run off the steps and practically leaped at him. He scooped her in his arms and buried his face in her hair. He felt her arms wrap around his neck tightly. They were getting soaked but they didn't seem to care.

"Don't ever pull a stunt like that again. I could have lost you," he told her, still very unnerved by her act.

"Don't ever tear off in your truck mad," she told him, trying to sound tough.

"You have a deal, sweetheart." He gently placed her on the ground, firmly held her with one arm and took his Stetson off with the other. With his lips on hers, he tasted the salt from her tears. She met his kiss willingly. He answered her with a need that was not sexual, but emotional. He felt his body relax, tasting forgiving warmth and desire in her kiss. He had never felt so much emotion in a kiss. It was as if their souls had met and become one.

"I didn't mean to scare you," she whispered softly.

"I know, sweetheart. I didn't mean to make you cry. I hate myself for making you shed tears over me," he told her, knowing in his heart that for the first time in his life, he meant it.

Madison swallowed hard and smiled. "I forgive you. You're here now."

"I am and we are both getting wet. Do you want to go for a ride?" Ty chuckled.

Chapter 12

Maddy turned the mixer off, lifted the beaters, and began to stir the chocolate pudding as Jill related all the latest town gossip she had gleaned from Mrs. Baxter.

Maddy tried to concentrate, but the visions of Ty's head thrashing back and forth on his truck seat kept her from hearing anything Jill said. She had done things with him last night that she had never done before. He had driven her out to the house and had seemed almost as nervous as she had felt as he pulled the truck over. He had slid down in his seat, pushed his Stetson back and tapped his finger on the steering wheel, reminding her of a kid on his first date, uncertain of what move to make next.

For a minute, she had thought he might be contemplating telling her the truth about their fake engagement. He seemed as if he were ready to say something very important, but as she watched him scratch his head then rub the back of his neck, she knew whatever it was, it would change everything. She couldn't lose him. That thought had shaken her to the core. So, as he turned to speak, her newfound fear spurred her into action. She had moved faster than she thought possible, tearing his Stetson from his head and silencing him with her lips, her tongue, her touch.

All she had thought was that she had to keep him from talking. It drove her forward, making her bolder than she had ever been. She had trailed kisses across his rugged jaw, down his chin, his neck, and back to his mouth when he tried to catch his breath. Her fingers had made short work of the snaps on his shirt and she had reveled in the feel of his warm skin under her fingers.

When he had whispered her name, it had driven her touch lower, undoing his jeans and dragging the denim down his thighs, then forcing him down in the seat. He had stared up at her with astonishment lighting his dark eyes. Astonished, but oh so very appreciative.

She had found him more than ready for her and lowered her mouth to the heated tip of his cock, tasting the flavor of his pre-cum on her tongue as she worked to learn the shape of him.

She had felt him try to sit up, and she had pushed him back down, keeping her hand on his chest. Taking him into her mouth, she worked to know the entire length, and was rewarded as any words that left his mouth were those of wonder and primal gasps and growls.

"Maddy!"

Jarred from her thoughts, she jerked her attention to Jill to see her sliding on her coat.

"I'm sorry."

"Aw, sweetie, it's okay. You just seemed lost in thought. I need to run to town and pick up a few more things."

Maddy looked down at the pudding, trying to hide her embarrassment . She had been miles away, reliving each kiss, each touch, each taste...

She sighed.

"Are you all right, Maddy?"

Maddy nodded, all the while picturing Ty's head thrashing on the truck seat as he called her name, his voice hoarse and rasping. "What? Oh, I'm fine."

"I worry about you. Maybe I shouldn't go."

"Go. I'm fine."

As Maddy watched Jill's SUV heading down the drive, she left the spatula in the bowl of pudding and made her way to the phone in the living room.

Dialing Beth's cell phone, she waited to hear her friend's voice. As she heard Beth's answering service instead of her friend, she could not help feeling something was terribly wrong. She replaced the receiver and returned to the kitchen to absently stir the pudding.

Her troubled thoughts turned darker. *Why would Beth's phone be turned off? That was as unheard of as taking the sun from the sky.* Unless her parents had somehow taken Beth's phone to track her here. Unless they were going to force her somehow to return and marry Teddy. Unless...

Arms slid around her from behind, causing her to jerk, a gasp springing from her lips at the feel of someone behind her.

"Whoa, Maddy."

"Ty?" She turned, seeing the man she had been dreaming of earlier now staring down at her and wearing a slash of chocolate pudding across his cheek.

She was more than relieved to see him standing there. He had left her sleeping this morning and as her gaze swept over him greedily, she realized she was starving for him.

He looked amazing in very fitted, very worn and slightly ripped jeans. A black t-shirt stretched across his chest and tightly over his biceps, making them appear even more muscular than they already were. Her stomach fluttered at the thought that those muscles were from hard work and not a gym at a country club. The flutter grew stronger as she recalled those strong arms reaching for her blindly as she had tasted every last drop of his red-hot release. Last night had been one of the best nights of her life and she reveled in the memory of those same arms holding her as she had fallen asleep.

She watched as he reached up, dragging a blunt finger through the pudding on his face, and brought it to his mouth. "Mmmm. You were a million miles away when I came in."

Not exactly a million.

"You snuck up on me."

"I didn't mean to startle you."

"What are you doing home?"

"Funny you should ask, since I'm blaming you for my lack of concentration."

"You didn't get a lot of sleep, did you?"

Those arms tightened, bringing her closer to feel every inch of hardness. "Um, no, I didn't. But that wasn't exactly what I was talking about...or thinking about. What were you thinking about just now?"

"Me?"

"Yeah. I stood in the doorway watching you for the longest time."

"You did? I didn't hear you come in."

"No, you were wrapped up in your thoughts with this faraway look in your eyes," he said with a grin that stopped Madison's heart. "Tell me you were thinking of me and you'll make my day."

Madison let out a small giggle. "Such an ego. You know I was thinking of you."

"Well, a guy can hope, can't he?" He pulled her into a kiss.

He tasted warm and sweet and Madison was sure she would get lost in the taste of him. "You taste good," he told her.

"I was just thinking the same about you."

She brought her fingertip across his cheek and swiped off more of the pudding. Instead of tasting it, she redeposited it on the tip of his nose.

Ty scrunched it in disgust and let go of her as she started to laugh. "So you think that's funny?"

"Well..."

As his eyes sparkled, Maddy felt her knees weaken at the sight of his reckless side. He was so sexy, chocolate pudding on his nose and all. He wiped his nose and removed the pudding then reached over and put it on Maddy's nose.

She flinched and in the process got the remainder of the pudding from the spatula onto Ty's chin and shirt. "Oops," she said, trying not to laugh. "Sorry."

Ty laughed and released her. "No, you're not." He stuck his hand in the bowl and scooped out some of the pudding.

Maddy felt her eyes go wide. She screeched as Ty lifted his hand. She was able somehow to move back to miss some, but not all of the pudding. The majority of it landed on her shoulder and down the front of her. She scooped up the glob of pudding on her shoulder and flung it back.

"That does it," Ty warned and grabbed the bowl of pudding.

Madison grabbed the bag closest to her, which luckily, was flour. She stuck her hand in and grabbed a handful.

"You wouldn't dare," he said, then let out a surprised laugh and stepped closer with his hand back in the bowl.

"Sure, I would." She flung the flour at him. "Ha, now you're a pastry."

"And I am going to turn you into dessert." He darted around the table toward her and flung the pudding at her. It hit her cheek, the glob falling down the front of her shirt. She flung back the glob on her shirt, hitting him in the chest.

He sent more pudding from the bowl at her and missed, hitting the fridge instead.

Madison grabbed another handful of flour and tossed it at him. It covered his black t-shirt and she laughed in surprise at the perfect hit.

Chuckling, Ty came toward her. "You are so mine." He threw more pudding and missed. Madison retaliated by throwing more flour and hitting him. She dodged again as he came at her. She watched in excitement as he set the nearly empty bowl of pudding on the table. Then he grabbed the bag of powdered sugar.

"Oh no," Madison exclaimed, darting to put the table between them.

"Oh yes, sweetheart." Ty tore the bag open wide. "My turn." He tossed the open bag across the table at her, coating her with white sugar.

Both Maddy and Ty were now covered in white powder. She flung another handful of flour at him. He retaliated with what was left in the bag of powdered sugar and coated her again.

Madison laughed at Ty's very pleased look. He dropped the empty bag on the table and began to stalk her around the table. Madison moved the other way to the open space. It was too late when she discovered that Ty had changed direction and was actually going in the direction she ran.

When her boot heel caught some of the flour on the floor, she slipped. Ty reached for her as the bag of flour dropped, causing him to slip and go down on the floor as well. He pulled her on top of him.

"Are you okay?" she asked, surprised and feeling the solidness of his form underneath her. There was no denying that Ty Kirkland was 'pure man'.

"I have a beautiful woman on top of me. Yeah, I'm doing just fine," he teased, his eyes darkening with desire.

Madison wiped some of the flour off of his face. Even though he resembled a powdered doughnut, her heart quickened with the feeling of being desired. She hesitated a moment, then brought her lips to his. Ty's arms wrapped around her waist pulling her hard against his muscled frame as his tongue parted her lips to deepen the kiss. She met his tongue with her own and savored the taste of him. Heat was suddenly coursing though her body.

He gently cupped her head, lifting her lips from his. "Careful, sweetheart, kisses like that could get you a lot more than you bargained for."

Madison looked at the sexy man covered with food in front of her. She shifted slightly, straddling his hips as she sat up. She could not remember anything that had ever been this much fun or sexually arousing. He was just terrific. Everything about him was terrific. She placed her hands flat on the floor on either side of his head and debated how much courage she had. She had never been this forward in her life. Her behavior lately had set a pattern. Ty Kirkland made it easy to be forward.

"So would this be better?" She ran her tongue up his neck where the spatula had gotten him earlier, tasting the blend of pudding and Ty himself.

Groaning, he shifted his body under her as his hands rested firmly on her hips. She caught his gaze with her own, and saw the yearning blazing in his eyes.

"Better for what? Me taking you up to the bedroom?" His voice, a husky whisper, caressed her spine and dampened her thong.

She felt a smile spread across her face and arched a brow.

"How about this?" She lowered her lips to the nape of his neck by his ear and, after placing a couple wet kisses there, brought her mouth to his ear. "Is this any better?" She purposely allowed her breath to caress his ear and neck feeling the fabric of his jeans tighten beneath her, hardening in arousal as another groan left him.

Ty sat up and held her tight as he gently placed her on the floor between his legs. She wrapped her arms around his neck as his lips found hers, coming down on them in a heated kiss of pure desire. Her body ached in need. He pulled away and looked her in the eyes. "You have no idea what you do to me."

"I was sitting on you. I think I have a pretty good idea." She kissed him again. His arms wrapped around her and she felt him tugging her shirt from her jeans. The instant his hands touched her bare back, her body ignited in longing. Their tongues entwined as she grabbed the hair at the back of his neck lacing her fingers through it. His hands moved slowly up her sides bringing a soft moan from deep inside her. She gasped when they slowly moved up over the lace of her bra to cup her breasts. *Who would have thought the touch of a man could hold so much power?*

She lost all sense of time and space as she felt Ty's fingers tease her hardening nipples through the lace bra. Squeezing her eyes shut, she knew the feel of his fingers stroking and exploring further. She felt a slight tug as he hooked a finger to the clasp, freeing her breasts. Her body responded to the touch of his hands on her; his thumbs circling her hard nipples.

Only as his touch left her did she open her eyes. She found he now stood before her and peering up, she watched as his jaw tightened and his fingers moved to unfasten his jeans. Reaching down, he held his hand out for her to grasp. Something in the way his dark eyes smoldered with heated passion let her know exactly what he had in mind. As she placed her hand in his, she watched the excited smirk play on his firm mouth.

He lifted her to her feet and backed her next to the kitchen table.

Maddy searched his flour and pudding encrusted face as she felt his fingers opening her jeans. In the silence, the sound of the tines of her zipper seemed louder than normal. His breath was coming harder, longer, deeper, then quicker. She held onto his forearms as he moved her to sit on the table.

"Ty?"

"It's okay," he whispered, as if reading her mind. "We are all alone."

"But someone could…"

He was already shaking his head. He lowered his mouth to hers as his fingers moved between her silky thighs, finding her damp and ready for him. She kicked off her boots and let her jeans and thong slide to the floor. She should have felt a bit unsure about this, but Ty's fingers felt so good, all she could think of was how she wanted to feel him inside her. He moaned and she tugged his jeans down. His hard, large cock danced before her eyes. Ty's finger teased over her clit and she bucked against his hand. He withdrew his fingers and pressed between her legs. Then he scooted her to the edge of the table and thrust himself deep into her. She moaned and reached for his waist.

His cock worked in and out of her and her hands cupped his ass, pressing him inside of her harder and fasater. His lips lowered to hers, his tongue prying her mouth open and then exploring it. Her tongue met his and her belly tightened. He gave a loud groan and his cock slammed into her hard. As his release shot inside her, she tightened her hold on his firm ass. Her body shook from her shoulders down as she climaxed. Her walls tightened around him and she threw her head back from the intensity.

She straightened her head and fought for breath as he rested his forehead against her shoulder.

"Unbelievable," he whispered and lifted his head. He planted a small kiss on her lips, then looked at her again. "That was really unbelievable."

Madison felt relief wash over her. "I could get used to that," she told him with a smile of her own.

Ty chuckled and gently brushed some of her hair back. "I'm glad to hear that. Why don't we discuss this in the shower?"

"I think that can be arranged. Consider it a date," she teased.

He lifted a brow. "The first of many, I hope."

He moved away and scooped her boots and jeans off the floor. Tucking them into one arm, he took her hand with the other and led her up the stairs.

Quickly, he tossed her stuff on his bedroom floor and led her into the bathroom. She shut the door tight, locking it. Turning, she stripped off the rest of her clothes and stood completely naked before him. She could tell his cock was rock-hard again and she found she could hardly wait. He stepped forward and closed the distance between them.

"God, you're beautiful," he whispered.

"And not nearly through with you."

She pulled his shirt over his head and tossed it to the floor. She stepped back so he could remove the rest of his clothes. His cock sprang to life despite the cool air of the bathroom. Reaching a hand out, she wrapped it around him and she began to stroke him. He wrapped her in his arms and moved her back toward the shower. Her lips trailed over his neck and jaw as he turned on the water. She wanted to drive him insane.

Ty could barely keep from groaning as her hand worked in a steady motion up and down his cock, while her lips and tongue teased the sensitive skin by his ear. He wanted to bury himself in her again and had every intention of doing it. After he adjusted the temperature, he gently stepped out of her hold and away from her.

"Get in." His voice was husky and her curvy frame moved into the shower and under the spray. He entered the shower and closed the glass door behind him. With smooth movements, he enveloped her in his arms beneath the spray. His cock throbbed as it pressed against her belly and his tongue plunged into her mouth. She gave a moan and wrapped her arms around his neck. He turned her slightly and rested her back against the wall of the shower. She flinched slightly.

"It's cold," she whimpered against his tongue. Sliding his hands over her hot, wet skin, he brought them down to her ass. He pulled his lips from hers and lifted her slowly. Her arms tightened around him and he brought her above his erection and lowered her over it. The pressing of his tip against her was torture and he thrust deep inside her. She moaned in pleasure and wrapped her legs around his waist.

She was so tight and always so wet for him. Ty couldn't get enough of her. He moved deeper inside her and started pumping in and out of her slick walls. Her pussy ground against him, meeting his movements with her own. As he picked up speed, his mouth reclaimed hers. He groaned as the pressure built in him. He wanted to come inside her again and again and planned on doing exactly that today.

Maddy loved the feeling of Ty's large, hard cock inside her and knew he would bring her to climax. The pressure built in her stomach and her body trembled as an orgasm overtook her body. "Ty," she called to him as she rode higher.

She clung to his shoulders as he continued to lift her with each thrust. In the distance, she heard a ringing.

Again.

And again.

The phone in the living room was ringing. She had no idea where the thought came from, but the vision of her parents swamped her. Her fingers slipped in their hold on his slick wet shoulders and she grasped at him almost in desperation. As he neared release, her arms locked tightly around his corded neck.

The ringing sounded again, and with each ring, she grew more fearful. Her fingers clutched at his hair, tugging as she felt the coiling in her stomach ignite with a burst, jerking her entire body as her channel groped him. His cock pulsed and his orgasm shot hot and deep inside her. He groaned loudly as he came. She knew an urging so intense, it zinged through her like a powerful jolt, her cries echoing off the tiles, again…again. With it came tears as she felt him relax his hold on her, gasping for breath. She grabbed for a stronger hold on him, her tears falling from her eyes only to be washed away by the steady stream of water from over his shoulder.

His arms moved around her, holding her close against him.

"Is that the phone?" he asked, sliding the shower door ajar.

"No," she answered quickly, her hand moving to stop him.

He looked back, peering down into her face. "Sorry. That was hardly the right thing to say at a time like this." He dropped a kiss on her wet lips. "Tell you what, let's get out of here and I'll make it up to you in my room."

Just as her breathing returned to normal, the phone rang again.

"Let it ring," she pleaded, trying to keep her voice light, seductive.

"I think I will. Whoever it is, I doubt anything they have to say would be more interesting than what we're talking about."

Her relief was quick and she flung her arms about his neck and hugged his wet body as if it would be the last time.

"Are you okay, Maddy?"

She nodded, trying to offer a smile. He lifted one dark brow and his gaze moved over the bruise still prominent on her smooth forehead.

"If I ask you to do something, will you?" he asked.

She slid her hands down his wet slick chest, skimming her fingernails across his taut abdomen and reveled in the breath he sucked in.

"Name it." She wondered if it would be something truly wicked.

"I, uh, I want you to go and see Dr. Phillips."

Her mouth opened to refuse. There was no way in hell she was going to get near a medical diagnostician. She could not take the chance that he might discover her condition was nonexistent. "I don't..."

"Don't worry, I didn't mean today. I'll make you an appointment for tomorrow."

"I don't like doctors, Ty."

"I don't either, but if I dumped my car in to the Medicine Bow, I think I'd want to at least have him check me out."

Stepping away from him, Maddy grabbed a towel. As she wrapped it around her, she knew her movements were as stilted as her voice.

"Jordan checked me out, didn't he? Didn't your mom say he was as good as a doctor?"

"Whoa, whoa." He was on her quickly, easing his arms around her body. "Easy there, princess."

"Don't…call…"

He pulled her against him and wrapped his arms around her form behind. "Maddy, what are you afraid of? I'll go with you."

"No!"

She fought the sensations as his mouth found the wet skin of her neck, his tongue sliding dangerously close to her ear. She couldn't stop the delicious shiver that coursed through her, buckling her knees. His moan mingled with hers and she knew somehow she would end up in his bed and at the doctor's.

As he walked her across the hall and into his room, she tried to think of a way, any way to get out of this. Finally, she felt his tongue darting inside of her ear and she gave up. Nodding her head as he moved her onto the bed, she promised him she would go.

Chapter 13

Ty moved quickly and quietly through the kitchen, sweeping up and wiping away any signs of the food fight from earlier. His thoughts were concentrated more on her than his cleaning mission. He had held her beside him as he rested flat on his back, sucking in deep breaths as his body had cooled for the fourth time. He had felt bone weary, yet his eyes had been wide open with concern. He had stared at the ceiling for the longest time, trying to figure out where her desperation had come from.

She had clung to him as if she were afraid he was about to disappear. Could she still be afraid he might walk out, like he had after their dust up?

Now, as he returned the dust pan and broom to the pantry, he heard the chirping beep from his pager. Plucking it from his belt loop, he peered down at the message.

911.

Jordan.

He pushed it back onto his belt and moved into the living room. Before he could pick up the receiver, the phone rang.

"Kirkland," he answered.

"Ty, it's Jordan," he heard.

"I was just going to call. What's the emergency?"

"I'm at the plant. You need to come over here."

"What's happened?"

169

"Nothing with the plant. Plant is fine."

"Mom and Dad okay?"

"This isn't about Mom or Dad. This about Madison Bellini."

"Jordan, I don't want to discuss this with you."

"Just get over here."

As Ty hung up, he felt an incredible urge to take the phone and throw it across the room. The tiredness he had felt earlier was now replaced with a trickle of dread. Snaking his hand across his neck, he rubbed furiously as he headed out.

* * * *

As he drove over the bridge, he scanned the wall until he passed the gaping and splintered hole where Maddy's car had left the pavement and plunged into the river. The sheriff had said her tires had caught in the wide pool of mud at the entrance and she had simply lost control.

He had gone along with that assumption in order to protect her. The sheriff did not have all the facts. He didn't know that Madison Bellini had just traveled hundreds of miles to threaten him and accuse him of ruining her life, even though they had never met. He also did not know that Ty had tried to impress her, seduce her, and had ended up arguing with her. Ty recalled stepping back into his office and seeing her holding up her hand to stall him as she brazenly read over his financial statement from the bank. That had made him furious. Then, as she had backed him into a corner, he had lashed out. She had become so upset, she had screamed at him, promising him that she would wreck any hopes he'd ever entertained of obtaining the contract and financial backing from her father and godfather. The same men who had treated him as he were something on the bottom of their expensive Italian loafers.

When he took off after her, he hadn't meant to scare her. He'd meant only to stop her and try and get her to calm down long enough to listen to reason. She had only picked up speed.

Just like their argument over Demon. He thought he had her backed into a corner, but she had only picked up steam. He should have remembered how Madison Bellini reacted to a fight. Amnesia or no amnesia, she was a force of nature.

Pulling up to his office, Ty stepped out of his truck and stretched, long and slow. Here was the bone weary tiredness that he had experienced earlier. God, she was incredible. Muscles ached...muscles he hadn't even known he had, until Maddy came along.

"Whew!" He pushed his breath out slowly and made his way to his office.

Jordan was waiting for him, with a bottle of whiskey and two glasses.

"What are we doing, Jordan? Playing poker?"

"Nope. Sit down, little brother."

"Oh, God," he moaned. "Is this gonna take long? I have a beautiful woman warming my bed and I'd like to get back to helping her do it."

Ty moved around the desk and stopped dead in his tracks at the sight before him. An expensive suitcase lay opened on the floor, a white frothy gown billowing out and over the sides.

"That looks like a..."

"Wedding dress?"

Ty felt a cold chill rake him from head to toe. He bent down and lifted the gown from the suitcase. It was a designer gown, and designed to fit one woman...his woman.

"Guess how much a dress like this costs?" Jordan asked him.

Ty could care less at the moment. "I don't know. A lot?"

"A whole hell of a lot. I looked it up on the web. This is an Alfred Sung. It's not even called a dress. Or a gown. Just a Sung. I looked it all up. These things run upwards of ten thousand dollars."

"This was your emergency?"

"Ty. She was carrying this in her luggage."

"So? Sometimes I carry a…first-aid kit, but that doesn't make me a surgeon."

Ty knew his words were as lame as the look on Jordan's face told him they were. Lifting the glass of whiskey, he sat back on the desk. "Okay. She totes a wedding dress with her. She is engaged to get married, you know."

"No. She *was* getting married."

Ty felt the drink slam into his windpipe at the same time those words slammed into his brain.

"What do you mean *was*?" His mind conjured up the desperate hold she'd had on him in the shower again. *Could she have gotten her memory back? Does she know we weren't really engaged?* "If you called me down here to tell me what a bastard I am again, I'm liable to beat the shit out of you."

"You'd try. Look, sit down. I pulled this up on the net."

"Aw, come on, Jordy. You can't believe the stuff you see on there."

"I typed in Madison Bellini," Jordan kept talking as if he either never heard Ty or was ignoring his protests. "Look!"

Ty felt the anger seeping up his neck to flame even the tips of his ears. Turning, he stared at the flat screen. "*The Alberta Sun.*"

"Read it."

"Runaway Bride Needs Relaxation," Ty read the words aloud. "There. You happy?"

"Read the story, Tarzan."

Ty made a throaty noise, hoping it sounded like the menacing warning it was intended as. "Family and friends were gathered to witness the joining of the Bellini and Von Housen fortunes. The wedding of the century, as it had been termed months before, entailed everything from the Alfred Sung gown to the peach and white rose wedding bundles and bouquet."

Ty sneered at the thought of peach roses, but read on.

"Standing before the altar, Miss Madison Bellini, heiress to the Bambardi and Bellini oil fortune shocked all assembled as she refused to marry Edward Von Housen III. Confusion and chaos reigned supreme as Miss Bellini fled the church, bouquet in hand and still in her wedding gown."

"See? Didn't you say something about her saying you were ruining her life?"

"Let me finish reading!" Ty held up his hand, reminiscent of the way Maddy had done to him upon their first meeting.

"When confronted by reporters, Mrs. Ivory Bellini excused Miss Bellini's astonishing behavior, saying Madison was experiencing bride's jitters and had sought relaxation at her favorite spa. However, reporters later discovered that Miss Bellini had not only run from the church, she had fled over the border and into the U.S. To date, no amount of questioning seems to shake Mrs. Bellini's steadfast assertion, which places her daughter at a nearby spa. Sources also now suspect a society cover-up. Both Bellini and Von Housen camps have sent out new invitations for the new wedding of the century. When confronted with the possibility that Miss Madison Bellini fled the country, the Bellini camp called the allegations categorically false. This just gets better and better, folks."

Ty leaned back and lifted his whiskey to his lips as Jordan scrolled down to a picture snapped of Maddy running from the church, her expensive gown hiked up to her knees, and her beat-up cowboy boots on display for all the wealthy society mavens to gawk at. He spewed his sip of whiskey.

* * * *

Ty leaned against the doorframe of his bedroom, staring at the woman in his bed. She was lying on her side, facing away from him, her dark hair spilling out across his pillows like an inviting dark pool. He'd read everything Jordan had dug up about her, from her earlier childhood to her debutante soirée to the fiasco of a wedding.

Edward Von Housen III. Teddy. The Teddy she had cast aside and had tried to shove away the morning he'd tried to wake her. Edward Von Housen, the biggest man whore in Alberta society according to *The Sun*. What he still didn't understand was what she had meant that day in his office when she had screamed at him, saying he had ruined her life.

How? To Ty, it appeared her life was already pretty much ruined. Which brought him to the bed and sliding under the covers. The thought of her driving her car off that bridge, trying to end it all made him want to kill Edward Von Housen. Sliding up behind her, Ty moved his arm around her, pulling her back against him. He was rewarded with a slight movement, a sound, a sigh, and his name dripping sweetly from her lips. He closed his eyes and held on.

* * * *

The next morning, Madison's thoughts were troubled and all centering on Ty, who kept his gaze locked on her all during breakfast. She had awakened in his arms and he had refused to let her up at first. He hadn't done any more than just hold her still next to him, as if he never wanted to let her go.

She had rested her head on his chest, enjoying the feel of his warm skin under her cheek and hearing the steady beating of his heart against her ear. He didn't speak, didn't kiss her, just held her. She thought back to yesterday when she had done the same thing to him. She had held on as if she feared turning him loose would mean letting him go forever.

Lying there, feeling the strength of his arms surround her, she had started to ask him a question, but he had pulled her to him again and whispered for her to just be still. Uneasiness had settled over her and it appeared he was affected by it as well.

Now, as she felt his eyes burning her face, she dared to peek at him through lowered lashes, her eggs all but forgotten. The look he gave her was anything but foreboding, and if his slow deliberate wink was any indication, he was thinking about their time in the kitchen from the day before.

She felt the color rise to heat her cheeks and could not suppress the grin that played at the corners of her lips.

"Well, now how did that happen?" Jill exclaimed as Madison slid a forkful of eggs into her mouth. "Why on earth would there be chocolate pudding on the ceiling?"

Madison's gaze flew to the ceiling, seeing what everyone now did, a slash of chocolate pudding. Her gaze slid to Ty. He was biting back a smile, trying to hide it behind a glass of milk. His eyes were alight with mischief.

"It's on the side of the fridge, too," Harold said, with obvious curiosity.

Jill turned quickly to follow where he was pointing. "What? Where?"

"By the cupboard there." Harold pointed to it. His gaze seemed to pin her before he turned to look at Ty, who seemed to be having a hard time looking his father in the eye.

"Ty, when I passed you yesterday, you said you were going to give Maddy a hand," Jill fussed as she began wiping the side of the fridge. "What did you two do, have a food fight?"

"Maybe," he answered, delivering another wink to heat Maddy's cheeks even further.

"That doesn't answer my question, does it?"

Maddy peered up at Jill, expecting her to be standing there with her hands on her hips, demanding an answer. She witnessed the wink she threw her husband instead. The woman wasn't mad. She was amused. "Did you play in it?"

Maddy slid her gaze to Ty and became all but ensnared in a look so sexual and bold, she almost lost the breath she was holding.

"Yes, ma'am. We sure did," he said plainly and clearly proud of himself.

Before any more could be said about the pudding slinging, Ty stood and tossed his napkin into his plate.

"Well, I have a very full day today. I made Maddy an appointment with Dr. Phillips."

Maddy jerked her gaze to his face, noting it was set in that stubborn square that would normally turn her on, but this...this was just not going to happen.

"I thought you were heading out—"

"To the plant, yeah, Dad, I am," Ty said, nodding to his father.

The lawyer in her sidled up to the suspicious female and she leaned back, regarding both men. Something was not right in Kirklandville.

"Then how is Maddy supposed to get to Dr. Phillips?"

"Jordan," he replied. "Your appointment is at ten o'clock. Jordan will come by and grab you. He said it was the least he could do for you for saving his life."

There it was. Refuse this and open that can of worms again. He had just thrown down a silent gauntlet.

She wiped the corner of her mouth as her mind worked furiously. This was easy. She would just call and cancel the appointment and plead sick for the day. It had always worked with her mother when Maddy had not wanted to go to school. Standing, she walked toward Ty, a smile lifting the corners of her mouth.

"So you'll be at the plant? I'll bring you lunch."

Ty reached for her, wrapping his arms around her waist. "I might be out in the field, so you don't need to worry about bringing me anything."

"A field? There's a field?"

"No." He chuckled. "I'll be out and about."

"Oh." She pouted, hoping he would notice.

"You okay, Maddy?" he asked, pushing back to take a look at her face.

She shook her head. "I'm just tired. I think I might go and lay down."

As she watched his features grow dark with concern, she almost felt guilty…almost.

"Tired? Tired how?"

She looked down and shrugged, perfecting her award winning sniffle and closing of the eyes for effect. She felt his palm riding her forehead.

"You don't feel hot. Mom, check her head, would you?"

"I'm fine, Ty. Go on to work. Don't worry about me. I've got a lot to do today."

"Oh, no! Mom?"

Maddy almost grinned as Jill came over, placing her hand on Maddy's forehead.

"Well?" Ty pressed her for an answer.

Maddy frowned, pushing her lips together in another pout.

"Well? I can't really tell. Maybe she should just rest today."

"I agree." Ty said the words she longed to hear. She bit back the smile that hovered. "Just as soon as you get back from the doctor's, you get yourself to bed."

Maddy felt her breath leave in a huff.

She had no more time to hedge as he moved his lips over her forehead. "Rest!"

"Yes, Mother."

He chuckled at her words and palmed her face in his hands. He smiled down into her upturned face. Slowly, he brought his mouth closer to hers, making her wait for the taste of him. She felt moisture pooling in her channel before his lips even landed. And by the time he tasted her lips, she was practically hanging onto his forearms for strength.

"I'll call you later."

She nodded, a bit dazed from the kiss. She opened her eyes to find he was already heading down the back steps, pushing his Stetson onto his head as he walked.

* * * *

Maddy waited until Jill and Harold left for their outing. *Strange, they couldn't really agree on where they were going.* Jill to the church and Harold to the plant. Moving toward the living room, she grabbed up the red leather phone book and flipped it open, finding the phone number for Dr. Phillips. Dialing, she waited until she heard a friendly voice on the other end.

"Dr. Phillips' office. This is Belva."

"Oh, yes, Belva, hello. This is Madison…" Should she say her last name? "I had an appointment to see the doctor today?"

"Oh, yes, Miss Bellini. For ten o'clock."

"Um, yes. I need to postpone that appointment. Something has come up."

"Oh, really? What came up?"

Maddy was taken aback at the question and found herself grasping for an answer. "Um, wedding plans. You know how those are. It's just one thing after another."

She was relieved to hear the woman laugh. "Yes, I sure do. However, it's too late to reschedule now, sweetie. We have a hard and fast rule around here. Besides, Dr. Phillips is already postponing his barber shop appointment to fit you in, so, we'd better not make him regret that."

"I hate that he's having to miss his hair appointment." Maddy stared at the receiver as if it had grown horns.

"Well, apparently, Ty was pretty adamant about him seeing you today."

"He was?"

"Yes, ma'am. Ty Kirkland himself made the appointment."

Ty Kirkland himself? What, was he a celebrity?

"Okay, Belva. I'll try to make it." Maddy felt her shoulders sag as she hung the receiver up.

"Calling Edward?" She heard from behind her. Turning, she found Jordan leaning against the doorframe.

Maddy knew her eyes were wide. They felt as if they were ready to pop from their sockets.

"What did you say?"

"I asked if you were calling Edward Von Housen III."

Chapter 14

"How long have you known?"

"About Von Housen or about the, uh, lack of memory loss?"

Maddy's fingers knotted together as she fought to find the right words. The look on his face was not the one she expected. There was no recrimination evident. He looked concerned.

"I can explain," she began, but that was as far she as she got. *Explain? How in the hell can I explain this? How can I ever make him understand?*

"I hope so. This ought to be good."

He was making fun of her? He was laughing at her?

"I...um was supposed to marry Teddy...Edward Von Housen. But I never loved him and he has one major flaw."

"He can't keep his pants on?"

"You know?" Maddy wondered if she looked as stunned as she felt.

"Yeah. Now, can we get to the other?"

"I...don't really have amnesia. I was confused...for about two hours."

Jordan's mouth dropped open in surprise. He looked like he was about to say something, but no words came out.

Oh! I've done it now.

"Let me finish. I overheard your brother and your dad talking about the trouble with the plant. Jordan, I know exactly what your brother's plan is."

"Oh, shit." His whisper reached her. "Why are you going along with it, then?"

"I...believe my father turned Ty down because of the Von Housens. He and the Von Housens made some kind of archaic pact where once the families were joined, Bambardi and Bellini would merge with them."

Maddy knew a release she had not expected at being able to voice her troubles like this. She wished she could be talking to Ty instead of Jordan.

"So, what? This is an act of rebellion?"

"What? No! I was groomed to be Edward's wife, ever since he swooped in and swept me off my feet. I just...didn't know all the particulars until it was too late."

"You mean almost too late?"

Suddenly, she began to wonder just how he knew the name Edward Von Housen. Had her parents tracked her, using Beth's phone? Were they outside now? She needed to find Ty.

"Where's Ty?"

"He's working."

"Jordan, how do you know about this?"

"I was doing some poking around on the computer."

"You..."

"Googled you. Great picture of you leaving the church, by the way."

"Okay. I ran out on my wedding and left my cheating hubby-to-be in front of a priest and a church full of people. I was heading to Texas until I learned about Kirkland Gas. I decided to see who had been responsible for pushing me into Teddy's bony fingers. I met Ty and saw for myself the bank statement."

"So you have known all along about the engagement?"

"Being fake? Yeah."

Jordan looked down at the living room floor, studying it. "Why are you letting this continue?"

"Because I know how badly Ty needs that contract."

"Even if I believed you…"

"Jordan, I'm a lawyer. I know my way around a financial statement. Ty is not going to be able to meet payroll unless something drastic happens. I'm that something drastic."

Jordan chuckled, nodding in agreement. "You've got that right. So, you're just willing to go along with this? What's in it for you?"

"I…I can't very well be forced to marry Teddy if I'm married to Ty."

Maddy had barely spoke above a whisper, but as Jordan raked his hand over his face, she knew he had heard her.

"I don't believe this." Jordan looked positively speechless. "Why him, Madison? You could have found anyone to thwart your father."

"Please don't think any less of me. Marrying Ty will give him what he wants most."

"Again. What are you getting out of this act of benevolence?"

"He saved my life, Jordan."

"Yeah, and you saved his brother's life. So far you're even."

"He…your whole family has taken me under their wing."

"That's not a good enough of a reason to marry my brother."

"What do you want me to say?"

"That you're falling in love with him?"

Maddy felt the breath leave her body in a whoosh.

Looking up, she found Jordan wearing a smirk of satisfaction. It irritated her. "I never said that."

"But you're not denying it."

Madison could tell Jordan was thoroughly enjoying himself. "Whose side are you on?"

"After what I've seen? My own, thank you. I see you and Ty together. He really likes you Maddy. Hell, he proved that the other night. He was pretty torn up over the mess he left you in. Trust me on this. I've known my brother a long time and I've never seen him get that upset over a woman's tears."

Madison digested his words. Could Ty really be feeling as twitterpated as she was?

"Can I give you some advice?" he asked, as he took another sip of his coffee. "Don't fight it, Maddy. You both have so much to offer the other. Maybe there's a reason you're together now. If Alicia had never hurt Ty and your ex-fiancé was not such a total idiot, you and Ty would never have met . Who knows? Maybe fate brought you together. Maybe fate will get you down that aisle."

"Jordan, we're not really engaged, remember?"

"Oh I realize that, but I also know what I see and I think you two would be really great together. So when you ask whose side I'm on? Well, Maddy, my dear, I'm on Cupid's. You about ready?"

Oh, God. How could I have forgotten the doctor visit? Again, her shoulders sagged. "Yeah."

"If you're a good girl, I'll ask him to give you a lollipop afterwards."

Maddy tried to hate him, she really did.

* * * *

She stepped into the filled to capacity waiting room at the doctor's office. She recognized Belva by her friendly voice as the woman waved her right through. *Great.* Maddy's thoughts were consumed with Ty and she knew she had to find him and tell him the truth. *Damn Jordan for being so inquisitive!*

Turning, she watched as Jordan picked up the new patient clipboard and waved her on into the exam room. At her look of askance, he said loud enough for everyone in the office to hear, "I'm putting you on Ty's insurance. By the time Belva gets these submitted, it'll be a done deal, right?"

Right? With everyone in the packed office listening intently, just how was she supposed to answer that?

"Right," she mumbled, turning to follow Belva down the small hallway. She was instructed up onto a padded table and left to wait.

Ty said he would be in the field. She wondered how one would get out to this field. She really needed to talk to him before Jordan let her secret out. What would he say when he learned she had known since virtually meeting him that he had been using her? Her mind conjured up visions of him moving over her as they lay in his bed late at night, as he made love to her slowly and silently, speaking with their eyes only as he took her higher and higher.

"Well, you are looking a bit flushed." She heard as the door closed. She had never even heard the man enter. "Maddy, is it?"

"Madison."

"Ty said Maddy," he told her flatly as he pulled up his stool and plucked out his penlight.

"Well, if Ty said Maddy, then Maddy it is."

"What seems to be the problem?"

"No problem."

"Ty sounded worried. So, let's try this once more. What seems to be the problem?"

She didn't know what to say. "I had a car accident and bumped my head."

"Someone tell you that?"

"Several people have told me that." She hedged the truth a bit, but until she could speak to Ty, she wasn't about to slip up and let the town doctor know she was a liar.

He checked her vital signs, then her eyes and ears for bleeding, in case she had received a concussion when her yellow Corvette had landed in the river.

"There sure has been a buzz in town over you," Dr. Phillips informed her as he wrote some notes on her chart. "It's good to see Ty finally settling down. You seem to be in great health despite your mishap. You're very lucky to have gotten away without so much as a bump. Any aches, pains? Tenderness anywhere?"

Each time he inquired, she shook her head.

"You know what, Maddy? I wouldn't worry too much about the amnesia. You seem to have some recollection, so I'm going to have to chalk it up to trauma. Your memory will eventually come back, probably sooner than you think."

Yes, her memory and her old life. Guilt seemed to bite at Maddy's conscience, but she just smiled at the doctor. She wished she could put everything from her life in Alberta behind her, but knew she would have to eventually face the music, especially if she was going to help Ty get the contract.

"Any vision problems?"

She almost laughed at his last question. Yes, her visions lately were causing her problems. Every time she closed her eyes, she saw Ty in some form of undress doing something delicious to her.

"You're flushed again."

"It's hot in here."

"It is not hot in here. Hmmm. Tell me, Maddy, do you and Ty plan to have a family right away? Or are you taking precautions?"

"Actually, I am on birth control."

"Good. Plenty of time for starting a family after the wedding."

Sure, Doc. I don't even know if Ty likes kids, let alone wants them. I've got to find him.

"Well, everything seems fine. How are the wedding plans? Belva said you were taking on more water than you can handle, pardon the pun. Are you getting plenty of rest?"

"Um, trying to. But you know how it is. Weddings have to be planned. They just don't happen." Her laughter sounded nervous even to her.

"Well, fine. If it gets to be too much, just call me. We don't want you passing out from exhaustion just planning the wedding. I suspect that is the cause of your getting flushed so easily. Worry can do that."

"I'll try."

"Okay. You're free to go," he said, heading to the exam room door and opening it. He led her out to the reception area chattering on a mile a minute. "Well, Maddy, it was a pleasure to meet you and I can hardly wait for the wedding, or for the little one to come. I brought Ty and Jordan into this world. Seems only fitting that I play catch for Ty's firstborn."

Play catch? Don't hold your breath, Doc. "I'll personally make sure you and Mrs. Phillips get an invitation."

"Excellent. Remember, take it easy. The next few weeks are going to be hectic and what you are experiencing is normal," he said then let out with a healthy chuckle.

Hardly normal.

"Thank you, Doctor," she said and turned to Jordan, who was sitting in the waiting room grinning.

"Hello, Madison, fancy meeting you here," greeted a familiar female voice. Madison's heart stopped.

"Hi, Mrs. Baxter," Madison said to the sweet busybody store owner. "How are you?"

"Oh, just getting my blood pressure checked and picking up Ernie's heart pills," she answered with a little smile on her face and tilted her head. "How are you feeling?"

Something was in Mrs. Baxter's tone that Madison could not read, something she found slightly annoying. "Fine, just here for a routine check-up."

"Oh, I'm sure it will be the first of many. Dr. Phillips is a wonderful doctor. You have no reason to worry, dear, he delivered both my children. Why, I bet he has delivered half this town."

"Mrs. Baxter, I'm not—"

"Mrs. Baxter, the doctor can see you now," Belva called out, drowning out anything Maddy would have said and ending the conversation.

"Well, you take it easy, dear," Mrs. Baxter ordered, hurrying behind the secretary.

Jordan walked up to Madison. "You ready?"

"Don't I have to pay something?" Madison asked, confused at how things were done here.

"No, I just told Belva to add you on Ty's benefits. She's gonna sit on the paperwork until the wedding. Her present."

"The wedding? But—"

"Come on."

"Where to now?" Madison asked, allowing Jordan to get the door for her as they left the doctor's office.

"Well, I think Ty said something about making you go home and rest."

"Jordan, I really need to find Ty and talk to him."

"I know, but he's all over today."

"The field?"

"Yeah. So, what did Dr. Phillips say?"

"He said that I'm in perfect health. The only thing I seem to be suffering from is guilt." Madison inhaled a deep breath and slowly exhaled. "Mrs. Baxter seemed a little weird. I don't know why she thought I would question Dr. Phillips. He seems like a good doctor."

"Mrs. Baxter is weird. She's the town gossip, which in itself shouldn't bother you. I just wish she would get her facts straight before she starts up the rumor mill."

* * * *

Ty moved down the aisle at the hardware store, scanning the seals and washers he needed to fix the water tap in his office bathroom. He knew what he needed, however his mind was engaged elsewhere. He knew that Maddy would be back home, hopefully resting. He had told her he was in the field today, which meant out and about in his mind. Truth be known, he had just returned from his meeting with the bank and had been staring at the picture of her on his computer, the one of her running out of that church. The office had been quiet, except for the sink in his private bathroom. The leaky faucet had bothered him long enough.

Besides, he had needed to get out of the office. Waiting for the phone call from the loan officer was eating him alive.

He needed this loan now more than ever. If Maddy ever regained her memory and realized their engagement was fake, she would no doubt think the same thing Jordan and his father thought—that he was only playing her to get that Bambardi and Bellini contract. If she ever thought he was anything like Edward and his business deal of a marriage, she would walk away from him. She'd be hurt. He would not have it. After what Jordan had forced him to look at last night, Ty knew more about his little Maddy than she did. He had wanted to protect her before and now, and after seeing exactly what had driven her over that bridge, he had come to a decision. He didn't need Bambardi and Bellini. The loan officer had gone over Ty's assets and had asked him about the gem mine, hinting he would consider the mine as adequate collateral for a very sizable loan. One that would see him clear for years.

At first, he had adamantly refused. He just couldn't see giving up his grandfather's legacy. But he had overextended by drilling for oil and so far, it was not panning out. So it was either use the gem mine or give up everything else. But now he'd give up everything to keep from hurting Maddy. To keep from losing Maddy.

The thing was, he loved her. She was incredible. Just thinking of the kisses they shared sent streaks of heat through him. Thinking of the other things they had done aroused him, making him want to run home and sink himself inside her again. He could get used to falling asleep in her arms after making love, then waking in the morning with her snuggled against him.

He felt a smile curve his lips and he realized how much he looked forward to going home to see her. He loved her smile and the way she scrunched her nose. The way they could talk with a comfortable ease.

"Hi, Ty, what brings you by?" a familiar voice said. Ty turned to see Mr. Merrit, owner of the hardware store for as long as Ty could remember. The hardware business had been passed down from his father, just like the plant had been handed down to him.

"Leaky seal on a tap at the plant. Figured I would sneak in and grab some new seals while I was thinking of it."

"Well, I hear double congratulations are in order," the older man said, patting Ty on the shoulder.

"Oh, you must mean about the wedding," Ty said, remembering that this was a small town and gossip was a favorite pass time. "Thank you, we are very excited."

"Imagine that, a wedding and a baby. Things seem to be looking up for you. It's no wonder you have your dad scrambling to get the house done," Mr. Merrit commented with a chuckle.

Baby? What the... "Baby?" Ty asked him, feeling a little confused. *Maddy wasn't pregnant, she couldn't be!* She had assured him she was on birth control the night he had first reached for a condom. She had taken the shiny packet from him, tossed it back into his bedside table drawer and shook her head. He was beginning to feel numb. He knew that birth control was not foolproof, but...

Ty swallowed hard.

Unless Maddy was pregnant before she ended up being pulled out of the river. Ty was not sure how he felt about her being pregnant with another man's baby. It was something he would have to accept, if he wanted to keep Maddy. *What must she be feeling right now?* And why hadn't Jordan paged him with the news?

"Ty, are you okay?" Mr. Merrit asked, cutting into Ty's swirling thoughts.

Ty looked up at Mr. Merrit. "Fine, just fine," he said, trying to keep the smile on his face.

Mr. Merrit put a hand on his shoulder. "You'll be just fine, son. Every man gets a little nervous before his wedding and even more so just before he becomes a father. Those are big steps in a man's life. You're a smart boy and I have heard nothing but wonderful things about your Madison from everyone, including your father. He's happier than can be over the fact he is going to be a grandpa."

"My father is?" Ty asked, wondering if he was the only one who didn't know about the baby.

"Oh yeah, you just missed him. He was over the moon when he heard the good news. He and your mother have waited a long time to be grandparents."

Ty knew that, but he still could not get over the fact Maddy was pregnant. "I better get these seals," he said, his mind reeling. Mr. Merrit took the seals. Ty was in a daze as he followed the older man to the cash counter. "So how did you all hear the news about the baby?"

"Ernie Baxter came in for some screws for his wife's quilting frame and your father was here. He was asking your father how excited he was about it," Mr. Merrit explained as he punched the purchase slowly into the register. "Your father seemed a little surprised at first. Had you and Madison not told your parents the news yet?"

Ty was speechless. Of course he had not told his parents the news. He had not even known the news. He needed to get to Maddy. Mr. Merrit seemed to be waiting for something, but Ty couldn't remember what.

"How much do I owe you?"

"Four dollars and sixty cents."

Ty pulled out a five-dollar bill and waited for his change and the receipt. "Thanks," he said to Mr. Merrit. He stuffed the change and the receipt into his pocket and left the store. He got in his truck and shut the door.

He needed quiet.

He needed to think.

Could she be pregnant with Teddy's baby? She hadn't been a virgin and the man had been her fiancé.

He started his truck. He knew he should turn left and head home. He knew Maddy would need him now more than ever. *Pregnant and not even remembering who the father was.* Again, why hadn't Jordan paged him?

He needed to get to her, hold her, tell her...what? What was he going to say to her when she looked up with those huge watery dark eyes and asked him about the father of the baby she was carrying? He had no knowledge of Edward Von Housen III, except for the fact the man was obviously a big whore.

Throwing the truck into drive, Ty tore out of the parking lot, squealing tires as he headed for the plant, his computer, and more questions than he had started out with this morning.

Three hours later found a surly and angry Ty Kirkland, leaning back in his chair, lifting a glass of whiskey and staring at the two women in the picture. On the left was Maddy, the woman he had fallen in love with and had just given up everything for. On the right was her best friend, Bethany, who he had just called and spoken with. The one who had just told him some startling news. The one Maddy had called just two days ago.

* * * *

Madison was busy helping Jill with dinner when her future father-in-law walked in the house with a large gift bag. It was a mint color with a teddy bear on it and yellow tissue paper sticking out of the top.

"Honey, I'm home," he teased playfully, walking into the kitchen and giving the white apron clad Jill a kiss on the lips. The intimacy and love they seemed to share after all their years of marriage warmed Maddy's heart. She wondered for an instant if there was any hope she and Ty would be able to have that. Something inside her wanted to believe in a fairytale ending, but the other side gently scolded that it was a marriage of convenience. Even though she loved him, it didn't mean they had enough to build a marriage on, other than business.

Okay, they had the sex part down, too. From the response she had been getting from Ty, there wasn't a problem in that department. She had to admit, her one time with Teddy had been nothing like she experienced with Ty.

Harold turned to Madison with the grandest of smiles. "There's my beautiful future daughter-in-law. How are you feeling, Maddy? Are you feeling okay?"

Madison found herself reminded of her attempt of getting out of her doctor's appointment and pleading sick. Yet, there was something in his tone that did not seem quite right.

"I'm fine, really."

"So you're feeling okay?"

"Fine, thank you." She cast a questioning look to Jill, who was studying her husband most intently.

Jill sent Maddy a puzzled glance and then turned her attention again on her husband. "I see you did some shopping."

He beamed proudly. "I picked a little something up today for our Maddy. I found out the best news today and I know you're going to be just as thrilled as I am." He passed the bag to Maddy and chuckled. "Go ahead and take a look. I sure hope you like them."

Maddy smiled at Harold. "I'm sure it will be lovely," she answered, taking the yellow tissue out of the bag. "It was very sweet of you."

She stuck her hand in the decorative bag and felt something soft and plush. She pulled out the knitted item, staring in total surprise at the little blue objects in her hand. "Booties?" She was not sure what to think. She was totally stunned as to why Harold would buy her such a gift.

"Baby booties." He seemed more than happy to clarify. "Aren't they adorable?"

"Harold, have you lost your mind?" Jill asked him, obviously as stunned as Maddy was becoming.

"Oh, I know. I should have waited until you and Ty made the announcement, but I couldn't wait." Harold brimmed over with a great deal of joy and pride.

"Told us what?" Jill asked her husband. "Maddy, what are you and Ty not telling us? By the baby booties, my guess is you are going to be parents."

"Oh dear, I..." Maddy really did feel ill, no pretending. She was positive she was going to throw up. This was the last thing she needed. Where would Harold have gotten such a crazy idea?

"I didn't mean to embarrass you, Maddy. However, it's a good thing you two are speeding up the wedding. I should have known something was up with that boy of mine. He's been walking around lately with his head in the clouds. I don't know when the last time was we all shared a meal together. He would rather be here taking care of you than at the plant."

"Harold, you're rambling."

"I just...I know by the way my boy looks at you that he loves you."

Maddy looked to Jill for help, but she looked as puzzled as Maddy felt. What could she say?

"Thank you for the baby booties," she stammered. "So, you heard I was pregnant?" She sent a silent prayer that no one had said anything to Ty. She would have to get to him before someone else did. "From whom did you get this tidbit of information?"

"Oh, it's all over town."

"Wh-what?" Maddy almost swayed.

"Oh, yeah. Ernie Baxter told Mr. Merrit and me at the hardware store today," Harold clarified. Ernie Baxter, husband of Mrs. Baxter, the gossip queen of Laramie. She recalled the strange words Mrs. Baxter had said at the doctor's office. *Oh, no.* And now she was shooting off her mouth about things that she knew nothing about.

The whole picture slowly came together in Maddy's mind. She not only wondered, but dreaded who else Mrs. Baxter had told this false news to.

"Okay, let me try to clear this up." Madison exhaled a long breath and struggled for composure. "Jordan took me to the doctor today for a check-up, as Ty requested. The doctor asked me about having children and Mrs. Baxter must have overheard and misunderstood."

Maddy couldn't help feel a twinge of regret at the disappointment on the face of Ty's father.

"So naturally, 'Busybody Baxter' assumed you were pregnant," Jill finished for Madison with the same expression she would have had after completing a jigsaw puzzle.

"That's my theory," Madison admitted. Thankfully, Ty *was* out in the field, where he would have been spared from hearing the shocking news.

"But you do plan on having kids, right?" Harold looked like he had just lost a million dollars.

She had no answer for him. *This was becoming more and more complicated. Where is Ty?* "Kids are certainly a possibility, but we need some time to get reacquainted again."

Okay, who am I kidding? We have to get to know each other for a first time.

"Only a possibility?" Jill asked, sounding worried.

Maddy was not prepared to field such questions. "No, I'm sure about kids. I would like at least a couple." Finally, something that was not a lie had left her mouth. She had to talk to Ty, that was becoming evident. "I'm sorry, but I'm not pregnant. So, no to the pregnancy and yes to kids…one day."

Oh the webs we weave, suddenly makes total sense.

"Oh, well then. I suppose we can wait to become grandparents for at least another few months, right, Harold?" Jill chimed in without missing a beat.

Maddy hated the fact that Harold looked a little disheartened. "No, you and Ty being happy is the main thing."

She smiled. Her stomach was starting to hurt, and she knew it was from guilt.

Jill must have picked up on it. "Well, let's just have dinner, and think of what a great life Ty and Maddy are going to have."

Harold nodded, coaxing a smile from Maddy. Sure, she and Ty would have a great life together, if great could be built on lies. She let out a sigh. "Actually, Ty should have been home by now. Is there a number where I can try calling him?"

Jill nodded and smiled. "Yes, in the living room by the phone."

She nodded and walked into the living room to the phone. She saw the phone list, started dialing Ty's office and prayed for the best.

"Kirkland," his sexy baritone answered.

Maddy felt her stomach flutter at the sound of his voice. "Hi, I just wanted to see how things were going there."

There was a bit of a pause. "Busy." His answer was short and to the point.

Maddy suddenly felt nervous and suffered a little ping of insecurity. "Your mom and I made meatloaf. I can do up a plate for you or…"

"Actually, I'm going to grab something in town and then come back out." He sounded distant and Madison wasn't sure what had brought on the change.

She forced herself to swallow back her insecurities. "Well, no worries, I have some things here to do. I'll wait up for you and we can talk when you get in."

"Actually, I don't really know if I'm even going to make it home." His answer was cool, and he sounded distracted.

And the workaholic tendencies surface.

"Well, maybe I will come by and see you tomorrow."

"Actually Maddy, I'll be just as busy. We will talk soon, but I have to go now."

She pulled the phone away from her ear, staring at it as a hundred different thoughts ran through her mind. She had been warned that Ty was a workaholic. But the man she had just spoken with, briefly, had sounded like a different person all together. He certainly did not sound as if he had heard about her pregnancy. He had sounded like he had the day she had first met him...distracted, busy, focused.

A sick feeling settled over her as she thought of Alicia and the short red suit and seductive make-up. *Was that why he sounded distracted? Is this another Teddy and Sophia episode?*

The sound of the a beep indicating the receiver was off the hook echoed in her mind. What was she saying? Any promise he had made her had been based on lies. Were lies. She had no business suspecting or even worrying about Alicia being with Ty. She certainly had no business being jealous of Alicia. She hung up, continuing to stare at it. This was going to be a marriage of convenience, but for something that was supposed to be convenient, it was becoming awfully complicated.

Chapter 15

Ty stared at the phone. Hearing her voice on the other end had just made his insides twist into a tighter knot of anger, betrayal, and confusion. Apparently, according to her friend Bethany, Maddy had called from his parents' house the same day he had fished her out of the river, meaning her pretense of not remembering was just that...a pretense.

And now she was pregnant, too? Or had been before she ran out of her own wedding. It didn't make any sense. Why would she fake losing her memory? Why go along with the fake engagement, unless she needed a husband and needed one pretty damn quick!

And what better way to make Edward Von Housen III pay than to marry the only man who could outbid him for the Bambardi and Bellini contract?

"He must have really pissed you off, Maddy," he said to the picture on the screen. Maddy smiled back, her arm draped around her friend Bethany at her graduation from law school. He thought back on the day he had met her, how he had caught her going over his financial statements. Now that he thought about it, she looked like a lawyer. At least she had that day, holding up her hand to silence him, as if she were used to commanding attention. She sure didn't look like a lawyer as she lay in his bed, though.

Had she known she was pregnant? Had that been the reason she had put up such a fuss about going to the doctor? Had that been the reason she had tossed his condom back in the table drawer? Damn, were all women liars? Conniving bitches who weren't happy until they took everything a man had to offer, only to spit in his face?

He heaved a heavy sigh, tossing the pen he had been clicking for the last ten minutes onto his desk. She had slowly become his world and he hadn't even seen it coming. He had even gone as far as to try and protect her, thinking she had tried to kill herself. Apparently, she was just a really careless driver.

He had shared things with her he never even thought about sharing with his parents or his own brother. The pain the break up with Alicia had caused had left a gaping hole in his heart and for a while, a very brief while, he had actually felt it healing, because of Maddy.

His mind drifted back to the house and how she had made him see it in a different light. She had made him open up and had actually reached inside him to soothe the hurt. Damn it, she had promised him a future.

"Damn it!" he exploded, flinging the pen across the room.

"Not who you were expecting?" Ty jerked his attention to the woman at the door.

Alicia all but draped her blonde body against the doorframe. This was not what he needed. Or was it?

"What do you want?"

Pushing herself forward, she moved like a cat, her hips swaying slowly and hypnotically. "Oh, Ty. I hate to see you looking so..."

"Angry? Pissed?"

"Alone." She slid onto his desk, her fingers moving to tease his lips.

He tossed his head to escape her touch. "Alicia, don't do this."

He held his breath, hoping she would stop, all the while knowing she would not. He would have to stop her. Lifting his hand, he swiped her hand from his mouth. Instead of taking the hint, she simply lowered it to tease the zipper of his jeans. With his eyes closed, he took in the smell of her perfume, the feel of her fingers as she found more and still more to tease. As he felt her slide the button from his waistband, he opened his eyes, meeting her heated gaze.

"Alicia, you're married. Stop it."

She chuckled. "Oh, Ty. I can't stop thinking of how it was with you. How we were...together."

"You might want to try."

"I have tried. It's no use. Tom is a dismal failure in bed."

"Then why did you marry him?"

"I was silly. I was angry with you and he was there, constantly stalking me, asking me out."

The mental picture of lanky momma's boy Tom Walsh stalking anyone was amusing and Ty gave way to the rumble of laughter. This whole situation was becoming funny to him. He stepped back from Alicia and raked her from head to toe. There had been a time in his life when seeing her like this, stretching her body across his desk would have sent his emotions soaring. Now all he could think was how ludicrous she looked. And how much make-up she wore.

"Tell me, Alicia, does it take a hammer and chisel to get that off?"

"To get what off?"

"That sugar sweet lipstick smile you have painted on your face."

He poured another drink and waited for her comeback. When he didn't get one, he peered back to find her nostrils flaring at him in stunned anger. "Oh, don't bother getting mad, Alicia. I couldn't care less."

"Ty, I just hate to see you like this. It's all over town, you know."

"What is?"

"That your little fiancée is pregnant. Quite the scandal."

"Still doesn't explain what you're doing here."

"I think that's rather obvious." Ty heard from the door to his office. Looking up, he found Maddy standing there holding a plate of food from home.

"Ladies, if you don't mind, I am really very busy."

"I can see that," Maddy seethed.

Ty jerked an angry gaze to the woman with the plate in her hands. *What did she have to be angry about? And why is she wearing my rain slicker? It isn't raining.*

"Alicia, take your ample ass off of my fiancé's desk and trot it on home to your husband."

Alicia swung back to seek Ty's help. Ty merely pointed to the door. He wanted them both to leave, however his morbid curiosity was getting the upper hand. He wanted to know exactly what Maddy had to say for herself. And he couldn't hear that until Alicia left.

"You're kidding me!" Alicia fumed, sliding from his desk to her high-heeled shoes. "You know, you must be stupid, Madison. If I had caught my handsome fiancé with his ex-lover twice, I think I would begin to cop a clue, sweetie."

"That's it!" Maddy turned to leave.

"Maddy! Get back here! Alicia, get the hell out!"

Ty was not sure why she did as he had commanded. She shook with fury and he knew she wanted to throw that plate of food at his head. "Alicia, I have never given you any reason to believe I might appreciate your behavior."

"Oh, really?" He watched as those painted lips formed a sneer. "Then explain that bulge in your jeans," she purred.

Maddy gasped in outrage, her gaze lowering to his zipper. He glared at her for looking. He also knew she would see no signs of him being aroused by Alicia. His laughter brought her gaze back to his face. He felt almost reckless, realizing she was jealous.

"Alicia, you never change," he said. "As usual, you've confused my cock for my wallet."

He watched as the color rose sharply on Maddy's cheeks and knew it was from anger. He watched as Alicia brushed past her to the door.

"Alicia, I'll bet if you go home and ask your husband, he'll show you the difference," Maddy remarked.

Alicia turned to deliver what Ty was sure would be a catty remark. However, Ty was in no mood to hear anymore from the bitch.

"Alicia, out!" he yelled suddenly, stopping any insulting words she would have spewed. "Don't come back!"

His voice reverberated his anger through the office and as Maddy stood there, she wasn't sure she wanted to turn around and witness the anger in his face. She wanted to run out and cry.

"Close the door, Maddy."

It took several deep and ragged breaths before she finally did as he said. Still her pride was stinging. This was the second time she had caught them together. He was very close to wearing his dinner.

"Turn around."

She took one more calming breath and turned, trying for an expression that would scream indifference. She even tried looking down her nose at him as she had with Alicia. As soon as her gaze found his face, she wavered. He was so handsome and she was starved for him. His expression was dark, almost angry, like the day she had first met him. He had affected her then with thoughts of peeling his shirt off and finding out if he tasted as good as he looked. Now after knowing his taste, that look pierced her to the core. She could feel his anger move over her as if it had hands.

Was he angry she had caught him and Alicia? Something was definitely wrong. She thought about taking a step closer and felt the thong of her merry widow slide across her bare backside. She had wanted to surprise her workaholic fiancé by showing up wearing the one piece of honeymoon confection she had seen him actually reach out and touch when she had brought them by. She had watched him as he had practically licked his lips in anticipation. She had put it on tonight and it was all she wore under his slicker. She was beginning to feel foolish now, standing here with him looking at her as if he could throttle her.

She watched as he sat back in his chair and lifted the glass to his mouth again.

"I'll just leave this," she said hurriedly, edging closer to the desk. She slid the plate on the corner's edge closest to her and began to back away. She imagined she could feel the heat radiating from his body. Hers began to weep.

"Come here, Maddy." His voice was low and deliberate, his words a challenge, almost as if he were daring her to get close enough for him to touch her. As she stared at him, he patted his thigh, calling her attention lower to his legs stretched wide before him. "Come here."

She moved around the desk, holding the slicker together as she did, lest he see what a fool she was making of herself by wearing next to nothing underneath it. She thought wistfully of the jeans and denim shirt she had brought in case she chickened out. They were just outside in the truck and she wished she had them on now. As she neared his outstretched legs, he reached for her hand, the one holding the slicker closed. She couldn't let go and she couldn't replace her hold with her other hand without alerting him to what she was doing. Reaching out with her other hand, she breathed a bit easier as he accepted, holding her fingers in his warm grasp.

She stared down at his upturned face. He was definitely working those dark brows of his. They were slashed across his forehead like he had the weight of the world on his shoulders.

"Is it raining outside?" he asked.

She shook her head too quickly, kicking herself mentally.

Too late, he reached for the slicker, peeling it open and exposing her to his gaze. She could feel his body heat and felt her own moisture slip down between her legs. Her body was actually weeping for him.

As he continued to stare at her, she shivered. Her heart was pounding in her chest and she almost trembled as he rose from his chair.

"I can see why you'd be chilly."

Maddy only had time to dart a glance upwards as the slicker was peeled completely from her body. Like lightning, his hands palmed her face, holding her still for his kiss. His face swooped down just as suddenly, his tongue ravenous as it filled her startled mouth.

He pulled her closer to feel the hardness behind his jeans, which she had caused, pressing against her belly. Grinding his hips against hers, he moved her to lean against the desk, his hands cupping her bare ass in each palm, kneading and teasing her to surrender.

She couldn't think. She could only feel, and this felt dangerous. She felt dangerous. He was insistent as he stroked her fevered skin, reaching lower to tease her channel from behind. The sensation jolted through her, forcing her forward as he continued to drive her mad with wanting. Her cheek landed against his chest and she held on as he delved further. She bit back the whimper as he turned her around. Once he lifted her hair, his mouth descended onto her neck, where he kissed, bit, and licked her nape. His kisses were primal. He was claiming her in a way he had never done before. His hands moved to grasp her hips, holding her against him as he ground his erection against her ass. One arm slid around her, his touch seeking to pull the bodice of her merry widow down. His other hand slipped down between her legs, moving them further apart.

As she heard him lower his zipper, the sound almost echoing in her brain, Maddy felt suspended in time. He nudged her forward and as she lowered herself over his desk, she felt him enter her from behind. The hot tip of his cock slid along her wet channel, seeking her and teasing her with the promise of filling her. He danced the tip over her, letting her know he wasn't ready to give her what she needed. He slid the tip in and out, making her squirm to feel more, until she was joining his movements in some desperate dance, reaching back as he teased her.

"Ty!" she called to him, begging him to penetrate her. "Ty, please!"

He finally answered her and she jerked. Slowly, she realized he had slipped his fingers inside her. He was making her crazy. Just as she felt she would scream from the urgency building within her, he slipped his cock inside her, filling her. She felt his hands riding her hips. He gripped her as he worked himself along her slick walls and his powerful thrusts wrung words from her lips as she reached for more.

Maddy had never experienced sex like this before. Her entire body was at his disposal and she squeezed her eyes shut as the pressure began to drive her over the edge. Fingers gripped the edge of the desk as she tried to meet him thrust for thrust. No words came, just loud grunts and moans as she climbed higher. He was holding her, filling her, driving her up, until she felt her body breaking apart. She called back to him as she felt his hot seed filling her.

She felt as if she would pass out. She rested her cheek on his desk as she tried to control her breathing and opened her eyes again. At first, she thought she was dreaming, seeing herself and Bethany at graduation. As her focus became clearer, she realized she was seeing just that. There she was in a picture on Ty's computer. She froze as she read the caption. *Runaway bride and her accomplice, pictured during happier times.*

He knows? She wanted to lift herself from his desk, but couldn't as his arms were wrapped around her and he was resting his head on her shoulder. She listened to his labored breathing as he tried to take in even more air.

"Ty?"

"What, Maddy?"

"Um…let me up."

"Yeah." He pushed his body from hers, giving her room to stand again. Before she could move away, he was there again. "We're going to talk about this."

She nodded, still staring at the picture. Her gaze landed on the notepad beneath her. Bethany's home phone number. She felt numbing heat moving up her neck as she heard Ty zipping his jeans behind her.

"I have to go," she blurted out, moving blindly past him, even as he tried to stop her.

"Go? Go where? Washington?"

"Let go of me, Ty!"

"It was nice of you to call Bethany and let her know you were all right. Especially since you couldn't seem to remember anything else."

So this was why he had appeared so angry. This was why he had been avoiding her. He knew she had been faking the amnesia.

"I…" Her words stuck in her throat as his fingers gripped her wrists, stopping her from moving away from him.

"Admit it."

"All right! I never had amnesia. I never lost my memory."

"No shit! I didn't want to believe it, you know. Your good friend Bethany told me you called her and I figured it out. It was the same day I fished you out of the river. So you've been lying this whole time." He released her with a slight shove, leaving her to catch herself on the edge of the desk. "Why? Just to get back at your father?"

"What? No!"

"No? You're a bright girl, Maddy." He moved to retrieve his glass of whiskey. "Marrying the Kirkland upstart would have embarrassed your father. That's what he called me, you know."

"Ty, I didn't..."

"You had it all worked out, didn't you? That little lawyer mind of yours. Marrying me would get back at all of them. Who better to raise Teddy's child than the man your father sees as some dirty cowboy. Is that how you see me, too? A dirty cowboy?"

She stared at him as his gaze raked her slowly from head to toe. "Did I do good just now? Was it what you wanted?"

Maddy knew her mouth was hanging open. "Wh-what?"

"Was it good for you, being taken like that? Did it make you feel nice and dirty?"

Her palm cracked loudly against his rugged jaw with speed and accuracy. Swiping up his rain slicker, she saw only the door and moved through it with alarming desperation and anger.

Ty fumed as he watched her from his office window. Seeing her storm out of his office had given him the feeling of déja vu. Only this time, she was climbing into his father's truck instead of her flashy yellow Corvette.

How much had happened since our first meeting? She would no doubt run back home and tell his family what an asshole he was. Grabbing up his keys, he headed out to follow her, just to make sure she didn't try to drown his father's truck.

After seeing her make the turn off that would take her back to his parents' house, Ty headed his truck and his broken heart towards Roper's.

Now, as he sat at the bar, peeling the label off his third beer, his thoughts centered on Maddy. It hadn't mattered how she had hurt him, he had heaved a sigh of relief as she had made it over the covered bridge and another as she had headed home. *Home.*

The voice beside him made him stop in mid-sip. "You drinking those like there's no tomorrow."

Jordan slid onto the stool beside him and signaled the bartender for two more.

"No tomorrow," Ty responded, staring at the beer bottle.

"According to the weather man, there is a tomorrow."

"Well, according to my computer screen, there isn't." Ty heard his own voice. Brusque, terse, unyielding.

"What's on your computer screen?"

"A picture of Maddy with her good friend, Bethany."

"Yeah?" Jordan asked. "So?"

"Bethany is her good friend. Such a good friend, in fact, that Maddy called her from the house the same day I fished her out of the Bow. The same day she was supposed to have lost her memory."

"Ouch." Jordan actually winced.

Ty's voice carried a warning as well as a challenge. "Do you see something funny in all of this? Something I've missed? She lied to me, Jordan."

"I know. She told me," Jordan said before turning up his beer.

Ty didn't believe he could have heard anything else that night which would have shocked him, but Jordan had just outdone himself.

"She...told you?"

"Yeah. Pretty cool, huh?"

"Pretty cool?"

"Yeah, her pretending to go along with your fake...engagement like that." Suddenly Jordan was looking as confused as Ty felt. "What happened? What have you done to her?"

"Me? She lied to *me*, Jordan."

"Yeah, to help you."

"Help me? She was helping herself."

"Oh, bullshit! You don't believe that."

"What? She was trying to get back at her family and that whore of a fiancé. She figured marrying a Kirkland would take care of it...and give that baby she's carrying a father."

"What? What baby?"

"She's pregnant, Jordan. It's all over town."

Ty waited for Jordan to gasp in shock. He never expected the grinding snicker. Looking over, he found Jordan was indeed snickering and fighting to keep his beer from spewing across the bar.

"I'm sorry," Jordan said through his laughter. "I wish you could have heard yourself just now. So grave." He affected the somber tone Ty had used. "She's pregnant, Jordan." He sighed. "She's no more pregnant than the man in the moon!"

"What?"

"Not pregnant. She doesn't need a father for her baby. She went along with the lie you told in order to help you get the money you need so badly."

"What?"

"She told me. She saw your financial statement and she could see how desperate you were. She said you wouldn't be able to make payroll if something drastic didn't happen."

"Drastic?"

"Like marrying money. And lots of it."

Ty lost the ability to blink or breathe.

Jordan wasn't finished. "She said it was her way of giving back some of the love we had shown her."

Her words, the same ones she had spoken at the jewelry store when she wanted to shower his mother and himself with presents. The night he bought her the ring. A ring that was nowhere near what she was probably used to. She had known then just what he was up against.

"I don't understand."

"She said it was because you saved her life. I got the feeling she was talking about more than the river rescue."

Again, her words came back to him. The ones she had spoken at the "house." She had wanted nothing more than for him to hold her. She had said it was enough to make her happy. He shook his head, trying to clear his thoughts. He remembered every word that had come out of her pretty, succulent, cherry-flavored lips. And somewhere amidst all of the lies, he had wanted to hear her tell him she loved him. But she never had.

"You know, I knew you would end up hurting her. Damn, you should have been honest with her."

"Well, obviously, she already knew."

"Then, what did you do to her?"

"Was she upset?"

"I wouldn't know. I haven't seen her. I got worried when she didn't come back from taking you some dinner. I was on my way to the plant to check on her and saw your truck here. Geez. Where else could she have gone?"

Ty stood, lifting his beer for the last swig. "She headed out to our place."

"Leave her alone, Ty."

Ty sat the empty beer bottle down deliberately. "Hell no! This ends tonight!"

Chapter 16

Not sure where her tears were coming from, Madison seemed to have a steady supply to go along with her broken heart. Her face was soaking wet as they were falling faster than she could swipe them away with Ty's slicker sleeve.

She had bypassed his parents' house, heading out here instead to get her head together before returning. Only, as she perched on the bumper of the truck staring at the dark beauty surrounding her, she knew her head was nowhere near together and if this kept up, she was going to be sick.

She had lost everything she had come to care about. She should've been honest with Ty from the beginning. No. If she had, there would have been no engagement.

"Okay, fake engagement," she said through fresh sobs. She had lied to him, his parents, his brother, the whole town. Sure, she had done it to try and help him. She had just wanted to help. Plus, she had fallen in love with him. She had fallen in love with the man who had tried to dupe her into marriage. She would have laughed if she weren't so miserable.

She wiped again at her tears. All was not lost. She would call her parents and tell them she would come back and marry Teddy once the contract with Kirkland Gas was signed and witnessed and the check was cashed.

She lifted her head to the stars above her, feeling an incredible ache welling up at the thought of Ty and how he had held her. How they had spent those quiet moments just looking up, seeing the same sky. She had been surprised at the improvements on the house since the last time she and Ty had come up. Jordan had let it slip that he and their dad had been doing some building on it. He certainly had. Walls were up, replacing the frame with rooms.

She felt her tears rolling down again as she realized she would not be living here with Ty, nor would she have her little garden. "Or a clothesline, so I can make the towels smell green and flowery."

She buried her head in her arms again and gave way to the torrent of tears. She felt a tug on her finger.

Again.

Looking up, she found Ty standing in front her, pulling the engagement ring from her finger.

Of course, he would want the ring back. He knew now he was going to need it to make payroll. Still, that didn't stop the hurt from going completely through her heart, ripping it to shreds.

"Just tell me one thing, Maddy."

She wanted to tell him to just go away and leave her alone, but he wasn't budging.

"What?"

"Why? Why go along with it?"

"I don't know anymore, Ty." She really couldn't think beyond her incredible loss. "What does it matter?" She swiped again at the tears.

"Maybe it matters to me."

"No, it doesn't. You just needed the money."

"No, Maddy. I didn't."

"I heard you tell your dad, Ty. I'm not stupid. No matter how this looks. I did have a reason."

"So did I."

"I know."

"You don't know. Damn it, girl. I watched you drive your car off the bridge. I thought for the longest time that you had tried to kill yourself. Hell, I couldn't tell anyone. They would have locked you up somewhere. You didn't have your memory. I couldn't let that happen to you. You needed protection, Maddy. And I needed to keep you safe until I figured out why."

"Well, I guess you figured it out."

"Maddy, are you saying I was right? Did you drive your car off that damn bridge on purpose?"

"No. I wouldn't kill myself. Certainly not over Teddy. I barely lost sleep over him. So, the fake engagement…you were trying to keep me from getting into trouble?"

She watched his brows slash down again, a clear sign he was either mad or confused. "Maddy, you don't remember, do you? I fished you out of the water and you said you were gonna marry a cowboy. I just went along with it."

"What?"

"Maddy, you hit your head pretty good on that steering wheel."

"But I remember you kissing me."

"I was giving you mouth to mouth."

"So you didn't lie to me just to get money?"

"No, I'm guilty as hell."

"I know. I heard you telling your dad…"

"That things were bad, yeah. I think they all thought at first I was marrying you for your connections. I couldn't exactly tell them they were right."

Maddy felt so tired, she could hardly lift her arm to swipe away more tears. She closed her eyes and sighed. She knew she couldn't stay here any longer. She would have to get the truck back and think about heading back to Alberta. Without looking at him, she told him her plans. "I'm going back to Canada and I'm going to make sure you get that contract."

"How do you plan on doing that?"

"The only way I can."

"No, ma'am. No, thank you."

Opening her eyes, she stared at the man in front of her. He had lowered himself to one knee and was taking her hand in his.

"What are you doing?"

"What I should have done all along. What I should have done to begin with. The truth is, Maddy, I love you. If you'll have me, for real, I think I want you to marry me."

She watched him slide the ring back onto her finger before it all blurred from watery eyes. She loved him. She wanted to be with him and live up to the commitment she made when she told him she would do what it took.

"So help me, Maddy, if you don't stop crying, I am going to kiss you breathless until I get a smile."

"But you love me?" Maddy felt a warm rush of surprise, and maybe even hope, race through her, as if her blood had suddenly started pumping again.

"Yes, and I don't want you to cry anymore. No more sad tears, sweetheart. I love you. You're wearing my heart on your sleeve. Would do me the honor of wearing my name for the next forty years or so?"

Maddy couldn't believe he was doing this. "Why are you doing this?" she asked, feeling like this was just a figment of her imagination.

"Because I want you to be my wife. I seem to have fallen in love with you and I know I'd be miserable without you." He hung his head, looking a little unsure. "I don't want it to be that way. I'm crazy about you and I mean every word I'm saying."

Madison wiped her tears with the cuffs of his slicker. "Well, I would be miserable without you too, so make it fifty and you have yourself a deal, cowboy."

He stood up leaning over to kiss her then pulled back to look at her. "Does this mean you love me, just a little?"

Maddy nodded.

He slipped his arms around her, his nose touching hers. "Good thing we have a wedding to go to, huh?"

She smiled, feeling that rush soar through her again as he pulled her against him.

* * * *

Ty stretched his naked body against the softness of Maddy's. He had carried her into the house and into what would be their bedroom. They had christened just about every room in the house by now and still he could keep going.

"Maddy," he whispered to the shower of dark hair fanning out over his arm. "Maddy?"

"Hmmm."

"Did we do the kitchen yet?"

He heard her laughter as he watched her shoulders shake. Reaching back, she smacked his arm. "Stop it."

"But I'm hungry," he teased, moving up against her to show her how hungry.

Rolling to her back, she met him halfway. He pulled her close and lifted her onto him. "I honestly didn't know that life could be like this," he whispered against her lips.

"I didn't either," she agreed, as her arms tightened around his neck. Ty felt her body relax and melt into his embrace.

It was a tender, warm kiss. Her lips were soft, yet demanding, meeting his with as much need for him as he had for her. As her lips parted slightly, he deepened the kiss and felt her desire for him wash away the fear, doubts and guilt, replacing them with a feeling of complete joy.

He pulled her closer, savoring every second. He knew he was not just falling in love with her; he *was* in love with her. He gently pulled his lips from hers and felt the gentle breeze cool them spontaneously. "I don't want anything to come between us," he whispered, knowing that their relationship was still very young even though it felt completely right.

Maddy gave him a puzzled look through her long dark lashes. "Nothing will, if we don't let it, Ty. I think we're going to be great together. We already are when you aren't being a jerk."

"Or you're being stubborn," he added with a grin.

She let out a small giggle, and even that small movement stirred his senses. "I can be stubborn."

Ty loved her, as crazy as it was, he truly did. "Tell me about it. But I don't think I would change that, even if I lose all the matches."

Maddy gave another giggle.

"Hey, look at me." Ty gently lifted her chin, bringing her gaze back up to his. "I know how lucky I am to have you. You're amazing, you're beautiful, you're smart, and you put up with all my flaws."

Maddy laughed, moving a hand from around his neck to the side of his head to run it through his hair. There was something intimate about it that Ty savored. "I have my fair share, but both our bad and good qualities seem to balance out. You've given me a whole new world. I feel like I really belong. That this is where I'm supposed to be."

Ty felt her fingers drift through his hair again, knowing in his soul that he could get used to this. He wanted to make love to her and give her so much more. Most of all he wanted to hold her just to feel her next to him. He wanted to roll over and know she was beside him. He bent his head down toward hers cupping her head as he watched her lashes flutter closed. Her lips greeted his like there would always be tomorrow, their full softness beckoning him to claim her. His tongue slipped easily into her mouth, tasting all she was. She was his, a loving, living, primal beauty, his mate in a way that swirled around in his heart and mind with a need to explore and explode.

He felt her body press up against his, sending heated desire through to his soul. He grew hard as the kiss intensified, loving the feel of her naked beneath him, moaning in pleasure while he buried himself deep inside her. Another moan left her, encouraging him to take things further. He slid his hands down, cupping her firm flesh in his hands. He pressed her to him as her hands slid down his chest, moving lower to his hips. She stroked lightly over the hot, throbbing ache in his cock.

A growl left him as he pressed it against her hand while his need silently begged to be released. He lifted his lips from hers, now slightly swollen, glistening from their kiss.

"What?" she asked, looking down at him.

"You like it on top, don't you?"

"I like it anyway I can get you."

He groaned as her lips took his in a hunger that was ready to send him over the edge. He felt her hands slide against his skin in a flaming caress, seeking his throbbing cock that pleaded to be touched.

Madison's hand, with silky, light accuracy, wrapped itself around his hardness causing him to grip her thighs in his hands. Beyond reason, he turned primal as he slid her up. He moved his hands to her hips pressing his thumbs gently on the bone as she caressed him, urging him to follow through with his desire. She stroked him, arousing him, causing him to grow even harder in her grasp. Ty had never felt this aroused. Madison pushed him to a new level, that level being pushed again as he felt how wet she was. "Maddy," he barely breathed as he pulled his lips from hers.

Her response was a whimper of need as her hand stroked over him with a feather touch. Grasping her hips he moved her over him, entering her in a single thrust and burying himself to the hilt.

"Yes," she whispered, as if feeling him inside her was a sudden relief.

It was an overwhelming relief for him as he slid his hands to her bottom and lifted her so he could move deeply within her. Slowly he moved in an even rhythm, feeling her tighten around him. He had never been so urgently in need of release and knew with every stroke it was going to be soon. He reclaimed her lips for a kiss just to have her pull away and struggle for breath as her soft scream of pleasure filled his ears. Her body tightened with such intensity that it was all he needed. He pressed her hard against him as a deep, throaty moan left him and he spilled his release in her. He was fighting for breath and close to passing out when he felt her arms wrap around his neck and her head rest against his shoulder.

"I love you," he whispered.

A small, satisfied smile played across her lips as she gave a nod in agreement. "Just so you know, I love you too."

Ty wrapped his arms around her, pulling her to him. He didn't care what it took, he would never let her go.

* * * *

Bright sunshine flooded through the open windows as Ty opened his eyes. Maddy was still asleep, curled up close to him. He brushed back her hair so he could gently kiss her cheek. It had been magical making love to her before holding her close all night. She looked so beautiful with her hair flowing down as he planted another kiss on her cheek.

He heard the sound of the newly hung front door opening.

"Ty?" he heard Jordan call out. Climbing to his feet, he dragged his jeans on and found his brother poking around the newly built rooms.

"Morning, brother. How was your night?" Jordan asked, taking in Ty's state of undress with a smirk.

Ty could not control the smile that crossed his face. "Incredible. But what are you doing here, giving us a wake up call?" he asked, glancing behind him to see if Maddy was stirring.

Ty noted the grim expression shadowing his brother's face. This did not look promising and Ty was sure he was not going to like the news. He knew somehow that something was dreadfully wrong.

"I think you need to wake Maddy," he answered, increasing Ty's fear with his tone.

"I'm awake," she groaned, moving up behind Ty. He felt her arms slide around him and he turned to kiss her good morning, glad she had slipped on his denim shirt. She gave him a smile that warmed him, despite the cool morning air.

"Good morning," he told her grinning. He leaned over and quickly kissed her lips with the briefest touch of his own.

"Well, now that you're both awake, I am, unfortunately, the bearer of bad news. Please remember not to shoot the messenger," Jordan told them. "The two of you have a big problem."

"No. No more problems," Maddy said after she yawned.

"Sorry. Not just a problem. A big problem." His features took on a grave expression. Ty felt real fear coursing through his veins.

Ty placed his hand on Maddy's as they exchanged a quick look of concern. She suddenly looked a little nervous as she pulled her bottom lip between her teeth. He gave her hand a reassuring squeeze before he focused his attention back to Jordan. "What's wrong? Are Mom and Dad okay?"

"Actually, Dad is fuming, Mom is silent and things are really tense. There's like an armada in the driveway. Maddy's parents are at the house—"

"No!" Maddy exclaimed, her fingers digging into Ty's arm. "Oh, no. This is not happening." Panic drenched every word she uttered as her pretty features turned to the same expression. "Jordan, I beg you, please tell me you're joking." Maddy sounded more devastated then Ty could have ever imagined.

"Sweetheart, relax. It'll be okay," Ty lied, hoping Maddy would calm down, but she was already pacing the unfinished floor. "Come here." He wrapped her in his arms, hoping to ease her misery. She had arrived in Wyoming and not only had she brought love for him, she had started to build a life for herself with him.

"That's not the worst of it," Jordan finally said, causing Ty to look up from his fiancée with an expression as dark as he felt.

He didn't stopped comforting the angel in his arms. "How much worse could it get?" Ty regretted asking as soon as the words left his mouth.

Maddy pulled her head up, ripping Ty's heart to see that silent tears were running down her face. "Oh. They didn't," Maddy exclaimed in a whisper.

Ty looked at Jordan who was staring at Maddy with the saddest look he had ever seen on his brother's face. "Yes, they did. They brought Teddy with them and they're all in the living room having coffee and arguing as we speak. Your father is furious, Maddy."

A sob finally escaped Maddy and she stepped out of Ty's arms and buried her face in her hands. Ty felt ill. It didn't help that a ray of sunlight bounced off the engagement ring on Maddy's finger.

"It could've been perfect," she cried out in the most heart-wrenching sobs Ty had ever heard.

With his fiancée's heart broken and a sudden guilty feeling for getting her into this mess, Ty felt this might be the worst moment of his life. He looked at Jordan and fought back the bile rising in his throat. All he could do was shake his head.

"I'm sorry, you two," Jordan said. Ty knew his brother was just as choked up about things as he was. "I'll try to calm things down at the house. That will give you two a minute." Jordan turned away, and Ty could tell by Jordan walked that he truly felt badly for them both.

Ty sighed heavily. *Hell, the truth was going to have to come out sometime, only this was the worst possible way for it to happen.* "Maddy…" His voice was husky and pained, reflecting the blow to his heart as it lost momentum. He could hear the raw emotion he was desperately trying to keep at bay.

"Ty, I don't know what to do," she whispered while trying to wipe her tears away with the sleeve of his denim shirt.

Ty wrapped her in his arms, unsure if it was for his benefit or hers. "You told me once that you were willing to work at it. Maddy, before we walk out the door and all hell breaks loose, please tell me you're still willing."

"I am, Ty, but you don't know my father. He's a force to be reckoned with." She tried to regain control herself. Ty was getting pissed.

"Well, so am I, sweetheart. And as much as I love you, I know you have the ability to be harsher than a tornado." He offered her the smallest of smiles, all he could muster up. "Shall we go face the music?"

"Not yet," Maddy told him, sounding far from her confident self.

Ty was sure, from her reaction, it was her family she had run away from. *The question was why?* "Maddy sweetheart, tell me what I can do to make this better. What's running through that pretty head of yours?"

"I cannot imagine any worse timing than this. It's a living nightmare and I have no clue how to fix it." Ty wasn't sure how to fix it either. Coming clean with both sets of parents seemed to be the only way. "I'm torn between the man I love, and him looking like a fake," she quietly confided, resembling a little girl instead of the society princess attorney Ty knew her to be.

"Maddy, it was my lie that got us into this," he gently reminded her, regretting it more by the minute. "Let me handle this."

"Oh, God. Ty, you don't get it. You have no idea how powerful my father is."

"No? After going toe to toe with his daughter, I think I've got a real good idea just how powerful. My wife, the powerhouse." He reached out drawing her in for a kiss.

She thwarted his attempted kiss, gently pulling back. "I'm not your wife yet," she teased gently.

"Yeah, I know, but in my heart you are." He cast her a smile just before his lips claimed hers in an attempt to breathe life back into her. She moved her arms around his neck as he gently drew her closer to him.

Madison pulled away slightly and looked up at him through her dark lashes. "I love you...so much."

Ty's soul filled with joy at the sincerity of her words. He felt the same, despite the short period of time they had known each other. "I know and I love you just as much. Now, what would you say to the idea of throwing your parents on a plane and calming mine down?"

Madison's lips brushed his with the faintest of kisses. "I would say my husband has a great plan."

Ty threw his head back and laughed. "But I'm not your husband yet."

Madison gave him a wink. "Yes, but my heart doesn't know that."

Chapter 17

Maddy followed Ty as they pulled their trucks up the driveway, steering them around the armada of vehicles.

"Oh, God," she almost whined at the parade of cars. The black stretch limousine and silver SUV blocked the drive, making it impossible to get close to the house without tearing up the yard, which was exactly what Ty did. Spinning his tires, he did manage to splatter mud all along the limo as he fought his way to the front door. Maddy almost laughed at his show of rebellion.

He stepped out, waiting for Maddy to climb out of his dad's truck and join him. Finally Maddy emerged, then lingered, putting off the moment when she would have to face her parents. Ty waited patiently, knowing full well that she was scared and worried, but filled with resolve. "I don't know what's going to happen," she said, drawing nearer to him. "A lot of awful things are going to be said."

She glanced down quickly at the sound of the front door banging open. She didn't want to know which one of her parents had come flying out of the house.

"Madison Bellini, so help me, you have really stepped in it this time. Are you trying to destroy your father with this little stunt?" her mother yelled, causing Madison to wince. Darting a glance to the man beside her, she saw Ty's jaw tighten, giving him the appearance of a man who was ready for a fight.

"Remember, I love you. I always will," she said as she turned toward the house and practically ran to where her mother was. She ignored him as he called out to her. Standing at the bottom of the steps, her mother wore her cream suit and looked more out of place than a rose in a vase full of daisies. "Mother, stop yelling. It's unbecoming," Madison snapped, digging in her heels and preparing for the worst.

"This, coming from my runaway daughter who is doing only heaven knows what with some common cowboy. Look at you, dressed in tight jeans and those hideous boots, like some rodeo hussy." To add insult, her mother crossed her arms and scowled.

"Do me a favor, Mother, and just shut up! Go in the house. I'll be right there," Madison told her, hoping to put some distance between her mother and the cowboy who was drawing near. She needed a couple of minutes alone with Ty.

Her mother gave her a scornful look, turned up her nose at Ty and stalked back up the steps and into the house. With each stomp of her cream-colored designer shoes, Maddy felt her resolve slipping and her heart sinking a little more. She had meant to stand up to her mother. Now she realized she had just made a tactical error in sending her back inside to reform and regroup with her father.

She felt like leaning into Ty as he stood by her.

"You going to be okay?" he finally asked quietly.

"I have you, and that makes all the difference," she told him, turning with a smile that she knew was coming across as less than sincere and no doubt revealed how scared she was inside. "Let's just do this," she mumbled, squaring her shoulders and taking his hand.

She took the steps with him, each one bringing her closer to the explosion that she dreaded. Ty reached out, grabbing the door for her. She looked up to give him one last brave smile.

"Madison! Thank heaven you're all right," her father greeted her, sounding relieved. He looked past Maddy and directly at Ty.

Her heart thumped when she saw the displeasure flicker across his face. "You must be Kirkland."

"Muffin," Teddy interrupted, rising from the sofa and plastering a smile on his face. "I have been worried sick! I've been beside myself with agony since you left me." His words sounded insincere as he moved toward her with his arms outstretched. "All is forgiven, Muffin. Let me prove to you that I can be a good husband."

Maddy wasn't sure if it was his words or the ridiculous smile that made her want to punch him.

"This ought to be good," she heard Ty comment dryly from behind her.

Teddy dropped his arms and turned. "I'm sorry," he said, lifting his nose. "My name is Edward Von Housen III. Miss Bellini's fiancé. And who might you be?" he asked in the snottiest tone Maddy had ever heard. She clenched her fist and curled it a couple times to stop herself from slapping Teddy's face.

Ty delivered a look that should have leveled Teddy. Maddy watched as Ty moved closer to Teddy. Seeing the two men standing together was almost comical, for they were as different as night and day. One was dressed in Wranglers, the other in Armani. "I might be Ty Kirkland, Maddy's new fiancé," he finally answered, his eyes never wavering.

"Muffin..." Teddy turned, a short incredulous burst of laughter leaving his thin lips. He was dismissing Ty completely, stepping closer to where she stood. She winced and stepped back.

Anger gave her strength. *How dare Teddy treat Ty as if he was beneath him? Ty was everything Teddy was not.* Ty stood tall and silent, his calm demeanor radiating control. The comparison between the two was stunning.

"Teddy, don't touch me, and by the stars above, do not call me Muffin again or I will hog tie your sorry ass right here in the living room."

"Madison!" her mother gasped.

From the corner of her eye, Maddy saw Ty and Jordan exchange amused snickers.

"Mother," Madison exclaimed, mimicking her mother's open-mouthed horror.

"That's enough!" her father roared. "I will not be ignored any longer, Madison. I want an explanation as to what is going on. These people seem to think you are marrying their hillbilly son." Taking a step toward her, he glanced at Teddy. "Take a seat, son. We will get this straightened out."

"I just want my Madison back home where she belongs," Teddy whined, pouting like a child.

"Madison, I'm waiting for your explanation as to why you humiliated everyone at your wedding, embarrassed your mother and me, then left Edward to go running out of the church just to end up in some cowboy's bed!" her father yelled.

Maddy remembered the sting to her pride that Teddy had caused, the pain she felt with his lying and cheating, the ridiculous way her parents had sheltered her and treated her like a fragile doll. Her heart pushed aside every other emotion to make room for her growing temper. Her anger rose like an erupting volcano.

"How dare you?" she hissed. "You have no idea what you are talking about," she accused in angered disbelief.

"Maddy is not to blame for any of this. I take full responsibility," Ty announced. An eerie silence fell over the room.

"Ty…" Madison tried to stop him from saying another word.

"No, Maddy. They want an explanation. I'm gonna give them one." There was harshness in his tone that Maddy had never heard before. "Mr. Bellini, you can call me anything you want, from a hillbilly to a redneck. Hell, I'm a cowboy, you aren't wrong there. On Maddy's behalf, though, I'd just like to say that she's her own woman, really smart, a lady who can make her own decisions. I'm also pleased to say that I have asked for her hand in marriage and she has accepted." Ty stood still, not backing down an inch.

"She already has a man to marry, a suitable match for someone with her money and breeding," her father snapped in a condescending tone.

Maddy watched and witnessed the mischievous light sparkling in Ty's dark eyes as he grinned. "Oh, we'll breed. Don't you worry." Ty backed up his words with a bold look, first to her, then back to her father, looking him dead in the eye. She watched as he took a step closer, shoving his fingers into the front pockets of his tight, faded jeans. "Your daughter stopped by on her way to…where were you going, sweetheart?"

"Texas," she mumbled, rolling her eyes. This was not the way to handle her father.

"Texas. It was love at first sight, well, for me anyway. She wasn't impressed, let me tell you. She was leaving and this was during a really bad rainstorm. She had a wreck on the covered bridge and her car veered off of it. She and that ridiculous sports car landed in the river. I jumped in after her and saved her life." He turned to Madison, sending her a smile that warmed her to her soul.

"What?" Maddy heard the shock from Ty's father. Turning, she watched as Jill tried to hush him up. "I thought you said you two met in Canada."

"I lied, Dad."

"Told you there was something fishy about this whole thing," Jill interjected.

Ty lifted Maddy's hand, his thumb stroking the engagement ring. "Well, I want us to have a relationship based on truth and honesty," he said, lifting her hand to his mouth and kissing it softly.

Maddy hesitated and gave a nod. "I wouldn't have it any other way."

Ty grinned again. Maddy felt her heart kick into overdrive, filling her with hope and a new, surprising calm. She watched Ty with adoration as he turned back to her father, casting a sour glance at Teddy as he did. "After I pulled your daughter out of the river, I realized she was suffering from amnesia. I told her that I was her fiancé."

"Oh, Ty." Jill's plaintiff cry echoed through the house.

"Sorry, Mom. I figured that a contract with his company would do Kirkland Gas a world of good. Bambardi and Bellini had already rejected my proposal, so I thought, what the hell?"

"'What the hell?' is right!" Maddy jerked her hand from his. "Ty Kirkland, you tell them the truth right this second!"

"I should charge you," Teddy yelped. "Please, like Madison would ever be engaged to the likes of you."

"Actually, Teddy, I am," Madison informed him, moving over to stand next to Ty. She then focused on her father. "Ty is not to blame here." Turning, she cast an apologetic glance at Ty's parents. "I never really had amnesia."

Jill laughed, causing everyone in the room to turn. "Oh, Lord. You two were made for each other."

"And Ty isn't telling you that the only reason…why he told everyone we were engaged—"

"And he isn't going to," Ty whispered urgently into her ear.

"But, Ty. They have to know the truth. They're your family."

"Yes, they are. And so are you, Madison Bellini."

"But—" Her words were stopped as he pulled her close, his warm breath against her.

"I don't care if they think the worst of me. I will not have anyone thinking badly of you."

"But, Ty—"

"Be still, princess."

"We never really believed the amnesia thing anyway," Jill reported.

"I did," Harold confessed.

"You knew?" Maddy asked in surprise, searching Jill's face in the hope of finding an answer.

"I believed the whole amnesia thing as much as I believed that you were really Ty's fiancée."

Harold stared on in shock. "Jill! You knew all of this and you didn't tell me?"

"You can't keep a secret." She slipped her arm around her husband. "I guess I figured if you kids were going to make a go of it, for whatever reason, I would jump on for the ride."

Madison gave them a smile. "I never thought I would end up loving both of you as much as I do."

Harold turned to Madison's parents. "I don't mean to be rude, but if you people don't have enough class or enough love in your heart to be happy for our children, I suggest you leave."

Her father gritted his teeth and growled, "Not without you, Madison!"

"Yes, Father, without me. I have a life here," she told him, reaching for Ty's hand. She needed to feel his skin against hers and his strength beside her.

"You wanted money through my daughter?" Franco Bellini demanded, as he scowled at Ty. "Very well. Just tell me how much."

Maddy waited for the fireworks, only to glance up and see the victorious grin plastered on Ty's face.

"Well, that was too easy." Her father's voice held a measure of victory all its own. "How much, Kirkland? Because you can't have my daughter."

Her father's glare fell on her with icy disdain. She glared back as she watched sardonic amusement twist his mouth into a smile of his own.

"He only wants you for the money, Madison. Can't you see that?"

"You don't know him."

"I know him alright. I will make this easy." His lips curled into a broader, demonic smile. Reaching into his suit coat, he pulled out his checkbook. "Let's just see how much he loves you, shall we? Kirkland, I'm writing this check to you for one million dollars." He signed his name and tore off the check.

Madison watched as Ty stared agape at her father, total disbelief etching the slashing dark brows.

"A million dollars?" Ty asked in disbelief. "You've got to be kidding me."

"I'm not kidding. Let go of my daughter's hand right now and I'll triple it. Take the check, forget this whole thing ever happened and my daughter in the process." Her father's tone was cool and determined as he wrote out the second check. *So this was how he did it. Controlled so many. Find out what they wanted most and exploit it. Then top it. Three million dollars?* Madison felt ill.

Her heart almost stopped beating as she watched Ty reach out and take hold of the bribe her father held out. He took the check, still holding her hand tightly in his. She looked at her father and saw only ruthless and primal victory in his eyes.

She knew what that meant. He had won. She pulled at her hand, loosening it from Ty's grasp, to save him from having to make the decision.

As his fingers tightened around hers and with careful deliberation, he crumpled the check with one hand and tossed it back at her father.

Ty's unflinching stare spoke volumes. The young lion had bested the old one. "Now, get out of this house."

Maddy felt the change come over him, felt his body harden, as if he was preparing for a fight.

"As I recall, this is your parents' home," her father reminded him bitterly.

Ty glared at her father with a steady gaze. "And as I recall, sir, my father already asked you to leave. According to Wyoming macho cowboy code, that gives me every right to show you the door. Don't make me have to do it."

"You hillbilly scum, don't even think of touching me." Her father sneered in total disdain.

Madison dropped Ty's hand. "I can't take this any longer, Ty. Please get them out of here. I'm going outside for some air. Let me know when they're gone." She kissed Ty's cheek and let her hand linger on his chest a moment, just to let her parents and Teddy know she had made her choice.

"Don't worry, sweetheart. They're just leaving," Ty assured her as she walked out the door and shut it behind her.

She heard the door open behind her as she ran lightly down the steps.

"Madison!" Teddy called, bringing her steps to a halt. "You still have a lot of explaining to do," he snapped in a tone that Madison disliked more than the man himself.

Madison turned and glared at him. "Bite my ass, Teddy!"

His fair features flushed with anger. It was official now. Madison knew the war was on.

"I believe I'll save that pleasure for the cowboy you've cock teased. That's about all you're good for, that and your bank account!" he yelled, grabbing her arm.

"Let go of me, you slimy weasel!" she protested as his fingers dug painfully into her upper arm. Maddy jerked and struggled, but Teddy was stronger than she would have guessed and his hold grew stronger and tightened. "Teddy, you're hurting me."

"You don't know the meaning of the word, Madison. You need to be put in your place." He rummaged through his pocket with his free hand as if looking for something. "That rich bitch attitude of yours is over and I'm not putting up with it anymore."

He moved, dragging her to the silver SUV and opened the driver's side door. The sound of something hitting it other than Teddy's hand on the handle caught her attention.

"Get in, you little bitch," he seethed, his smooth voice resembling that of a demon. He gave her a hard shove, pushing her into the vehicle.

Losing her balance, her ribs slammed painfully against the steering wheel. She crawled and scooted quickly toward the passenger door, hoping to make an escape. Desperation clawed at her throat as she felt her hair being pulled roughly, forcing her back. Teddy's hand twisted in her hair, causing her to abandon her escape.

"You're not going anywhere, except with me!"

After she felt him settle in behind her, she tried once more to move toward the passenger door. Her outstretched fingers could almost reach the handle. She heard the driver's side door shut and the hand holding her hair tightened viciously, causing her near panic. She felt something hard against her head.

"What the hell do you have in your hand?" she screamed at him in temper. "It's hurting me."

As Maddy heard the key turn the engine over, she tried once more to free herself. She struggled and again felt the metal touch her head.

"That's it, you naïve little bitch. Keep fighting and pushing the barrel closer to your head. Once it goes off, you'll know what really hurts."

Oh my God! He has a gun.

Chapter 18

"Teddy, please!"

His sharp bark of laughter sounded demonic. "Oh, don't worry, Maddy," he said her name as if he were spitting something nasty from his mouth. "My days of trying to please are over."

Trapped in the SUV, Maddy felt complete horror as Teddy brought it to a stop in the parking lot of Ty's family's gas plant.

Oh, God. She needed Ty. She needed a miracle.

"What are we doing here?"

Teddy's laugh was mocking and cynical. "You haven't figured it out yet? You should know by now, Muffin. I never leave anything to chance. Really, you should have been at my house for the past week. Thanks to your spectacle during our wedding, I have been ridiculed in the press. I could have weathered that, but for one thing."

"What?"

"The money, you stupid bitch." Viciously shaking her head, he yelled in her ear, "Without you, I get nothing! Nada! Do you think for one second I can let that happen? That I can allow this to go on? Do you know what I did on the jet, while your father ranted and your mother filed her nails? I listened. Every time your father took another call and found out more information on Kirkland, I was listening. I overheard your father mention Kirkland Gas and I knew that cowboy had done something to get you to agree to marry him, instead of me. I just couldn't figure out what."

"Teddy, please." Maddy felt tears spring to her eyes as he moved the barrel of the gun to press into the base of her skull.

"As soon as we landed, I opted to rent my own vehicle. Do you know why?"

What was he asking?

"Wh-why?"

"I plugged Kirkland Gas into my palm pilot and got the location. It even gives me this nifty little map!"

Maddy knew he had snapped and her fear swamped her.

"I decided since you would rather make your new fiancé the richest man in the northern hemisphere, I would take out either you or my competition. But as I stood there in that quaint little abode watching you fawn all over him while I was being ordered about by your father, I knew what I wanted to do."

"Kill me?"

"Finally! You had me worried there, Muffin. Yes, kill you. Brilliant, huh?"

"Teddy, you don't have to do this—"

"But, Muffin, you're taking away all of my fun!"

She heard him open the driver's side door, knew the chime that beeped as he moved away from her. His grip on her hair pulled her backwards, forcing her to climb awkwardly without being able to see what she was doing.

She finally managed to dart a fervent and desperate glance along the steering column, down to the ignition. Her hopes crashed as she realized he had taken the keys out. She was trembling so badly she could barely stand as her feet found the pavement.

The hand tightened again, bringing fresh tears.

"Let me explain my logic to you as we walk." Teddy gave her a shove, moving her toward the building. "See, if I kill you, then you can't marry the cowboy, which means he doesn't get the contract."

"Teddy, please. He doesn't want the contract."

"I heard him with my own ears, Muffin."

"He was lying!"

"And you are going to marry him?" His laughter sounded bitter to Maddy. "You would never marry a liar, remember?"

"Oh, God. Teddy, he lied because he was trying to protect me."

"How wonderful. Still, I can't allow this union to take place, Muffin. You know that. Once my father gets the contract, I can marry Sophia and we can be happy. Oh, you won't be invited to the wedding, but I will pay regular visits to your grave."

"Teddy, your father doesn't need the contract with my father. He's the richest man in Alberta!"

"Was!"

"What?"

"He made some very bad choices. His latest, in particular was falling into bed with your godfather. He sank every penny we had into Bambardi and Bellini. Only your godfather screwed my father. He has nothing. We have nothing. Marrying you was the only way to reap any of the rewards."

Once they reached the door, Teddy opened it, shoving her in with the gun at her ribs. "Teddy, if it's money you want, you can have it."

"Do you know how it felt watching your father write that check for three million dollars? That's my money he was using to pay off that cowboy of yours. Mine!"

"You can have the money. It doesn't mean anything to me."

"It doesn't mean anything to you? I didn't mean anything to you. For fuck sakes, Madison, does anything means anything to you?"

Teddy stopped abruptly, pushing his twisted face closer to hers. His eyes, wide and maniacal, searched hers.

"Ah," he seethed. She watched his mouth twist into a grimace just before he shoved her hard, sending her staggering down the corridor ahead of him. "It's that stupid, ignorant cowboy, isn't it?"

Maddy couldn't answer as a sob rose in her throat. She pictured Ty. She needed Ty. She was never going to see Ty again.

"You're insane, Teddy. You need help. I can get you help."

Teddy gave a disgusted snort as they walked through the hallway. "Insane, am I? I didn't drive my car off a bridge and pretend to have amnesia. Just which one of us is insane?"

"It doesn't have to be like this, Teddy."

He shook his head in frustration, then glared scornfully at her. "Tell me, Muffin, how else should it be? You need to pay. You need to be punished. Where's the phone? I need you to make a call for me. I need for you to call the press and tell them you can't live without me."

Oh he is crazy.

"Anything. Just let me go."

"Phone!"

Maddy pointed to the office. She felt the pressure as he nudged the barrel of the gun into her back.

Madison moved to the handle and turned the knob.

Locked!

Her back hurt where the hard metal of the gun kept pushing into it as did a spot low on her ribs where it had been for most of the ride out to the plant.

"For Christ sake, Madison, what the hell is the problem?" he yelled again, pressing the gun to her.

"The door is locked."

He shoved her out of the way, her back hitting the wall beside the door.

"Then we will have to unlock it," he grumbled more to himself than for Maddy's benefit, she was sure.

She wanted to sink to her knees and send up a prayer. *Teddy was serious. Seriously insane. Where was a miracle when a girl really needed one?*

A noise at the end of the hall caused Maddy to turn. Her heart soared, almost choking her air as she found Ty and Jordan moving toward them. Her relief faded quickly as Teddy turned, aiming the gun at both men.

Maddy tried to speak, but fear and tears seemed to lump in her throat making speech impossible and breathing near nonexistent.

"Just put the gun down." Ty's voice broke through the buzzing she heard in her ears. He sounded so calm.

Calm was the last thing Maddy was feeling currently, especially with Teddy's aim on the two men unwavering.

"No! Come closer and I will shoot you both," he hissed the words like a rattlesnake getting ready to strike.

Taking his threat seriously, both men stopped. Maddy watched as a wicked smile spread across Teddy's lips. His arm snaked around her, more quickly than she thought possible. He grabbed her, inducing a small shriek to break through the barrier in her throat. He wrapped an arm tightly around her collarbone and pressed the gun to her ribs.

"Teddy, let me go." Madison didn't even recognize her voice. It had washed away to resemble a whining plea.

"Teddy, let Maddy go," Ty gently requested, his eyes darting between Teddy and the gun digging into Madison's ribs.

"Please, Teddy."

"Shut up, you filthy little bitch!" He was mad and the hard metal seemed to press harder against her ribs to the point it was now painful.

Maddy felt something inside of her snap. She felt nothing for Teddy, not even pity. Now all she could feel was anger flowing through her veins. Anger, ruled by determination. She was not going to let him hurt Ty or Jordan.

Lifting her leg, she drove her boot heel against the instep of Teddy's foot. Surprised, he stumbled back. He not only released Madison, he accidentally pulled the trigger on the gun. The gun fired loudly, the bullet hitting a pipe before ricocheting and landing in the floor in front of Ty.

Teddy lunged toward Madison, causing her to step back. Thrusting her leg forward, Maddy tripped Teddy, who fell face down onto the floor. Both Ty and Jordan moved toward them as Teddy struggled to get up. Considering the nose-dive he had taken, Maddy was amazed he still clutched the gun. Jordan roughly placed his boot in the middle of Teddy's back, shoving him down.

She felt Ty touch her arm. "Maddy, get out of here."

"Not without you."

Teddy struggled beneath the weight of Jordan's boot.

"We all need to get out," Jordan added. "I smell gas."

"Shit!" Ty hissed. "If he fires that gun, we're all dead."

Ty lifted his boot heel and connected quickly and soundly against the side of Teddy's head. Teddy uttered a grunt and fell back into the floor.

Jordan loosened the man's grip on the firearm and stepped off his back.

"Ty. Can we shut the gas off?"

"I'll do it. Get her out of here."

"Ty, I won't go without you."

He moved away from her, his palm hitting a large red button on the wall. A loud danger signal sounded, reminding Madison of an air raid siren from a war movie. "You have to go, Maddy. Get out of here, now!" he yelled, hitting switches and turning a valve.

237

Just as she was about to protest, he turned, grabbing her arm.

"Let's go, honey," Ty ordered, moving her hurriedly toward the doors. As they reached them, a sprinkler system kicked on and a new alarm rang a high-pitched warning. Another loud noise rumbled, echoing through the air along with the blare from the siren.

Ty pulled her through the doors at a run. Shoving her along in front of him, he ran away from the building. Before she could fathom where they would run to, she felt his hands on her shoulders as he pushed her forward, throwing her to the ground. As Ty's strong body covered her, her breath left her.

"Ty? Jordan."

"He's out. He's got Teddy."

She could hear the sound of emergency vehicles approaching. The ground gave a tremble before a loud bang sounded. Maddy had never been so scared in her entire life.

"I love you, Maddy," Ty whispered into her ear.

She held on, praying those would not be the last words she ever heard from him. Time felt suspended as they waited for the blast that was sure to come.

Sirens sounded louder as they screamed past her and Ty and into the parking lot.

Finally, she lifted her head. "Ty?"

"I got you. We're okay."

"I was so afraid. I thought you were going to die." She choked out the words in a whisper.

"Not today, Maddy."

Shouts were heard above and around them as another rumble was heard. Pushing her head down, he covered her again. She held her breath for what felt like an eternity, finally hearing the sounds of heavy rain hitting the ground around her.

"What the hell?" Ty exclaimed. Something landed in her hair. Looking up, she dared to dart a glance up. Something black was oozing down his forehead and lower off his broad shoulders.

"Ty!" Maddy heard Jordan call out as she stared up at the man she loved. She heard footsteps approaching quickly as Jordan began pounding Ty on the back excitedly.

"You did it, little brother!"

"Are we alive?"

"Boy, you not only saved the office, you hit oil!"

"What?" Maddy asked, looking again to the black ooze.

Ty rolled away from her and helped her to sit up. She looked around at the chaos surrounding them. Fire trucks, ambulance, police cars, one stretch limo and three Kirkland trucks and they were all being showered with oil. Sure enough, oil was spurting up from a break in the roof.

"Jordan, go find Mom and Dad and tell them we're safe."

Jordan laughed as he moved away.

Ty moved his arms around her and pushed her back onto the oil-spattered ground.

"What are you doing?"

"Just looking at you. I came very close to losing you."

"I'm not going anywhere."

"Except under me," he joked as he pressed his need closer.

"Thank you for saving me."

"Which time?"

He was correct. From the first time she had almost drowned, he had been saving her. Whether he knew it or not, he had not only saved her life, he had saved her heart as well.

"All of them."

Ty pulled her closer to him. "It was the least I could do since I'm marrying you."

Madison gave a laugh. "About our wedding, other than my mother, do you think anyone would object if I wore cowboy boots?"

Ty threw his head back and laughed hard before looking back at her. "No, I would think it would be just perfect."

Madison leaned into Ty. "Like you are for me." She kissed him, grateful for all they had and hopeful for all everything still to come.